CU00905960

Bryan Drake was born in Devonshire. His first career was with the RAF, as an Air Electronics Officer on the Vulcan B2 Bomber Force. In 1982, he joined a high tech defence electronics company as a sales engineer, and in the ensuing posts, experienced the pressures of big company politics, aggressive tendering, take-overs and travelling unwisely.

He became Marketing Director of the Defence Systems Group in the early nineties, followed by five years as the Regional Director of their United Arab Emirates' facility.

Bryan now lives in Paphos, Cyprus, as a marketing consultant for the Middle East. This allows him to spend time on his first love – writing. Although his non-fiction work has been published previously, this is his first novel, which reveals the lighter side of working in a fascinating, but difficult and highly competitive business.

His hobbies include tennis, keep fit, music and travel.

RICHARD'S WAY

Bryan Drake

Richard's Way

Vanguard Press

VANGUARD PAPERBACK

© Copyright 2003
Bryan Drake

The right of Bryan Drake to be identified as author of
this work has been asserted by him in accordance with the
Copyright, Designs and Patents Act 1988

All Rights Reserved

No reproduction, copy or transmission of this publication
may be made without written permission.
No paragraph of this publication may be reproduced,
copied or transmitted save with the written permission or in
accordance with the provisions
of the Copyright Act 1956 (as amended).

Any person who does any unauthorised act in relation to
this publication may be liable to criminal
prosecution and civil claims for damage.

A CIP catalogue record for this title is
available from the British Library
ISBN 1 843860 92 9

Vanguard Press is an imprint of
Pegasus Elliot MacKenzie Publishers Ltd.

www.pegasuspublishers.com

First Published in 2003

Vanguard Press
Sheraton House Castle Park
Cambridge England

Printed & Bound in Great Britain

Dedication

To by daughters

Caroline and Kate

(In case they should meet a 'Richard'.)

Chapter One

Today is an important milestone in Richard Bryant's career. He's about to give his first presentation to the Management Board of his employers, *AGC Electronics plc*. Sinking into the plush leather settee outside the Conference Room, he senses the bitter taste of fear. His throat is dry. His chest tightens, making breathing difficult and laboured. For the umpteenth time in the last hour, he takes the dog-eared script from his smart new leather briefcase. He fumbles with the pages. To his horror, he sees that they are no longer in the right order. Panic sets in; they'll call for him any minute now. After several shuffles, he now finds that page four is missing altogether.

He lunges a clammy hand into the case, scooping out the contents in a wild search for the missing folio. In the turmoil, his laser pointer ejects itself onto the parquet floor. He watches helplessly as the device disintegrates into several parts and the battery rolls under a gigantic display cabinet.

The door swings open. 'The Board's ready for you, Mr Bryant.' The Finance Director appears in the guise of Jack the Ripper and beckons menacingly.

The floor feels like rubber. The auditorium appears much larger than he remembers. Someone has turned the lights up to full brilliance. Richard knows he's walking awkwardly. They'll think he's drunk. He fixes his eyes steadfastly on the lectern, studiously avoiding contact with the esteemed audience. Yet, suddenly he is blessed with the gift of almost limitless peripheral vision. The CEO is watching his every clumsy step and frowning disapprovingly over his thick horn-rimmed specs. The Chairman is eating a carrot. The Engineering Director has turned up in shorts. The Production Manager is knitting a jumper. There's even a duck sitting in the audience.

It takes what seems a lifetime to stagger to the podium. He heaves an asthmatic sigh of relief on reaching the top step, when his briefcase flies open, sending its contents crashing noisily onto the floor. Mouth open, Richard watches as the crystal trophy he saw outside in the display cabinet splinters into a million pieces. This is quickly followed by a large bottle of red ink. Then a packet of flour. A pair of white lace panties. A frog.

He just stands there, trembling, like a whippet with dysentery. With Herculean effort he grabs the wooden rail and heaves himself onto the dais. He tries to speak, but all that emanates from his parched throat is a hoarse burbling sound. The first slide flashes onto the screen. But it's not even his. He recognises it as Miss January, Playboy 1997. By now he's sweating profusely. He feels the urgent need to urinate.

Someone in the audience is cooking bacon over a primus stove. The hall starts to fill with mouth-watering, hickory smoke. The fire alarm sounds. The ringing becomes louder and more urgent, and then stops as suddenly as it had begun.

'Wake up Richard, it's seven o'clock. Come on, up you get. The bacon and eggs are on the hob. Thought you'd like a good old fry up today. After all, it's not every day you get to address the *AGC* Board.'

It was with unbelievable relief that Richard forced open his eyes to see Becky, in an extremely brief red silk top and matching pelmet, placing a cup of steaming liquid on the bedside table.

'You look like shit.' She planted a moist kiss on his even moister cheek. 'Look alive – this is your special day.

Don't worry – you'll have them eating out of your hand.'

What should be plainly evident is that such a loveable, thirty something, ever cheery, pint size, attentive, gorgeous, blonde is not Richard's wife. She is in fact, Becky Martin, a co-worker at *AGC Electronics*, his closest friend, live-in tenant and self-confessed lesbian.

Richard loves the fairer sex. They are his primary hobby (well above squash, water sports, music, travel and reading). But he's a hopeless case. He tries so hard to understand and please his girlfriends. He always treats them with the utmost kindness and consideration, dines them in fine restaurants and woos them sympathetically. Oblivious to their good fortune, they soon abandon him for some hideous, unscrupulous creep who treats them badly, handles them roughly and displays the sensitivity of a Tasmanian devil.

Richard had also been somewhat imprudent over the choice of his ex-wife Maggie. After a whirlwind courtship, they were married in Tooting Registry Office and set off for a honeymoon in romantic Sorrento. By day two, she had succumbed to the ungainly charms of the owner of the 'Bella Vista Hotel' and decided to stay. Possibly, she had been influenced by the screening of *Shirley Valentine* during their flight from Stanstead. You can imagine Richard's ignominy, having to return home alone from his honeymoon. However, he was determined not to become embittered and took solace in the knowledge that Maggie hated pasta, garlic and opera, and was expecting a bald headed, ugly, greasy, Diego bambino for Christmas.

Richard ate the hearty breakfast. It would line his stomach and reduce the chances of nervously throwing up over the lectern. Becky chatted away, attempting to take his mind off the ordeal.

'Don't be intimidated by them. They're no different to you. They just earn a hell of a lot more and live in huge houses with servants and things. Imagine them shopping in

Tesco with their flies wide open. They're just men. That's of course, apart from the HR Director, Penelope – and I might even be wrong about her.'

'But I had this terrible dream. It was so real. Do you know…'

'Richard. Shut the flip up. You've absolutely nothing to worry about. Apart from your career, this flat and your livelihood of course. Come on, cheer up. I'll run you to the station. I'm sure the commuters will welcome with open arms such a ball of fun on the 8.16 to Waterloo.'

During the forty-minute journey, Richard, having satisfied himself that page four had not vanished into thin air, eventually stopped fretting about the presentation. His thoughts turned to Becky. He couldn't imagine anyone nicer to live with. She was caring, tidy, bubbly and a talented cook. Above all, their friendship had never been tarnished by sex, lust, rivalry or jealousy. Never mind, one couldn't have everything. However, Richard couldn't help wondering why such an exquisite and feminine beauty didn't fancy men. One day he might broach the subject. When the time was right.

He was still clinging tightly to his briefcase when the train arrived at its destination. So tightly in fact, he'd lost most of the feeling of his fingers. It was a typically grey London day. Richard decided to hike the thirty-minute journey to Holborn, find a café near the *AGC* Company HQ and arrive at reception shortly before ten.

Everything was going according to plan until he met Paul Hamilton at the entrance to *AGC* Towers. Paul was the Corporate Marketing Director and Richard's difficult and extremely contrary boss.

'Richard. How nice to see you in UK for a change. Chairman's delayed for half an hour so I thought we'd run through your presentation together.'

What the Director really meant was: 'Your travel

14

expenses are too high and I am going to pick my way through your briefing and cause you an enormous amount of grief.'

By the time the Chairman arrived, Richard's jaw ached from gritting his teeth over the many arbitrary changes to his script and the forced removal of the four key slides from his presentation. He drew some comfort by recalling a television advert from his youth. It went something like-: 'Have a Rowntree's fruit gum – they don't make adults disappear, just more tolerable.' Now Paul Hamilton was an overtly ambitious yet cautious man. He insisted that nothing controversial should ever be shown to the Board – like anything useful, factual or quantifiable. This included those slides depicting the level and phasing of the funding needed to launch the new *Aphrodite* Radar product.

It was therefore with intense relief when Richard was eventually called into the Conference Room. The destructive interference of the previous half hour had turned any nervousness into abject annoyance. By the time he reached the podium he was in crusading mood. After all – this was his chance for him to change the Company's pedestrian and miserly habits. What did he have to lose? His briefing took on almost evangelical tones. The more he sensed he had their interest, the braver he became. Only Paul Hamilton appeared to be squirming uncomfortably in his seat.

'So you see, there's a vast market for solid-state, three-dimensional area radars. We're talking of potential orders of nearly three billion pounds over the next five years. And that figure doesn't include the USA and its traditional customers – a market historically that has been denied to us. With *Aphrodite*, we've a clear technology lead, a working prototype and a long and successful record of selling reliable radar systems world-wide. To retain this position, we must invest. We can't afford to wait until we win a contract in order to complete development. Similarly, to remain competitive, production start-up costs must be spread over several contracts. Time is of the essence. We've a strong technical lead – but delaying funding would mean this advantage would soon be squandered away.'

By the time Richard concluded the presentation, he could sense that the majority of the audience was onside. He was now ready to take on the world. 'Your questions please, lady and gentlemen.'

'You haven't told us exactly how much seed-corn funding you actually want.' The Chairman was quick to spot the forced omission.

Richard took the confiscated slides from his briefcase. 'You will see, this graph illustrates the recommended spend profile over the next two years. A total of ten million pounds is needed to launch this product and the costs can be spread evenly over that period. We need to develop the product now or we'll never meet customer delivery expectations and *Elsa* will be the beneficiary. Slide two shows the detailed Statement of Work. The final two slides illustrate world markets by value, timing and my assessment of our chances of success.'

'Thank you, that's very clear now.' The Chairman nodded supportively but was no doubt thinking 'Why the hell didn't he tell us that before?'

'You said the French Company, *Elsa* will be our main competitor for the first two key bids. Can we beat the Frogs?' Lady Penelope raised her token xenophobic question whilst smiling knowingly at the CEO.

'*Elsa's EL97* technology lags behind our *Aphrodite* by more than a year. *Elsa* also has a reputation for dumping their equipment on the market at give-away prices and then charging the earth for spares and maintenance. Conversely, I believe our reputation is good – we've many systems operational and working well after twenty years and we provide fixed prices for spares and servicing. That said, *Elsa* enjoys the highest level of political support and uses the most influential and unscrupulous agents that money can buy. You can never underestimate the French.'

What Richard omitted to tell them was that the greatest threat came from *Elsa's* treacherous and deceitful salesman, Henri Latour – 'the Fox', who would sell his own *grandemere* to win an order.

After several more questions and the usual ritual dance, the Board grudgingly approved the funding and Richard escaped as quickly as possible to avoid meeting up with Paul Hamilton. He returned to the site for a pre-tender meeting with the Contracts Department, affectionately known as the *Business Avoidance Directorate*. Their department manager, Dave O'Leary, thought all salesmen were a waste of space and that most customers were stupid and existed solely to distract him from his real purpose in life. Whatever that was.

That evening, Becky created a mouth-watering chicken pasta dish whilst they shared a bottle of red plonk and chattered about everything and anything. 'Apparently, Liz Jarvis told me that Paul Hamilton came to the site after your presentation. He threatened to fire the security guard, reduced one secretary to tears and rejected four expense claims and five travel applications. Apparently he was also looking for you but couldn't find you.'

'Nothing out of the ordinary then.' Richard opened the second bottle. 'Not bad wine this, for £3 a bottle. Bulgarian. I was determined not to buy French. But you see, Paul has one or two serious deficiencies – he can't make a decision and he's hopeless at his job. The last thing he wanted to happen today was for the Board to fund the *Aphrodite* project. Now both he and I will be accountable for its success and meeting the sales targets. Anyway, as Fawlty Towers has approved the funds, he'll just have to live with it. So, let's close the stable door and talk about something more interesting like the sexy new engineer I saw in Lab Two today.'

'She's called Kate. She's twenty-eight, single, likes riding, classical music, squash and hang gliding. Lives alone in Guildford, keeps Burmese cats and has just terminated a tempestuous, long term relationship.'

'Male or female?'

'Richard!'

'The cats.'

'Ha ha. Very funny. I didn't ask her about her sexual orientation.'

Neither remembered going to their separate beds that night. This wasn't at all surprising, as they'd guzzled four bottles of wine and sampled the assorted dregs of any bottle containing alcohol left over from the previous Saturday's party.

At least there were no more nightmares. When Richard emerged from his coma, he vowed never to drink, smoke or chase women ever again. Well, perhaps he'd find time to cast an eye over Kate Webber. He needed to visit the Engineering Lab later that morning anyway.

Chapter Two

It was mid morning by the time that Richard had ploughed his way through the mountain of faxes and mail. He disliked being deskbound, much preferring to conduct any business face to face. He believed that the internal telephone system was a much abused and intrusive facility that made it far too easy for people to decline or dither over the simplest request. By moving around the site, he found that people were more willing to give him their time. It also allowed him to circumvent the occasional officious secretary who believed her sole mission in life was to prevent anyone interrupting her boss.

As Richard shuffled through the morning mail, he rued the blight of modern office machines that made it so easy for people to generate info copies for every man and his dog. After all, just a few years before, the 'knowledge is power' brigade had ruled his business world. That said, he was guilty of making extensive use of the info copy when dealing with the indecisive Paul Hamilton. He would, as a matter of habit, inundate Paul with copies of everything he wrote (excepting, of course, anything useful or that could enhance the Director's power base). Amongst this multiplicity of these useless documents, Richard would slip in a 'real' memo. Buried deep in this missive, would be a typical request for authorisation:

'I therefore intend to visit Oman next week, agree these changes with the client and release the next batch of funding to the engineering group.'

Even if the bungling Mr Hamilton ever read the

memo, by the time he said 'no', it invariably would be too late. It was fortunate that just about everything Richard sent him, Paul studiously ignored anyway.

Richard left his desk strewn with untidy piles of paper and made his way to the Engineering Block. He was wearing one of his dappier suits that day – just in case he should accidentally bump into the alluring Kate Webber.

'Good to see someone visiting us from the sharp end.' The tall, slightly hunched, speaker was Clive Deacon, a fifty-something, self-effacing radar expert. They worked well together. Richard, the extrovert, charismatic, risk-taking, free agent and Clive, a salt-of-the-earth, cautious, traditionalist who was exceedingly married. Clive had spent his whole working life with *AGC* and was an acknowledged expert in his subject. He found Richard's coltish energy stimulating and envied his freedom.

'Well, someone's got to see how you're spending all the Company's money,' Richard responded.

'Good to hear the Board approved the funding yesterday. Coming to my tiny office for a cuppa?'

They spent the next hour discussing *Aphrodite*, arranging customer visits and brainstorming the way ahead. They then adjourned to the Development Lab for Richard to see the new working prototype modules.

Before leaving the area, Richard thought it would be only polite to introduce himself to their most recent recruit and crossed towards the bench where Kate Webber was wading her way through the Company Engineering Procedures. She looked even more stunning at close range – about five foot seven, slightly built with high cheek bones and short wavy blonde hair.

'Hope I'm not interrupting. Richard Bryant from Sales. Just thought I'd say hello.'

'Oh so you're Richard Bryant'. As she spoke he was further enchanted by her impish smile and bright green eyes.

'You've actually heard of me?'

'Of course. You're the Radar sales guy, mid-thirties, single, travels a lot, can wield a squash racquet. You're also into hang gliding and live with Becky who's just a friend.'

'I'm humbled and flattered. But you're wrong about the hang gliding. I do a bit of micro-lighting though. Funny thing, I heard the same about you.'

'That's also untrue. I'm scared of heights.'

'Classical music?'

She mouthed a taunting grin. 'You seem to be pretty well informed too.'

'Well, we classical music buffs are a rare breed around here. What kind?'

'All kinds, really. Verdi, Bizet, Tchaikosky, Prokofiev – you know, the usual.'

'How about Wagner?'

'My favourite actually, but most people wince if I so much as mention his name.'

'Well, that's an amazing coincidence. I'm planning to see *Tristan and Isolde* one evening next week at the *Coliseum*. I really hate going on my own. Would you care to join me?

'Now then, it happens to be my favourite opera. Let me see,' she flicked the pages of her pristine diary. 'Next week. Yes, I'm free Monday, Tuesday, oh and Wednesday, Thursday and, that's amazing, Friday and… yes, and the whole of the weekend.'

'Great. I'll try and get tickets for next Friday or Saturday. It starts about 5pm and takes about four hours, if I remember correctly. Anyway, I know an extremely pleasant Greek restaurant nearby in St Martin's Lane.'

'So, what they said about you is true then. You don't waste any time, do you?

They chatted easily for another few more minutes. Richard decided it would be prudent to leave – after all he

21

had her reputation to consider. His steps were light as he floated out of the Engineering Department and made his way back to his office to book seats for *Tristan* and tackle the rest of the day's chores with renewed vigour. He'd just met a really beautiful, intelligent, classy and discerning female. Perhaps this one would be different.

It was late afternoon when Paul Hamilton's PA rang to tell him Mr Hamilton wished to speak with him.

'Gosh, he's still there on a Friday afternoon?' He knew Paul's PA, Pat, well and had often cheered her up after her thoughtless boss had reduced her to tears. He'd frequently send a cheeky greetings card or a Dilbert cartoon with the boss, the object of derision and mirth, carefully modified to resemble Paul.

'Shush. He'll hear you one of these days.'

'Oh yes and that would devastate our close master–slave relationship. How's the old goat today anyway Pat?' Richard switched on his speakerphone knowing that it would be several minutes before Paul deigned to come on the line…

He could easily have finished the Times crossword and War and Peace by the time Paul spoke. Despite the fact the site had a strict no smoking policy, Richard took out his coffee jar ashtray from the desk and lit a Davidoff Virginian. He occupied an office in a building well away from the site headquarters. Anyone in the position of authority who could object to his smoking wouldn't visit his office. They'd get their secretary to send for him instead. He also took additional delight from the knowledge that Paul was a fervent anti-smoker.

'Ah Richard. Good to find you in the office. I've got a little task for you that should keep you out of trouble for a while.'

Richard groaned to himself. Thank goodness it was not next Friday. He taunted Paul by not responding.

'Are you there? Richard. Hello. Hello'

He took another couple of slow puffs on the Davidoff. 'Yes, of course Paul, I was waiting patiently for you to give me the instruction.'

'Mmm. Now, the *Aphrodite* Product Plan. Needs a lot of work. We need to generate a sort of simple Executive Summary – something all the Board members can understand. The body of the document needs a lot more padding. Make it more readable. It's far too brisk. And tone down all the technical stuff. It just confuses people. Also, we must have much more information on the French system. What you've got is far too superficial. You know the kind of thing, a detailed specification. Real intelligence. Are you still there?'

'Yes, I'm still listening'

'Well, that's it really. Just work on it and e-mail me the completed revision by Tuesday noon. You'd better start work on it over the weekend?'

'Of course Paul. But bear in mind that the French system is in very early development. So our assumption is they'll be working towards achieving exactly the same specification as *Aphrodite*. That's because the key potential customers have already based their requirement on our system ...'

'Richard, I know all that. Just crack on with it. On my desk Tuesday at the latest.'

'Of course, Paul. You know I never miss a deadline. Have a nice weekend'.

'Just a minute Richard, I found that in last week's expenses you left a charge for a newspaper on your hotel bill in the Qatar *Sheraton*.'

'Did I? Gosh, I must have missed that one. Strike it through or should I send a cheque to Accounts?'

'Don't be flippant Richard. I've already removed it. Just be more careful in future. Attention to detail and all that. Crack on.'

The phone went dead. Paul never ended a telephone

conversation properly. He just suddenly stopped speaking. Richard smiled to himself. The hotel bill in question totalled around 6,600QRs (£1,200). How could anyone be bothered to focus on 50p in such a sum?

Fortunately, Richard intended to have a quiet weekend anyway. Becky was going to Southampton to see her parents. So producing a new Product Plan would be little more than a minor inconvenience. He had a knack with words and a good grasp of all the necessary data. He knew he could shuffle the previous Plan around on his computer, pad it out a bit and then knock out the 'Noddy's Guide' for the Board. Should only take couple of hours. Plenty of time left for the important things in life, such as squash, red wine, chasing women and catching up on his sleep.

In the event, he stayed in the office until seven, finished the new Plan and left to enjoy a full weekend as he pleased. He decided that he would e-mail the plan to Paul a minute or two before noon on Tuesday. After all, it would be a mistake to make it look too easy.

The week could not go quick enough for Richard. But at long last, it was Saturday and he was driving up the A3 to London, Kate Webber chatting easily at his side. She was wearing a smart black little number, which he later found out was from the Gucci stable. In fact, he discovered that she had bought most of her wardrobe from the American Gucci outlet factories over the past four years. Her ex-fiancé, Marvin had insisted they holidayed in California two or three times each year. He was ten years older than Kate and had a well-paid position with a large fund management company in the City. He loved the West Coast's easy lifestyle and weather. Unfortunately, he loved gambling even more and during the many excursions into Nevada, he managed to lose all his money, his job and their home to the Casinos of Vegas, Reno and Laughlin. Kate acknowledged that this was the main cause of their break-up, although it became evident from many of the things she told him, that Marvin had treated her badly. She admitted that he had a few other minor imperfections. He drank too much, was a workaholic and a devoted womaniser.

'So how about you Richard?'

'Hardly ever gamble. I'm a prudent lush. I work only to live and never, ever chase women.'

'Come on Richard, You know exactly what I mean. Tell me all about you.'

'Nothing to report really. Married five years ago for three whole days. Lost my wife on honeymoon to some oily hotel owner in Sorrento. No other long term relationships since then, unless a fortnight qualifies. You know, it always starts off fine. In fact girls often take the initiative. Then, just about the time I think there's potential; some roughneck comes and sweeps them off their feet. On the other hand, I think part of the problem is that I travel frequently and unwisely. In fact, spending the past week in the UK is the exception rather than the rule. I don't think many gals in a relationship want to spend so much time on their own. It's also difficult to plan anything as I frequently have to go at short notice.'

'So what was different about last week?'

'Oh, I sent a Travel Application for Thailand to Paul Hamilton on Monday. By the time he got around to telling me not to be so stupid, it was Friday and too late to send me anywhere else. Anyway, he thinks he's punishing me if he makes me stay in the UK. In truth, I needed to visit our Ministry and the Defence Research Agency anyway and I had no intention of giving up the chance of taking you to see *Tristan*.'

They were completely at ease in each other's company, bouncing off each other's wry humour. Richard parked in the Festival Hall car park. As they walked the short distance to the Coliseum hand in hand, they were oblivious to the pressing demands from some vagrants camped out on the Hungerford footbridge for 'the price of a tea'.

This was the first time that either of them had seen *Tristan* – a moving story of unbridled love, intrigue and treachery. The story is set in Cornwall where *Tristan and Isolde's* existing love is brightened further by their accidentally drinking a love potion. The opera follows their passionate relationship until, after a brief enforced separation, they meet with their tragic deaths in Brittany. As Wagner takes several hours to retell this simple legend, they were both famished by the time they reached *Beotys*. Richard used this Greek-Cypriot restaurant regularly for business lunches (and evening romances whenever the opportunity arose). He knew he was always guaranteed a convivial and a discreet welcome.

'Mr Bryant, how good to see you again. You're looking very well. And your lovely companion. I believe this is your first visit to Beotys, Madam. Welcome.'

Yiannis showed them to a small table, slightly apart from the others.

'Will this table be all right for you Mr Bryant?' Yiannis knew full well this was Richard's favourite table. But Yiannis always observed the same ritual, even when, during one Farnborough Air Show, Richard had taken four different girls there on four sequential nights.

Fine wine, an appetising dinner, the romantic setting and attentive service contributed further to their perfect day. It was three in the morning by the time they reached Kate's flat in Guildford. By now both felt elated but exhausted.

'Would you like to come in for a drink before driving back to Farnham, Richard?' Kate volunteered.

'No more alcohol, but I could really murder a coffee if it's not too late for you.'

'Well, I wasn't intending to rush out of bed this morning. Come on up.'

As he expected, Kate's flat was impeccably clean and tidy. They were greeted by two identical black Burmese cats, except that one was wearing a blue collar and the other red. Richard thought they were black but Kate insisted that, according to their pedigree, they were in fact chocolate. The lounge dining room was sparsely but tastefully furnished. There were a few ornaments. Two photographs in silver frames perched on a small Regency table; one of Kate's graduation, the other he assumed was of her parents. A large bookcase was neatly stacked with novels, autobiographies, travel and cookery books.

Kate returned from the kitchen with two mugs of coffee, which she placed on the low table in front of the three-seater settee.

It was at such times as these that Richard felt at his least confident. If he moved too quickly, he could be considered pushy and 'after only one thing'. If he moved too slowly, he could be seen as weak willie-woofter. His technique therefore was to let the girl make her intentions clear, take his lead from them and be incredibly attentive and responsive to their needs. He need not have worried. Half way through his coffee Kate caught him completely off guard.

'Richard, I thoroughly enjoyed today. I like you a lot and have done ever since I met you. I'm not ready for another relationship but I'd really like you to spend the night with me. Just sex, no commitment though.' She spoke softly and naturally as if she were ordering another glass of champagne.

Richard felt as if he had been hit on the head with a hammer. He was particularly astonished by the matter of fact way Kate had broached the subject. This was the last thing he expected of her on their first date. He was about to respond with, 'Come on Kate, say what you mean' but thought better of it.

Instead, he reached forward and lightly brushed her

cheek. His hand moved slowly and imperceptibly to stroke the nape of her neck as he drew her towards him and pressed his lips tenderly to hers. The kiss was long and lingering as they savoured, relished and tried to prolong the enchantment of those first few precious moments. They each began to caress each other's bodies in a slow, deliberate attempt to extend and intensify each other's pleasure. Richard speculated that she had probably not slept with anyone since she broke up with Marvin, some four months ago. It took only minutes before Kate began panting softly with delight. Her reaction immediately drove Richard to reach even greater heights of passion. Their lovemaking suddenly became urgent, driven by a relentless and burning desire and culminating together in one shuddering, breathless crescendo. The neutered cats, by now clearly bored by the whole performance, had curled up together and fallen asleep in an armchair.

Richard and Kate both slept soundly, wrapped in each other's arms. At dawn, Kate awoke first and her soft caresses soon excited Richard. But this time, they made love purposefully, no longer driven by the wild impatience of discovery that they had experienced the night before.

Becky was vacuuming the carpet when Richard opened the door to their flat.

'That was a very long opera. Or did we lose our way home?' she mocked.

'Hi Bex, what an amazing twenty four hours.'

'Are you hungry or did she give you breakfast?'

'We weren't exactly thinking of food. I'm not really hungry but I thought I'd treat you to lunch at the *Bird and Ferret*. Unless you have other plans?'

'No plans. Just cleaning the flat from top to bottom, doing the laundry, washing the dishes – you know, women's work. Of course you can buy me lunch. Then you can tell me all about your little excursion. I want to know every minuscule detail, mind.'

'I didn't think you were that much of a Wagner fan and I've taken you to *Beotys* several times.'

'OK Richard, I'll let you skip those bits. Just tell me what happened at her place.'

Richard spent the rest of Sunday with Becky and took great delight in failing to satisfy her persistent curiosity. He made one quick call to Kate to let her know he had arrived home safely. Remembering her warning about involvement, he was careful to make the call brief. 'Anyway Kate, I really enjoyed yesterday immensely. No doubt I'll run in to you at the site this week before I fly out to the Middle East.'

'Thanks again Richard. I had a great time yesterday too. If I don't see you before, have a good trip.'

Chapter Three

It was early on Tuesday morning when Richard collected Clive from his home on their way to Heathrow airport. He had not seen Kate since their day of opera and passion, although Becky had told him Ms Webber had an enormous grin on her face all day on Monday. However, he put that down to Bex just having a bit of her usual, wicked but harmless fun.

Clive was feeling somewhat battered. He had been in the doghouse for the past three days; ever since he had told Annie (his spouse, greatest critic and jailer) he'd be away for about a week. However, about the time they joined the M25 morning tailback, he began to visibly relax at the thought of the week ahead – interesting work, sun, entertainment and freedom. He knew that whenever he travelled with Richard, they would work hard by day and play hard at night.

The Pink Elephant long-term car park was almost full and they had to search for one of the last few spaces. It was beginning to drizzle as the courtesy coach entered the airport tunnel and the prospect of guaranteed sun seemed even more attractive. Richard evaded the long queues of expectant holidaymakers at check-in, guiding Clive to the Executive desk and placing his treasured Frequent Flyer Gold Card on the counter.

'Two for sunny Dubai.'

'Lucky you,' smiled the pretty girl at the check-in as she tapped their details effortlessly into the computer. 'Really nice place. I spent a holiday at Jumeirah Beach

three years ago but I gather it's changed even more in...
Oh Mr Bryant, it appears that your reservation was
cancelled by phone yesterday evening.'

Richard turned to Clive. 'That'll be bloody Latour up
to his tricks again. His agents would have found out about
our meeting tomorrow. He knows the flights are heavily
booked and has damn well cancelled my booking.'

'I'm afraid the flight is full Mr Bryant. The best I can
do is to waitlist you. I suggest you take your hold baggage
through to our lounge and check again with the desk at
about ten o'clock. Good luck. She turned to Clive. 'Here's
your boarding card Mr Deacon, and your invitation to the
lounge. Have a good flight.'

The airport was so busy that a long queue had formed
even on the Fast Track channel through passport control
and hand baggage checks.

'I just need to buy some *Eternity* for Annie.' They had
just reached the Duty Free section and Clive was already
beginning to feel guilty.

'Leave it until Dubai, Clive. It'll be much cheaper.
Come on, it's a zoo out here. I'll treat you to a relaxing
glass of Bucks Fizz in the lounge.'

Despite the Bucks Fizz, Richard was still feeling
uneasy. If he missed the flight they would forfeit the
precious opening in the General's busy diary. He knew that
missing appointments in the Middle East resulted in long
delays in rescheduling another meeting. It was hard
enough to set up an appointment in the first place. He also
knew that Clive would not be happy to meet with the
General and his staff alone. Despite Clive's extensive
technical expertise, he was not well versed in the ways of
Middle East culture and business customs.

Almost an hour had passed when Richard was paged
to report to the Reception desk. During that time he had
collected, fidgeted with and discarded five national
newspapers, taken several trips to the breakfast buffet and

the cloakroom, and made a number of frustrated phone calls.

'Mr Bryant. Good news. We've found you a seat on the flight to Dubai. You will also be pleased to hear that we've upgraded you and your travelling companion to First. Please give your hold baggage to this gentleman. Enjoy your flight.'

Fifteen-love, thought Richard. One over on the Fox this time.

This was the first time Clive had travelled First Class. He seemed determined to sample all the available goodies during the six-hour flight. He took out three personal videos, ate a five-course meal, drank several glasses of champagne and examined the contents of his complimentary wash bag like a child with his Christmas stocking. He couldn't resist buying Annie a gold pendant from the duty free trolley.

'Clive, we're going to the Gold Capital of the world!' Richard counselled to no avail.

It was late evening when they landed at Dubai airport. As they joined the airfield circuit, the lights of the city were clearly visible. They could make out the plethora of elaborate resort hotels bordering the Arabian Gulf, the lights of the Trade Centre and other numerous skyscrapers. They had a clear view of the harbour which was cluttered with dhows and contrasted starkly with the massive container ships at the nearby Port Rashid.

Dubai's International Airport is modern, clean, ultra-efficient and large. Even when using the extensive moving walkways, it took them over fifteen minutes from disembarking to reach the immigration desk. Processing through passport control and customs was almost instantaneous in the newly completed terminal. As they left the air-conditioned building, they were subjected to the shock of the baking night air. It was still humid and over

40° Celsius.

The taxi sped unhindered along the eight lane highways and they checked in at the Crowne Plaza hotel, just forty minutes from landing.

'Mister Richard, so nice to see you again. Welcome back to Dubai.' The smartly dressed Filipina receptionist smiled eagerly as Richard approached the desk. 'Oh, and I have message for you. A Mister Captain Mohammed rang. I made note for you.' She passed Richard a neat encrypted note saying that *ther meetin was delade until noone.*

Richard passed the note to Clive. 'I don't believe the call came from Mohammed. This probably has the hand of the Fox again. Don't worry; their staff officer's in the office by six thirty, so I will check it out then. Let's have a quick drink in the Club Lounge and get some kip.'

Richard's intuition had been correct, Captain Mohammed had left no such message and the meeting was still scheduled for nine-thirty.

Their Indian taxi driver needed frequent directions to the Al Rashid Tower block, the venue for their meeting with the General Ahmed and his staff. Despite Dubai's excellent road system, once they reached the busy downtown area near the Creek, traffic was reduced to a crawl. Richard had allowed for this and they still had time to take coffee in a small café in the Al Rashid building before taking the express lift to the twentieth floor for their scheduled meeting.

When they arrived in the office suite, four of the General's trusted officers were camped out in the Reception area. Richard had just finished making the necessary introductions, when the Army Commander bustled in. General Ahmed had an immense amount of energy, worked night and day and was always rushing from one meeting to the next. Despite this, he'd the ability to switch his mind rapidly to the topic of the moment and possessed a memory that any elephant would envy. His greeting was warm and sincere and they soon adjourned to the Conference Room for Clive's presentation.

After observing the Arab ritual of talking trivialities for several minutes before discussing business, Clive was invited to make his presentation. He may well have been seriously henpecked at home but when briefing on technical matters he was confident, outgoing and assertive. If only Annie could see him now. His presentation was, as usual, first rate. He took a number of searching questions in his stride and it was evident from their reaction, he'd clearly earned the confidence of his audience.

Richard was not surprised that the General declined an offer to lunch. On principle, he'd never accept even the smallest favour from any potential contractor. He departed with his team, thanking them with open sincerity for their useful discussions and Clive's excellent briefing.

They were making their way back to the hotel, when Richard's mobile rang.

'Hi Richard, heard you're in town. Finger firmly on the local pulse and all that. Actually, came up from Abu Dhabi crack of sparrows today. Should be free about one. Can we meet?'

'Sure Bob. We're on our way back to the Crowne Plaza. How about joining us for lunch in the Italian?

'Great. Fancy a spag-bol. One 'tis. See you then.'

Richard pocketed his phone. 'That was Colonel Bob Archer. He's the Defence Attaché up from Abu Dhabi. I'd better explain. UAE is the only country in the world with two British Embassies, but there's only one Ambassador and one DA. So, Bob travels up once a week to brief the Consul General in Dubai. He's a bit quaint but very pleasant and has a good grip on what's happening around and about.'

Colonel Bob was punctual, as always. The small Italian coffee shop was busy, packed with an assortment of businessmen in lightweight suits, casually dressed tourists and a number of Arabs in their sparkling white dish-dashes.

'Thanks for joining us Bob. It's always good to see you and we do need to catch up on the changes here. I'd also value your views on how the Air Defence competition is going. This is Clive Deacon; by the way, he's the brains behind our visit.'

'Always ready for a lunch, courtesy of *AGC*. Welcome to the heat, Clive. I've heard good things about you on the grapevine.'

They ordered and Bob dropped his voice to avoid being overheard by the adjacent diners. 'I believe the Frogs are up to their tricks again.'

Richard nodded and told him about the airline cancellation and the spurious note at the hotel. 'What else have they been up to then Bob?'

'Oh, the usual. They've been spreading gossip about the problems with your radars in Oman and the UK. Claim they have a lead of one year on the design. I think their agents have bought a copy of your early technical drafts so they'll have their technocrats pulling that apart looking for information and any weaknesses. On the political front, they're bringing in some high ranking Ministers to make extravagant claims about *Elsa* and offering favours of special technology transfer.'

'All's fair in love and competitive defence contracting then.'

'Yes Richard, but I have to say they're good at the wheeler dealing. We Brits could learn a lot from them. When we're playing cricket, they are majoring in karate. HMG sent eight different Ministers out in the last year and most of them couldn't spell radar. I also think the majority of them had to consult a map to find UAE before they came anyway.'

'That good eh. What can we do?'

'Not much really, except more of what you're doing

now. Play it with a straight bat. Continue keeping the customer informed – including any problems you find. I'll wind the Ambassador up and see if we can improve our political lobby.'

'Much as I thought Bob, but thanks for the information.'

'Just one more thing. Picked up from one of the French Embassy staff that *Elsa*'s having serious problems with their new Air Defence installation in Turkey. Thought you might like to know that.'

'Thanks Bob, that is good news.'

'Now, if you have the time, come down to Abu Dhabi and brief the Ambo – I'm sure he'd appreciate it and we haven't seen you down in the Capital for a few months. He's holding a Reception in his garden tomorrow evening. You're both invited of course. Anyway, that's it. Let's talk about happier things. . How's your love life these days Richard? Still a shambles?'

By the time Richard and Clive arrived at the receiving line for the Ambassador's Reception, there were already several guests sipping cocktails in the large and well-groomed garden. The area had been skilfully illuminated with a combination of small floodlights strategically placed amongst the shrubs and some white fairy lights hanging from the branches of the taller trees.

'Thanks for the briefing today; it was timely and most useful.' Her Britannic Majesty's Ambassador, Phillip Gray, shook their hands cordially. 'I'll do everything I can to improve the UK lobby.'

Richard pecked Helen Gray on both cheeks. 'Looking as delightful as ever,' he remarked with honesty. He really liked Helen and they had frequently found some light relief in each other's company during the more boring of Embassy functions.

'Richard, it's been so long. I thought you'd abandoned me. Enjoy the party and make sure you find some time for me during the evening.'

Just before descending the few steps into the garden, Richard scanned the assembled guests. 'Ah Clive, there's Squadron Leader Alan Elliott, one of the Brit exchange officers, come and meet him.'

'God. It's Richard Bryant. Who let you in? I thought this was a high class do.'

'Nice to see you too Alan. Can't be high class or you wouldn't be here. This is our radar expert, Clive Deacon.'

'Richard looking after you OK? Dragged you into any bad places yet?'

They talked about their visit, the problems with the French, Alan's hobby of driving along old riverbeds, or wadi bashing as he called it, and girls.

'So how's your situation with the fair sex, Richard? Still a bloody disaster?'

'Time to leave this man.' Richard steered Clive to meet a gathering from the British Business Group. Just as he completed the introductions, Richard was amazed to see none other than the Fox, leering over the embassy beauty and communications officer, Zoë Clark. Richard really liked Zoë too. And there she was, being verbally and visually abused by this lowlife Frog. Latour was the personification of the clichéd Frenchman. He was a short, swarthy figure with piggy eyes, an equine nose and walrus moustache. Richard thought he looked like the classic French onion seller. Henri had tried hard during the last few years to perfect his English. But he had been raised in the belief that English was a barbaric language and had avoided using its guttural tones until forced by the necessity of a career in international sales. So when he became flustered, angry or excited he would lapse into Franglaise This deficiency, together with the hundred years war, Nelson, the Channel tunnel and British food did much to contribute to Latour's hatred of the arrogant, warmongering English.

Some five minutes later Richard felt a cold clammy hand on his arm. 'Mon ami. I'm so surprised to zee you in zee Emirates. Don't you know they 'ave already selected our *EL97* for zeir Air Defence Requirement? Or perhaps you are here trying to sell something else now?'

'Henri. I'm just as surprised to see you. I thought you'd be in Turkey sorting out your failures of the AD system you supplied them?'

'It eez no problem. You 'ave been meesinformed. The Turkeez know our systems are zee best in zee world. Now tell me Richard, you're a man of zee world. Why eez it you're lovely English girls prefer we French? Eez it because the British are such poor loovers?'

'Sorry Henri you're mistaken. Our girls are friendly to just everyone and everything. You know how much the English even love their animals. Of course, some people are not used to being treated so hospitably. They often read far too much into the charms and considerate good manners of our girls and get the wrong message. So anyway my friend, how is Madam Latour and your four enfants?'

Richard knew full well how much Latour envied his freedom, imagining that he bedded a different female every night. Let him stew, he thought. They continued their barbed game of verbal tennis until Henri retired, slightly injured to skulk in a corner in an attempt to find some solace with the French Attaché and his lady companion.

Richard looked to see how Clive was coping with the Business Group but need not have worried. Clive had supped several glasses of champagne and was confidently entertaining the businessmen with stories and jokes. If only Annie… This time, he felt a warm, affectionate, delicate hand gently tug his arm.

'Hello Ricky. You didn't let me know you were in town.'

'Zoë. I was just going to look for you. I'm really

supposed to be in Dubai but we came down to brief the Ambo today and stayed over for the Reception.'

'We?'

'Yes I've got an engineer in tow. He's fine but likes to be in bed by eleven.'

'Sounds just like you Rick.'

'Oh, very droll. He likes to sleep alone. And, by the way, I thought you were a discerning lady. Half an hour ago I saw you gazing longingly into the eyes of Henri Latour and hanging on his every word.'

'You know I'm putty in his hands. Come on, you know I can't stand the chap. Just doing my diplomatic duty. But he did invite me to the jazz club later tonight.'

'And?'

'Why Ricky, I do believe you're jealous. I said I was going out with you tonight.'

'Well done Zoë. Where shall we go?'

'Thought we'd go and taunt him at a table for two in the jazz club.'

Clive was content to 'call it a night' immediately after the reception and took a taxi back to the hotel. Richard and Zoë found a table at the jazz club where they flirted outrageously, paying only slight attention to the professional South African jazz quartet syncopating a few yards away. They were slightly aware of the presence of a bored Henri Latour seated at a corner table with three swarthy males and made a special effort to ensure he could see what an enjoyable time they were having. Zoë was a compact, twenty five year old, attractive Liverpudlian redhead who took life by the throat and clearly enjoyed her single status. She had an army of admirers but showed no sign of becoming hitched to any of them. Richard enjoyed her company immensely. He especially enjoyed the part when they always went back to her flat for a nightcap and ended up in bed together. Zoë was a willing, experienced, talented and energetic lover.

The remainder of their visit went much according to plan. Back in Dubai, they met with the General Manager of the *AGC* local support company and had several lengthy discussions with the Army technocrats. During their off duty time, they sampled both the high and low life of the vibrant modern city which is still in the process of defining its new identity. Clive made five visits to the *Gold Souq* and three to the *City Centre* shopping mall to purchase sufficient placatory trinkets.

.

Chapter Four

It was almost noon on Sunday when Richard arrived back at his Farnham flat. The lovely Becky was listening to the latest Shania Twain album and reading Michael Crichton's *Disclosure*.

'Hi there sweetie, you're back early,' she beamed as he opened the door.

'Hi Bex. Couldn't wait to see you. Oh, that's an interesting book you're reading. Would you like to try the plot out on Paul Hamilton for me?'

'I don't think so somehow. I'd rather have my tongue nailed to the floor and set on fire with a blowtorch. How was your trip? Bonk anyone I know?'

'Becky! What do you think I'm like? Of course I didn't. Absolutely no one you could possibly know. Any plans for today?'

'No. Had a girlies night out last night. Drank too much, ended up in a club. Male stripper and all that. Drank some more. Threw up. Apparently Sandra made sure I got home safely and I slept over there on the rug next to the bookcase.'

'I can see I shouldn't leave you home alone. Got enough energy for a Chinese tonight Bex?'

'Sure, providing she's young and gorgeous.'

'Ha bloody ha. I'm talking about eating at *The Peking Duck*.'

'Love to. But a quiet evening please. Just one bottle between us – OK?'

Richard emptied most of the contents of his luggage

into the washing machine. They watched the video of Bridget Jones's Diary. He accused Becky of being as dippy as Ms Jones. She told him he behaved like the guy who Hugh Grant played – sex mad and hopeless at it.

The Peking Duck was upmarket compared with most Chinese restaurants in the UK. The lighting was subdued, the music soft (Western rather than Yingtong) and the food light and delicately flavoured. They shared a crispy duck starter and then picked over a 'Meal for Two' sampler Menu. On delivery of the third bottle of wine, they both resolved it to be their last. They laughed some more about Bridget Jones then Becky interrogated Richard relentlessly about his escapades in the Emirates. Half way through the fourth bottle, Richard admitted to the existence of a Zoë. He was then under extreme duress to provide the most minuscule and private details of their night together.

'So this is how you get your kicks young lady?'

What a pity Bex thought of him as the brother that she never had.

Paul Hamilton was always at his most unpleasant on Monday mornings. It was as if he had spent the whole weekend psyching himself up to vent his spleen on anyone who might dare challenge his thin veneer of competence. He thought that 'young Bryant' was a particular good target for harassment. Paul never really understood Richard and was convinced that he did not put enough effort into his work. He knew Richard rarely stayed in the office late and never appeared stressed? And he was always tripping off to here, there and everywhere. However, he did manage to get his work done so well and on time. Paul was also completely confused by the odd assortment of girls Richard squired around and wondered what on earth they ever saw in him.

Sad Mr Hamilton on the other hand, ate, lived and slept work to keep his head barely above water. He was forced to slave long hours to deal inadequately with his workload. His daily struggle was primarily caused by his inability to prioritise anything or even discard what was obviously superfluous information. He prevaricated over anything that looked difficult or begged a decision. Thus, Paul's in tray grew larger by the day until, eventually, panic set in and he farmed it out randomly to his unfortunate subordinates.

Paul was also ill at ease in female company. Women completely bewildered him. This frequently brought out the most hostile and unpleasant facets of his disagreeable character as he taunted and bullied, in an attempt to hide this insecurity. Despite his unfortunate nature, he had been married for over twenty years to an absolute star, Sarah who should have won several Oscars for her regular appearances in the role of the cheerful, uncomplaining wife. In sharp contrast, the convivial, easygoing, fun-loving Richard could only keep his spouse for three days. Where was justice?

By eleven Paul had reduced his PA, Pat, to tears. If Pat hadn't been desperate for the job, she would have quit when she was assigned to Paul in his new role as Marketing Director some three months before. She suspected that the more experienced PAs had dived for cover when they heard of the vacancy.

Paul had just bawled her out for accepting a meeting for him with the Chairman on a day he had planned to be somewhere else. In fact, the fault was entirely Paul's, as he had not deigned to tell her about a prearranged appointment at Twickenham

'Pat get me Bryant on the phone.'

Paul then disappeared for five minutes whilst Richard did his best to placate Pat and then switched to speakerphone to await Paul's return.

'Hello Richard. How was the UAE? Bring the order back with you?'

Deafening silence.

'Richard are you there? Hello. Pat where is the wretched man?'

'Oh hello Paul, I thought we must have been cut off after I spoke with Pat.'

'I was asking about your holiday in the UAE.'

'Very busy. Saw all the right people. The General's got his staff drafting the tender. Our local partners are on board and the Embassy is supportive. Clive Deacon did an excellent briefing. The General seemed very happy. Oh, and it was hot.'

'I didn't ring up for a weather forecast. When are we going to get the order?

'I guess you haven't had chance to read the visit report I emailed earlier today.' Richard always produced his reports on his laptop in almost real time. Paul, on the other hand, created his several days after meetings with consequential glaring gaps and inaccuracies in the information. 'You'll see the meetings with both General Ahmed and our support company confirmed that we should expect the order in around thirty months time.'

'That's not soon enough.'

'But Paul, the Board approved the funding based on that forecast. That's also the timing the customer is stuck with. The General would not wish to admit it publicly, but that is when the Chief of Staff has phased it into the Army's budget.'

'Well, I expect you to do better and bring it forward.'

Richard admired his doodle of a dagger jutting from the Marketing Director's back.

'Hello. Are you there?'

'Yes of course. You were telling me I must try to change the Emirates' phased defence budget.'

'Don't be flippant Richard. We need to launch this product and get it on the world market.'

'I'm putting some pressure on the UK customer to

make a selection soon on the grounds that he will be able to control the specification and thereby save money. By the way, have you any comments on the revised Product Plan I sent you before I left for the UAE Paul?'

'Richard, I've a million other things to do as well as reading your Product Plan. I'll get around to it when I do. Must go now.' *Click.*

'Goodbye you old git.' Richard hoped the click was Paul replacing his receiver.

What a start to Monday morning! It could only get better from hereon.

If having a menopausal boss wasn't enough, Dave O'Leary was wearing his *even more difficult than usual* Contract Manager's hat to the point where he was starting to undermine Richard's efforts to win business. For some odd reason, it seemed that O'Leary had invited Richard to his office in order to irritate him. O'Leary was adamant that the Division should switch product development to the civil radar market. He argued that this was a more lucrative business opportunity because of the vast number of commercial airfields around the world. Richard was quick to pour cold water on his suggestion for a number of reasons. He argued that, until they completed *Aphrodite's* development, they did not have any state-of-the-art radar product. Richard also told him about the large number of strong competitors in the civil market, especially from the USA. These companies had the right infrastructure and expertise to build, sell, distribute and support such products. Richard knew that O'Leary underestimated the breadth of changes necessary to make such a major transformation. This was not surprising as he rarely left his office, let alone the site. Richard put this down to the fact that Dave O'Leary was afraid that he might find a substitute in his seat when he returned. Finally, Richard pointed out that the history books were full of companies who went out of business because they thought that the grass was greener on the other side of the fence. He contended that the way forward was to complete the development of *Aphrodite,* win the key competitions and then look for niche derivatives for selected parts of the civil market. He stressed that they would then need to find a suitable partner with background in selling and supporting civil radars.

Such logic did not convince Dave O'Leary who continued banging the drum relentlessly and calling Richard short-sighted and introspective. Richard was particularly concerned that if O'Leary continued such a campaign, it might find some senior support. He knew some of the dinosaurs in Head Office felt more comfortable dealing with civil products in preference to the unpalatable defence business. There were also those who believed that any change was preferable to taken accountability for current strategies. Penelope Field, the HR Director for one. Sir Anthony Laycock, the political lobbyist for *AGC* might believe that supporting such a campaign might detract from his apparent failure to lobby the politicians effectively. He seemed to have difficulty even getting MPs to give him an audience anyway. Fortunately, for the time being, Paul Hamilton had not yet heard O'Leary's theories; that would be tomorrow's problem. In the meantime Richard encouraged the engineers to spend or commit the approved funds as fast as they could.

Later that afternoon, Richard felt it was time to test the water again with Kate. He needed to spend an hour with Clive bouncing around a few ideas in preparation for any problems perpetrated by Messrs Hamilton and O'Leary. But first he had to listen to Clive's soliloquy on Annie.

'She really liked the presents. It was just as well really

as she had a terrible week. The washing machine had sprung a leak on Wednesday and a tyre blew on Thursday. She locked herself out of the house on Friday morning and it cost fifty pounds to get a locksmith to open the door. Oh, and she heard some strange noises on Friday night.' Poor Clive. He just couldn't win. There wasn't much hope that Annie, at age fifty-two, would change for the better. The ever-helpful Richard suggested he should consider buying a puppy to keep her company.

As he left Clive's office, he saw Kate at the coffee machine.

'Hi Kate. How's tricks?'

'Oh, hello Richard. Good to see you back from your travels. I'm fine. Fancy a cuppa at my bench?' Her greeting was enthusiastic. 'Clive said he had a good trip. I'm going to be working on the *Aphrodite* development project, so perhaps I will be able to come with you next time.'

'I'd like that very much Kate,' he lied, concerned about the prospect of having to ignore Zoë and others. 'Fancy having dinner with me tonight and brightening up my Monday? '

'Yes, of course. I'd love to.'

'Any preferences? You know Guildford better than I do.'

'Yes, my place. I'll dazzle you with my cooking. Eight OK?'

'Eight will do nicely. Look forward to it. See you later.'

It was raining again, when Richard drove by way of the A31, Hog's Back, to Guildford. The traffic was light and, due to his eagerness to see Kate, he arrived near her flat twenty minutes early. He parked the car, spent half an hour in the nearby *Swan and Signet* pub and by this means arrived at her flat with impeccable timing for dinner.

As she opened the door, he juggled awkwardly with

the huge bunch of long-stemmed carnations (he thought roses might be too intense for Kate) and three bottles of Brown Brothers Cabernet Sauvignon.

'Do we have to drink all this tonight?' Kate placed a wet lingering kiss on his lips as he struggled to return the compliment without releasing his grip on the wine.'

'Goodness no. We'll just have a glass each out of the first bottle and lay down the rest for a special occasion.'

'Well just in case, put the bottles on the cabinet next to the dining table. Perhaps you should open one and let it breath. I'll try and find a vase big enough for these beautiful flowers. Thank you so much Richard. It's a long time since I received such a thoughtful gesture.'

As he was uncorking the bottle he felt Kate's presence close behind him.

'Now then Richard, the prawn starter thingy is cooling in the fridge, the chicken casserole is heating in the oven and will take at least an hour, her voice was soft and purring. 'The cheese and biscuits are all prepared. So we'll have to think of some way of passing the time until dinner is ready.' With that, she reached forward and kissed tenderly on his neck. It was only seconds before she swiftly unbuttoned and removed his shirt and began running her hands over his naked chest. Richard tried to turn to face her but she whispered for him to stay. With one hand, she removed her top and began pressing herself against his back. Whilst still teasing his chest, she kicked off her shoes and stepped out of her miniskirt. She moved her hands lower and began brushing her hands up and down his groin. He felt his zip being opened slowly and her teasing fingers reach inside. By now she was swaying against him and whimpering softly.

Unable to resist her further, Richard turned and began kissing her eagerly on the lips. They sank slowly to the floor where they made love, driven by what had become obsessive desire. Two bemused Burmese cats looked on but soon became bored and returned to the kitchen to guard the cooker.

Kate proved to be a proficient lover but average cook. Her runny prawn creation had been overdosed with lemon and the casserole was bland. He nevertheless thoroughly enjoyed her easy company, Wagner's *Lohengin* playing softly in the background, the selection of continental cheeses and the Aussie Cabernet. He discovered that her father had been a high-flying member of the Diplomatic Corps. She'd been sent to boarding school from the age of seven, spending her vacations in odd, often inhospitable, corners of the globe. Her academic career was also unusual, achieving a first in English Literature, Physics and Sociology.

Thank you Kate.' He helped her to stack the dishes. 'That was wonderful.' He carefully omitted to say what '*that*' was.

'It's been all my pleasure,' she replied throwing her arms around him and kissing him in that expectant way again.

The woman's insatiable, thought Richard, as he decided that it would be unkind and churlish to refuse such an enthusiastic advance.

'You look knackered.'

'Thanks Becky, I think the prawns disagreed with me.'

'Seems to me that you and Kate are becoming an entity.' Becky's voice was mocking and light but with a slight undertone of disapproval. Only someone who knew her as well as Richard could have detected the hidden message but he decided this was not the right time to pursue the reason for her censure.

'Now you know me better than that Bex. And neither is Kate interested in a relationship.'

'Yeh, yeh. And I'm Mary Poppins. Oh look there's another pink elephant flying past our window.'

'Come on, I thought I was giving you a lift to work today.'

'I'm ready. After all I had eight hours sleep last night. Do try and get that soppy self satisfied look off your face before we get to the office.'

The journey was stop-start as they reached the busy outskirts of Farnborough.

'See they've started getting ready already for the Air Show. It'll be chaos around here in four month's time and we'll be part of it.' Becky's job as the PR manager in *AGC* carried with it the burden of planning, organising and attending the major defence exhibitions.

'I hate Farnborough week,' she added. 'It's always so intense with all the Company bigwigs putting their oar in. They're always changing their minds and bringing unscheduled guests into the busy chalet and demanding lunch. And then there's the exhibition stand. As if you can please everybody. Last ti…'

'Bex, please. It's not for another four months. Talk about something nice.'

'Well, there's this girl in engineering called Kate …'

'But she is nice, Bex. Her cooking isn't exactly haute cuisine but she's extremely good company, we've similar interests…'

'Oh she's a tart too then. And, don't tell me Ritchie, and bonks like a bunny rabbit.'

'If you've not tried it, don't knock it. I can't wait to drop you off at the site today beautiful lady. Remind me never to give you the moral high ground ever again.' He reached across and fondly squeezed her hand.' To his surprise, Becky held on to his hand and planted a lingering kiss on his cheek. He heard the toot of a car horn from behind and realised that the traffic light had turned to green.

'I think you ought to see this memo before you do

anything else.' Liz Jarvis had been the Marketing department's secretary since Pontius was a pilot. She treated Richard like a son and protected him accordingly. 'I'll get your coffee. Did you sleep last night? You do look a bit tired and drawn today.'

'Thanks Liz. Black will be fine.' He picked up the two-page memo and began reading. Half of the first page just contained addressees – most of the Board members including, of course, Paul Hamilton and Lady Penelope, Sir Anthony Laycock, Harry Black (Engineering Director), most of the finance department, operations, logistic support and uncle Tom Cobbly and all.

From – David P O'Leary
Subject – Aphrodite Funding.

Richard read quickly – Believed the Board of *AGC* plc had been misled to approve the funding of ten million pounds. This memo sets out to outline an alternative outline strategy… greater benefit to the business… switch to civil product development… huge potential… worldwide market… defence market receding… blah, blah, blah.

'What a load of cobblers.' Richard dropped the memo onto his desk in disgust as Liz placed the mug of coffee on his desk.

'He does seem to be trying to spread his influence, that Mr O'Leary, doesn't he? And him writing to all those important people like that. And it's your programme Richard.' Liz was the mistress of the understatement.

'Well that will set the moggy amongst the pigeons Liz. If Paul Hamilton rings, I've thrown myself off Tower Bridge or emigrated to Australia, or both.'

As he sipped his coffee, Richard contemplated the options. Should he wait to defend his position? Should he go and talk to Dave O'Leary again? No, he decided, attack is the best form of defence. He would write to the same addressees pointing out the glaring holes in the supercilious Contract Manager's arguments. He would draw their attention to all the reasoned arguments in the Product Plan and give examples of the many recent failures in civil diversification.

Richard knew his subject well and it only took him half an hour to finish the first draft. 'I'm off to engineering,' he called to Liz as he was leaving the office. ' I'll be with Clive Deacon. Back in an hour.'

'Have you seen this?' Richard waved O'Leary's memo at Clive.

'No, I don't think so. What is it?'

'Have a look Clive. Tell me what you think.'

Clive read the memo slowly and painstakingly whilst Richard sat on the edge of his seat.

Eventually, Clive placed the memo on the desk. 'I guess this will reopen the whole question of *Aphrodite* funding.'

'That's putting it mildly Clive. There are a few people who'll have a field day on this one. It'll give them a new purpose in life – let's screw up the core Radar business that it has taken *AGC* thirty years to achieve their market dominance. So what does O'Leary want us to do? Just challenge the American and European companies who have donkey's years of experience in the civil market and we'll be using military standard components which cost ten times as much. We'll then apply unproven technology, an unsuitable manufacturing base and distribution system and all this with absolutely no knowledge of the customer and his real requirements.'

'Well yes, it would be a bit difficult to change.' The seriousness of the memo had not yet fully captured Clive's crusading spirit.

'Difficult! I thought you would be as damned upset as I am when someone with no brains and a stupid grin starts meddling like this in our patch.'

'Well… yes… I…'

'Have a look at this Clive. It's still only a rough draft

and I'd be grateful if I could have your inputs. I plan to send it out to all the addressees by e-mail marked URGENT by mid morning.'

'Isn't that rushing things a bit?'

'No, we need to head off the problem in its infancy. Someone has to tell the Board the truth. We've made military radars for thirty years. We are good at designing and manufacturing military radars. Our core business and customer base is... yes, military radars. There's a damn good market out there for...'

'You're right Richard. I'll get a few of my guys together here and we'll try and give you as much technical ammo as possible. See you in about an hour.'

Within the hour, Clive arrived at Richard's office with a number of technical arguments to add as an attachment to the draft. Richard quickly made the revisions and produced a final copy on e-mail. He made one last check of the address list and text and hit *SEND*. All he could do now was to sit back and wait to see their reaction.

.

Chapter Five

It took two days before most of the addressees woke up to the content of Dave O'Leary and Richard's missives. Someone must have eventually alerted Paul Hamilton, because on Wednesday morning he called Richard. This, in itself, was unusual as he rarely dialled a number, preferring to delegate such a menial task to others.

'Now Richard, have you seen the diversification memo from Dave O'Leary? It seems to me he is making some pretty valid points.'

'But Paul, have you read mine? I've already countered all of his spurious arguments. O'Leary's merely trying to cash in on the popular myth that changing from defence to civil products is simple and would produce instantaneous results. He ignores the numerous competitors in the new market. He has no sales background and seldom meets customers, except to upset them by niggling over trifling points in the contracts. Speaking as the one who has responsibility of selling our products, I contend his memo is full of flawed logic and subjective nonsense…'

'Richard stop. Why are you so negative? I can tell you now that some of the Board members are taking this very seriously…'

'Yes, Penelope Field, Sir Anthony, the Product Support Dir…'

'Let me finish. The Board members are taking this very seriously so it's not just a case of calling it nonsense. We have to do a proper appraisal.'

Richard lit a Davidoff.

'Hello. Hello. Richard are you still there?'

'Of course Paul, I was waiting for you to finish. What form will this appraisal take; the one *we* are going to produce?'

'Well, that'll need careful thought. I'll call you again in a few days when I've had more discussions this end.'

'Before you do that, I'd like to bring Clive Deacon along to your office so we can thrash out the technical and sales aspects. So we can all sing from the same hymn sheet. I need your backing on this one Paul if we are going to meet future order intake budgets.'

'I suppose so. But I can't possibly see you today. I've some visitors from *Jane's Defence Magazine* this afternoon. Come tomorrow at eight.' *Click.*

Following the click, Richard made a typical caustic comment and then called Clive to tell him the good news.

'Pick you up at six then Clive. Bring all the bumph and your sense of humour – you'll need it.'

Richard and Clive arrived at Paul's outer office at five to eight. Paul turned up at ten to nine.

'Oh good, you're already here then. You'd better come in. Pat sort out some coffee, I'm parched. Now you'll have to make this quick as I've another meeting at ten.'

Richard led. 'You've seen the memos. Where would you like us to start?'

'Well. At the beginning of course. Tell me why you're so opposed to O'Leary's ideas and why you don't believe they are workable. At least he's thinking laterally about our business. He doesn't just drift on in the same old tin pot way. Pat, get me Roger Benton on the phone.'

'So Paul, I'll run through the eleven points on my memo. Then I'll hand over to Clive to fill in the technical bits.'

'Right, just don't be negative... hang on. Oh. Hi Roger, how are you? Yes, I'm just calling to say that Sarah and I would love to come for the weekend. Yes, I'll bring my clubs. I'll leave early on Friday…' Paul talked for over five minutes before firmly replacing the receiver. 'Right then, crack on; we haven't got much time. Where's the coffee Pat. Are you growing the beans?'

'I've just brewed you a fresh pot Mr Hamilton and I've put a few biscuits on the tray.'

'Right, close the door. If Penelope Field or Sir Anthony call, put them through.'

It was difficult to present logical arguments with Paul periodically going off at wild tangents. It soon became clear that he'd a sneaking respect for O'Leary as if he saw in him the wide boy and shallow rebel he could admire. To avoid making any decisions, Paul decided he should accompany Richard to see their two potential launch clients – the Royal Air Force and the Emirates. Now Richard was not bothered at the prospect of taking Paul to meetings in London but the thought of spending several days with him in the Emirates…

'Just fit it in with my diary and sort out the programme with Pat. Anyway, my visitor arrives in five minutes so that's it then. Meeting closed. Think laterally. Don't just defend your corner.' And with that, they were abruptly and summarily dismissed.

'Can you take the train back please, Clive, I'm off to have a heads up with Wing Commander Ian Tucker at the RAF's Procurement Branch. I need to carry out a damage limitation exercise before I take Paul to meet his boss.'

MoD(PE) Rad 2 appeared in black lettering on a pine plinth screwed unevenly to the open door of Ian Tucker's office.

Without lifting his eyes from a salmon pink file on his desk, he called to Richard, 'Come on in you old scoundrel. S'pose you're meeting a bird later and you're just using me to fill in an hour as usual.'

'You're just jealous 'cos your wife lives in Northwood and you have to go home every night after work.'

'Anyway Richard, very pleased to see you again. How was Dubai? Get your leg over? How was the General? Fancy a coffee?'

'Hot, possibly, fine and yes please, NATO standard with one sugar.'

Such was the strength of their relationship, that Richard was able to tell Ian openly about his problems and Paul's intended visit to his boss.

'Oh, so pious, procrastinating Paul is going to pay us a visit. Don't you worry; the boss and I will take care of him. Ted doesn't rate Paul much either. He'll reassure him again that we plan to place the contract in about eighteen months and of our overwhelming confidence in *AGC* etcetera, etcetera. Frankly Richard, we wouldn't be at all happy if your company switched your products to civil market. We must give work to British companies so they will continue to support research. So leave it with me. Anyway, how's your personal life; still a mess?'

'Hi Becky. How was your day?'

`Really good. I'm going to be the publicity manager for the Asian Aerospace Exhibition in Singapore next month. You'll be going won't you?'

'Too right Hun. It's my favourite. I love Singapore and something delicious has happened to me every time I've been there.'

'Oh you must tell me more. Have you eaten?'

'Nope. Let's send out for a Pizza?'

'Great minds. Hawaiian I think, what about you?'

'Boring old Margarita please.'

'Right, you open the wine. I'll call Giovanni.'

Under extreme duress and after their second bottle, Richard admitted to having a fling with a Filipina singer on his first visit to Singapore. She sang like a bird and made love like a rattlesnake. On the next visit he met this Malaysian waitress who liked to give him second helpings of everything.

'Still collecting flags of the world then Richard.'

'I never really set out to. It's just that…'

'Richard. This is me, Becky you're talking to. Don't put on this air of innocence – I was just sitting there, minding my own business, when crash, bang, wallop, suddenly out of thin air this gorgeous creature appeared…'

'Now then young lady, how come you know so much about this subject? You told me you weren't into that sort of nonsense.'

'Good point. But nothing in life is that straightforward. You still don't know everything about me Richard. Don't judge a book by its cover and all that. Perhaps, one day… really good Pizza this. Quite warm for the time of year isn't it? Read any good books lately?'

Richard was about to leave the office when, what he thought must be the ghost of Dave O'Leary appeared at his door. He choked back his initial reaction, to enquire if the apparition had lost his way and needed directions.

'Well Dave, this is a surprise. Have you come to see me?'

'Yeh, your boss said I should come over and see if I could persuade you to take a more sensible line on this diversification thing.' His accent was broad Essex. Richard studied the lolling stocky, mid-twentyish, figure. He observed the blank stare in his piggy eyes, the mocking downturn of his mouth, the pretentious quiff in his hair, his whole demeanour and body language – that all shrieked *supercilious*.

'Won't you come in. I'll make a coffee or tea if you wish?'

'Na, shouldn't take long. Anyways, I've got a job interview at six.'

'Oh, are you leaving us Dave?'

'Na, course not. I mean to say I'm interviewing for a new Contracts Assistant.'

The fact that Dave always seemed to have several staff vacancies and was forever interviewing for replacements, spoke volumes about his mismanagement style.

'So what are we going to do about it then, Richard?'

'Do about what, Dave?'

'Well, you know, about stopping us wasting money on *Aphrodite* and getting into the more lucrative civil market. All the airports. There's 'undreds of them, all over the world.'

'Come on Dave. You know my views. *Aphrodite* is the right product for the market and in the right timescale. It's the market we know and the Company has been successful in for over thirty years. The UK defence budget may have been cut back a little, but they still spend billions on equipment. The new area radar project is high on that list…'

They went around the buoy several times until O'Leary, believing he had carried out Paul's edict, left abruptly to attempt to sweet talk some poor, unsuspecting and unfortunate candidate into joining his department.

That evening, Richard drove to Guildford for a pre-bonding meal with Kate in a smart but cosy Italian Trattoria. He really couldn't believe his good fortune. He was guaranteed a hot bed for the night. Kate never pried into his other conquests or relationships. She never nagged and always seemed relaxed and in good humour. Above all, she put her all-embracing, vigorous, enthusiasm into everything she did. This girl was too good to be true.

Now that he knew her better, Richard felt he could safely broach the subject of spending a mucky weekend together, without making it sound too much like the dreaded word *relationship*. So over dinner he suggested they spent the following weekend together in Amsterdam.

'That would be super Richard. D'you know, I've never been there. I hear it's very lively and just about anything goes.'

'I've been several times on business but never with a pretty lady.'

'Must be the only place left then Richard.'

They spent the rest of the evening and night, in what was by now an extremely predictable way. This time, however, their lovemaking exhibited the added zest of exhilaration and anticipation over the weekend ahead.

It was a particularly stormy Thursday evening when a rain-soaked Richard burst into the flat.

'What a day, Bex. I'm soaked. Had to park half way to Alton. They really should do something about the parking around here.'

'So not so good eh? Come and sit down and tell Auntie Becky all.'

'You'd never believe it. You know I planned this wonderful weekend away with Kate.'

'You mean the dirty weekend in the sex capital of the world?'

'Yes, yes hilarious. And you know, I've paid for the tickets and the hotel and everything. Well, you wouldn't believe it, but she came to my office today to tell me that bloody Marvin is on the scene again and wants to make a fresh start. So that's it. Over. Finito. Caput. And about four hundred pounds down the drain.'

'Why don't you still go?'

'Oh come on Bex. I really don't fancy that. I'd be miserable.'

'I'll come with you if you like.'

'Would you really? Are you serious?'

'Of course, Richard. I never joke about a free holiday I've never been to Amsterdam. And besides, I'm sure we'll

60

have fun.'

'But I've already booked one cosy room with a double bed.'

'We'll manage. I'll borrow my grandmother's bolster to put between us.'

'You're a poppet Bex. I don't know what I'd do without you sometimes.'

'Yeh, well I might get stood up one day; but I guess you wouldn't mind that. Just shut the flip up whinging and open a bottle of wine.'

Before leaving for Amsterdam, Richard had the pleasure of joining Paul for their meeting with Group Captain Ted Green at the Ministry. Ted was a broad Lancastrian of the 'call a spade a bloody shovel' persuasion.

'Come right in you two. Don't stand on ceremony. The coffee's instant and milk's plastic, but after all, this is the MoD.'

Richard deliberately left all the talking to Paul, who felt acutely out of place in the Ministry of Defence. This made him obviously ill at ease and twitchier than ever.

'Well Ted, we really appreciate you giving us your valuable time like this and I always... how's your lovely lady wife... golf handicap... Hope you will be able to visit *AGC* at the site...' Richard cringed at Paul's uneasy and rambling opening.

'Yes the wife's fine thanks. Well, she was te last time I saw her. Her chain te kitchen sink is titanium ye see. Now, you want an update on t'e Radar programme I gather?'

'Well, we would appreciate that very much. The Board is concerned...'

'Ye don't have te worry lad. T'e programme's under control. Bean counters have agreed budget. It's in Long Term Costings. Customer needs it. Contract in eighteen months I should say. About time I should leave this stupid job and join t'e real world again.'

Paul continued to ask the same question in several different ways. Thankfully, the torture was over in half an hour. Paul overdid the fond farewells and insisted Richard joined him for a 'wash-up' in a nearby café before they went their separate ways. Richard was convinced from Paul's account of what Ted had told them, that they had clearly attended different meetings.

It was early on sunny Saturday morning when Richard and Bex arrived at the Den Helder Hotel, a ten-minute walk from the Amsterdam Centrum. The Den Helder was a small, family run hotel on five storeys with just four bedrooms on each floor. They were able to occupy their 'room at the top' immediately and were both enchanted by its quaint, olde-worlde charm. The furniture, prints and pottery were classical Dutch. The curtains and heavy bedding were of bright white linen. The overall effect was just perfect for a weekend affair of the heart. He looked across at Bex 'the untouchable'. This might completely destroy his reputation but he wouldn't let it spoil the weekend.

Becky suggested they invest in a canal trip to get the feel of the place,

'Good idea and the weather's perfect – but I can't go along with the view that it's an *investment*. That's a salesman's word – it's a *spend*.'

'Yes Richard, but this one's definitely on me. So its an investment!'

'Well in that case, that's definitely an investment.'

Following this early morning philosophical discussion, they set out to investigate Amsterdam. After the cruise they must have hiked around most of the City. Bex was keen to visit the super-deluxe department store, Magna Plaza but fortunately did not find any worthy investments. They visited the Torture Museum, which revealed Becky's hidden sadistic nature, particularly when genitalia formed part of the plot. They took lunch in a canal side café and then set off to see the Dutch Masters in the *Rijksmuseum* and *VanGogh* Galleries. They queued for forty minutes to view Anne Frank's House. So it was late afternoon when the happy and exhausted pair returned to the hotel by way of the *Bloemenmarkt* where Richard bought Becky an enormous bouquet of flowers. The sight of sheer pleasure in her eyes and smile that beamed from ear to ear more than rewarded him.

It turned out that Richard had invested in two bottles of bubbly at the Duty Free, which they emptied before setting off for their evening's adventure. They lingered over an Indonesian meal and two bottles of rough Australian red at the *Bandung* restaurant then left to sample the city's nightlife. Predictably, they followed the footsteps of all inquisitive visitors and walked the canal-side red light district. They both remarked on how dishy many of the girls looked. By the third circuit it was past eleven and Becky admitted she really wanted to see a live sex show. They bought tickets for the next performance and whiled away the hour's wait in a crowded nearby bar which reeked of cigarette smoke and marijuana. By the time they left the bar, they both felt a little high. The theatre held about two hundred patrons seated in plush red armchairs. Some department store muzak wafted from the surround sound system. Drinks were served from trays similar to those used by ice cream vendors at more conventional shows. There was a choice – beer or wine. Bex made the mistake of choosing wine, which she said tasted like blackcurrant-flavoured vinegar.

The auditorium lights dimmed. The curtains were drawn back to the background music of Götterdammerung to reveal a scantily leather clad Brünnhilde. Soon Siegfried enters with horned helmet and little else to woo and then beds the fair maiden, much to Becky's amusement, to the *Ride* of the Valkyries. Between each act there was a short intermission to allow noisy scene changing. There followed escapades of doctors and nurses, Tarzan and Jane, master and slave and a few others.

'But they never finish,' complained Becky loudly after one cameo.

'Bex, they do five shows a night. If they finished there'd be nothing to see by the third performance.'

It was one in the morning when the couple, still laughing uncontrollably as they recalled the many humorous parts of the show, reached their hotel room. Becky went to change in the bathroom whilst Richard slipped into the small double bed in a pair of boxer shorts. He smiled to himself when she reappeared in a large tee shirt, boxers and football socks.

'That the latest birth control Bex?'

'The socks?'

'No the whole lot. You needn't worry, I've had far too much to drink to molest anyone tonight.'

What was true at one o'clock in the morning became slow torture when he awoke at eight with Becky's warm body close to his. She looked even more innocent and vulnerable asleep. Richard reflected on his appalling track record with his women. He knew he was no Brad Pitt but was fairly sure he looked younger and better than Jack Nicholson in *As Good as it Gets*. And the birds still cooed over good old Jack. Just a week ago, he remembered how Kate had been all over him like glue. But their beautiful arrangement had been snuffed out as quickly as it began – and by a *Marvin* of all things. Then there was his ex – Maggie who after such a whirlwind start… his mind continued to wander when he was aware of Bex stirring slightly. As she turned over, her arm came to rest across his naked waist. This was too much! He felt he was losing control. Here he was in Amsterdam, on Sunday morning, in bed with a gorgeous, stimulating but impregnable beauty. He gazed longingly at the desirable Bex, his mentor, his favourite person, his closest friend. After five minutes, he could stand it no longer and eased himself reluctantly from under her arm and took a lengthy and very cold shower.

'Richard, Wing Commander Tucker's on the line,' Liz called from the next office.

'Got it,' he shouted. 'Thanks.'

'Hi Ian, you're in early. Boss having a purge?'

'Something like that. We've got a bit of a flap on with budgets again. You know, more revisions and cuts. I am pretty sure that the Radar requirement will not be one of the sacrificial lambs this time.'

'That's a relief so soon after our last meeting.'

'But I really rang to say we've received an interesting document attacking *Aphrodite* yesterday. It's about four pages of alleged deficiencies. I'll fax you a copy if you stand by the machine to make sure no one else picks it up.'

'Sure, I'll go there as soon as we finish. Do you know who sent it?

'No but I guess it's Frog anonymous. Who else would do such a thing? Look, I assure you, we really don't believe any of this stuff but you need to give me all the necessary ammo to head off any disbelievers here. Don't mention the document when you reply. Just write to me as if it's a routine progress report on the *Aphrodite* development. Just make sure it covers all the points in the fax, but in a different order, of course.'

'Grateful as always Ian. Will go straight to the fax now and ring you back when I have it.'

'See you soon, Richard. Good luck.'

'Thanks Ian. I'll buy you lunch next time I'm in town.'

Two minutes later, the document appeared on the fax machine Richard rapidly scanned the pages. *Aphrodite*... early development. Unproven technology... sensitivity of antenna units low... high noise factor...inadequate deinterleaving algorithms. Just as he had expected. Latour was trying to put them on the defensive despite the glaring inaccuracy of the accusations. He made two copies of the offending document and made his way to see Clive.

'Morning Clive, not planning a quiet day, I hope. The Fox has been up to his tricks again.'

Clive read the contents laboriously, pondering over each of the accusations. After Richard had sat quietly for ten minutes, he could wait no longer.

'So Clive, what do you think? Can we contest all the points convincingly?'

'I'm down as far as number eight and there's absolutely no problem so far.'

After a further few minutes, Clive assured Richard that all the criticisms in the fax were unfounded and he could prepare a defensive paper within two days.

'We must assume that all our other potential customers would've received the same rubbish. So if you can give me the technical bones, I will do the marketing bit and turn it into an innocent looking progress report.'

'OK Richard, in that case, I'll give you the first draft tomorrow so you can start the marketing touch to turn hard facts into readable fiction. I guess the Sales Department have to justify its high salaries, big offices and fast cars somehow.'

'But you could always transfer across to Sales, Clive. Then you too would benefit from the wisdom and guidance of Mr Paul Hamilton.'

'Thank you Richard. Now you really are joking. I'd rather starve. And can you imagine Annie agreeing to me trotting around the world like you?'

Chapter Six

As Richard checked into the *Dubai Al-Deira Beach Resort*, he felt the heavy burden and trepidation over the week ahead. Paul's PA had sent a message to the hotel to say that Sir Anthony would also be joining Paul's visit to give some additional high-level support. High-level mischief more like, thought Richard. Just as well he had taken the precaution of travelling ahead of the duo to set up the meetings and prepare the ground.

He knew the Lebanese Marketing Director at the *Al-Deira* well and asked the receptionist to page her.

'Richard, I was expecting you. You're on the Exec floor of course and I've had you upgraded to a suite.' Hanna bustled out from the back office beaming. 'Come, let me buy you a welcome drink.'

Amazing, thought Richard. The girl's thirty-eight and looks twenty-five. As he followed her to the café-bar, he admired her waif-like figure, her flowing raven hair and slow, swaying gait. They sat on plush low chairs at a corner table. Hanna leaned forward and asked what he would like in her purring Franco-Arabic accented English.

'The usual,' grinned Richard. 'And just a Cappuccino for now.'

'Oh, I think we can manage that. Tom's on his travels again and I finish here at five, so amazingly I'm completely free tonight. How about you?'

Richard wondered how on earth husband Tom could spend so much time away from this gorgeous creature. He'd met Hanna on his previous visit. She was friendly and appeared to be lonely. They had dined and discoed and, on his last evening, had made love in her swimming pool and again in the Jacuzzi. She told him she'd spent the last six weeks with her parents in Beirut whilst Tom took a cruise around the Greek Islands.

'Just a bit of shop Hanna. I'll need a senior suite for Sir Anthony Laycock. I've already booked an Exec suite for my boss. They're both arriving on Saturday. If you value my life, can you please make sure they're especially well looked after? Both are impossible to please but it might just make their visit slightly bearable for me.'

'Of course, Richard. I'll give them my personal attention. We at the *Dubai Al-Deira*, always aim to please.'

'Oh, and believe me, Hanna, you do, you really do. But you should delegate the job of looking after them if possible. They're both really a bit of a pain in the rear.'

'I'll definitely sort something out for you, my darling. Now, why don't I meet you in the car park at, say ten past five, and we'll go for a swim at my place and we'll eat in.'

'Wonderful, Hanna. You're rapidly giving me the strength to face the week ahead.'

Much of the evening went as predicted. After several sundowners, they swam in the sixteen-metre pool which had been cooled to a pleasant twenty-five degrees. Not bad considering the shade temperature was forty-eight degrees. It was past ten o'clock when the Sri-Lankan maid served them a typical Lebanese meal. Whilst Richard ate heartily from the assortment of chilled vegetables and hot, spicy meats, Hanna merely picked at the green salad. They drank two bottles of fine *Knudsen Erath* Lebanese wine and, after the meal, lingered over several Irish coffees.

Eventually, Hanna suggested they take brandy in the lounge. She told the maid to just stack the dishwasher and then go on home to her husband. They sank into the large plush settee and savoured the warm vapour as they sipped the fine Cognac. It soon became clear to Richard that Tom had not been around for duties for several weeks. Hanna's need was clearly urgent as she kissed, teasing him with her darting tongue. She quickly unbuttoned his shirt, kissing his chest as she swiftly changed position to kneel in front of him. Within minutes she had unzipped and expertly removed his trousers and boxers and resumed her frenzied kissing of his body. Her head moved lower as her darting tongue searched and teased around his groin. Just at the point that Richard felt he was about to climax, she pulled him to the floor and held him close to her, gently stroking his hair and murmuring sweet nothings. After about five minutes, she resumed her harried tonguing, stopping again just before he climaxed. This ritual was repeated three more times before they coupled, rapidly resulting in an uncontrolled and frantic crescendo.

They lay quietly in each other's arms for an hour.

'I need a coffee, how about you?' Hanna pulled the flimsy silk dress over her head and made her way into the hall. Within seconds there was a deafening crash. Richard jumped to his feet and hurried towards the noise. Hanna was lying on her back on the stone kitchen floor, the kettle, water and broken china all around her. She was out cold.

What a quandary! Here he was with a married woman, barely covered by the brief silk dress and lying unconscious on the floor. He couldn't call an ambulance. He didn't know the address or even the name of the area in this rapidly growing city. He could hardly knock on a neighbour's door and seek help without inviting even more trouble for them both. It was two in the morning. What on earth was he to do?

It took about ten minutes for Richard to gather his thoughts and for Hanna to show some early signs of confused consciousness. It was impossible to make any sense of what she was saying as she'd lapsed into her native tongue and seemed oblivious to his questions. Richard hurried to the lounge, gathered her scattered underwear and began to dress her. More used to removing lady's clothing, he'd underestimated how difficulty it was to dress a semi-conscious person; even someone as light as Hanna. As he struggled to position her, limp arms and legs flopped in all directions. Eventually he was satisfied that she could be seen in public. He called the hotel and asked for the location of the casualty hospital. Richard then searched for her keys and drove the car to the side entrance of the villa. Hoping that the neighbours were fast asleep, he bundled her into the rear seat of the car, fastened the seat belt and drove cautiously in the direction of the hospital. The last thing he wanted now was to be stopped by the police for even a minor traffic offence. Strange thoughts darted through his mind as he recalled reading in the *Gulf News* that the Dubai police were having one of their safety campaigns and pulling motorists over to congratulate them on their good driving habits.

Once at the hospital, things began to take on a semblance of order. Two Indian porters manoeuvred Hanna into a chair and wheeled her into the modern Casualty Department. Richard had to provide them with a signed imprint of his American Express card before any treatment could begin.

'I'm afraid we've had to report this to the police. They will need to take details and make a report.' The duty sister looked sympathetic.

'Sure, I guessed that you had to do so when someone brings in a person who is out for the count.'

'Fortunately, she has regained some degree of consciousness but I doubt if they will be able to take a statement from her until the morning.'

Richard hoped if he called their local partner, he would be able to help. So he rang Shaikh Faruk, apologised profusely for disturbing him and told him of his predicament. Faruk laughed out loud and said that he wasn't in the slightest surprised and would do what he could.

Ten minutes later, two uniformed policemen arrived. Fortunately one understood English well and appeared to be friendly. The other was sullen and standoffish. They were given the use of one of the doctor's offices.

'Now this lady. She is your wife or your sister?'

'No, she's a friend.'

'I see. A friend.'

'Yes.'

'Well, perhaps you can tell me how you came into possession of your friend in her injured and unconscious state.'

'Yes, she went to make some coffee, fainted and must have hit her head on the floor. I was in another room and heard the fall.'

'Where was this?'

'At her home.'

'At her home. Where is that?'

'It's in Jumeirah.'

'Address?'

'I'm not exactly sure.'

'What time did this happen?'

'About two o'clock this morning.'

'About two o'clock this morning.' He laboured the phrase as he copied the details in Arabic into his notebook. 'She was making coffee for you at two in the morning?'

'Yes, that's correct.'

'Was there anyone else present?'

'No the maid had just left for home.'

The laboured questions continued for more than an hour. Often the same question was asked in a different way. Richard could not detect from the poker-faced interrogator what was going through his mind. The other policeman looked bored and seemed pleased to be called away to take a phone call at the Receptionist's desk. Richard presumed that he did not understand English. But it was eventually he, not the one who asked a thousand questions, who drew the proceeding to a close. In nigh perfect English he explained that they could not take a statement from the lady until the morning. He said that under normal practice, Richard should have been detained in the cells but as Shaikh Faruk had vouched for him, he would just need to surrender his passport.

The following morning it was soon diagnosed that Hanna had suffered from extremely low blood pressure, which they put down to her eating less than it would take to keep a budgerigar alive. She was wired up for a brain scan and kept under observation for another twenty-four hours before being allowed to return home.

Richard spent most of the next two days arranging the visit and briefing the would-be victims of Paul's visit on the likely topics that would be raised. He also took the opportunity to deliver copies of the *Aphrodite Progress Report* to the General and their Logistic Support partners. During the evenings, he managed to spend some time with Hanna who had wisely taken a week off work to convalesce from her fall. Fortunately, although she had slight bruising to the back of the head, she said that the result of the electroencephalogram was normal.

'Bet you didn't have low blood pressure earlier in the evening,' Richard commented with a broad grin.

She promised Richard faithfully that she'd eat more sensibly in the future and let him make the coffee.

Richard insisted that her maid stayed in the villa overnight for the next few days just in case she should have a relapse. He had his own problems arriving in a few hours' time.

Richard had hired a chauffeur driven Jaguar to take the visitors around for their three-day visit. He arrived at the busy airport fifteen minutes before the flight from London's scheduled landing time. Richard instructed the driver to stay with the car and made his way to the Arrival Hall. He disliked meeting VIPs at Dubai airport, as it was too easy to miss people in the milling crowd. He noticed that as many as twenty people would frequently meet one single Indian or Pakistani passenger. Another frustration was that whenever he found a spot where he could see the arrivals, someone would invariably come and stand in front of him.

When the visitors still hadn't emerged after forty minutes, Richard became concerned. They had travelled First Class and should have been well ahead of some other passengers he had seen emerging with rat-class tags some twenty minutes earlier. It would have been easier to herd cats or a pack of cub-scouts.

He eventually tracked them down on Paul's mobile phone. They had somehow managed to exit through the Departure Terminal entrance.

'We've been looking all over for you for ages. Where have you been?' Paul grizzled.

'Well, I've been standing at the Arrival's exit door for about an hour. However, if you can tell me where you are, I'll come and find you.'

'How do I know? I've never been to this airport, have I?'

'What can you see?'

'Lots of people with bags checking in.'

'Can you see any specific airline?'

'I can see BA and Gulf Air...'

'OK, stay there. I'll be there in about two minutes.'

'Good, I look forward to that.' *Click*

'Stupid prat.'

After Richard had located his charges and successfully tracked down the driver, who was by now on his seventh circuit of the airport, they headed for the *Al-Deira*.

'Staying in the Sultanate of Oman are we?' Paul asked sarcastically. 'Couldn't you find somewhere near the airport?'

'Yes Paul. There's the airport hotel of course but I think you will find this more comfortable, convenient for the meetings, shops and restaurants.'

'Where's the golf course? Sir Anthony and I would like to play.'

'Very near. Tell me when, and I'll arrange it for you.'

Whilst they talked handicaps in the back, Richard surreptitiously phoned the hotel and told them of the VIP's imminent arrival.

Right on cue, Aldo, the *Al-Deira* General Manager was waiting to greet the visitors at the hotel entrance. Richard made the introductions.

'You're most welcome and I will do everything possible to make your stay as comfortable…'

'Jolly good,' interrupted Paul. 'Can we check in?'

'No need, I have all your details from Mr Richard. Can I offer you a welcome drink at the bar?'

'No thanks. It's a bit early for us. We'll go straight to our rooms now.'

Richard glanced at his watch to make sure it really was seven in the evening.

'The hotel looks quite new,' was Sir Anthony's total contribution to the conversation.

As they reached their rooms, Richard presented them with a well-prepared briefing pack showing the detailed programme with annexes showing personality briefs and succinct descriptions of the relevant issues for each meeting.

That evening Paul wanted to eat in a Japanese restaurant. Sir Anthony said that was fine by him. Richard was not a fan but, as they say in France, *that's life!*

They met in the Club Lounge where Richard ran through the programme over a glass of full-bodied Chilean Cabernet. Paul drank Perrier and Sir Anthony a whisky on the rocks. It was clear that neither had bothered to look at the briefing pack.

'So at ten o'clock tomorrow, I thought we could start

the programme with Shaikh Faruk, the owner of our local partner company. He'll give you his latest view of the programme and how *Aphrodite* is rated. Then, Commander Army, General Ahmed, is available at two, tomorrow afternoon. In the evening, Charles Wilkins, the Consul General, has invited us all to dinner at the Residence. On Monday, I have planned a trip to Abu Dhabi for you to meet with the Deputy Commander Air. The Ambassador has asked us all to lunch along with the Defence Attaché – Colonel Bob Archer and the Head of the British Business Group – Tony Drew. That should get us back to Dubai in the early evening. Finally, I've booked your golf for a 7 o'clock start on Tuesday at the Creek and your flight leaves at four.'

Paul was frowning. 'I'm not happy with much of that. I don't like Faruk. He's the slime-ball who came to my office last year. Thinks he knows everything about business in the Emirates. It's essential that I speak to the Ambassador before I see the Commander; I need Phillip Gray's views before I see General Ahmed. Finally, I don't want to see the Deputy Commander. Don't you know that the Commander, Brigadier Salah is a personal friend of mine? I want to see him, not his sidekick.'

'Well Paul, Shaikh Faruk has helped the Company win hundreds of millions of business over the past few years and will feel slighted if you don't see him. He's extremely influential and I'd rather have him on our side than working against us. The Ambo has already shuffled his programme around to accommodate you. And Commander Air Force is in New York and sends his apologies.'

'Mmm. We'll see. Well come on then, time we left if we're going to eat tonight.'

As they reached the lobby, Paul suddenly enthused. 'Look there's Henri Latour.'

Without further ado, Paul made a beeline towards the

wicked rival.

'Henri. Mon ami. How the devil are you? It's so good to see you. You must join us for dinner…'

Richard wondered if he should feign a heart attack or operate the fire alarm. What on earth was Paul up to now? Perhaps he should have included a sheet on Latour in the Briefing Pack – don't talk to this dreadful Frog – he's crooked, sly and deceitful and our main competitor!

'Henri, I don't think you've met our Knight of the Realm, Sir Anthony Laycock. He's our political lobbyist.'

They shook hands. Latour seized his advantage.

'Of course. I'd love to join you for zee dinner. It eez all my pleasure.'

Richard made sure he sat opposite Henri in the Japanese restaurant so he could watch every sly move. He was particularly dismayed to watch Paul confer with Henri to choose a bottle of French *Hermitage*.

'Oh, how about a Japanese wine, Paul. Have you tried the Japanese *Suntory Chardonnay*, it would go well with fish?' Richard quickly interposed.

'It eez like gnat's peeze, Paul. You stiek with zee *Hermitage*. We French know how to treat our grapes and our weemen.'

'You mean press 'em hard and lay them down Henri?'

'Ha ha, Richard you are zee fonee one.'

Not to be outdone, Richard declined the wine and ordered a pint of beer and listened in horror as Paul talked openly about their plans for *Aphrodite*.

'So what is your assessment Henri?' Paul asked whilst they awaited the main course.'

'Seemple Paul. Zee Dubians want *Elsa* and are prepared to wait. They know zee French stayed with zem when ze Briteesh pulled out of zee area and abandoned them in ze seventies. Zee General tells me that he will delay ze contract for three years for *Elsa*. And you must realise that ze French government will pay all our development costs. I don't think your Ministry is as generous. So we av a price advanteege and will beat you in your own country as well.'

Richard sat quietly, biting his tongue. He knew Paul would believe every word so there was no point in adding fuel to the untimely debate. Sir Anthony nodded occasionally and grunted approval, more to show he was awake than to contribute to the conversation. The two and a half hours in the restaurant seemed like an eternity to Richard and it was with great relief they said goodbye to Latour outside of the restaurant.

During the journey back to their hotel, Paul nagged Richard incessantly about the important intelligence that Henri had provided.

'Look Paul, Latour is a salesman. What's worse he's a French Salesman. I certainly wouldn't buy a second-hand car from him and his success rate in sales is pretty dismal to date. He's going out on a limb for this one. It's probably his last chance. He's using you. All I ask, is you wait until the end of the visit to judge the real situation. Keep an open mind 'til then.'

Richard was grateful that Paul chose to sulk the remainder of the journey.

'I suggest we meet in the lobby at nine-thirty,' was Richard's final contribution to a disastrous evening.

As soon as Richard reached his room, he rang Hanna.

'Sorry Hanna it's so late but the kiddies have only just gone to bed.'

'Don't worry; it's not even midnight. Just tell the taxi driver Jumeirah Park Villas, Seaview, Number 18.'

'See you in twenty minutes.'

Richard was amazed that the taxi was driven straight to the villa without a single prompt. However, he was less surprised when he learned that the Pakistani driver had lived in Dubai for thirty years.

'Come in sweetie, I missed you.' Hanna was looking

her young self again.

'Me too, Hanna. I've had a hell of an evening. Can I have a swift brandy please?'

'Of course come and relax.'

'How's the head?'

'Fine now. Just a bit of a lump but the headache's gone. Guess I was lucky I hit the stone floor shoulder first.'

'No more scares like that please. I might have a heart attack next time.'

Richard spent the night with Hanna and was soon reassured that the fall had not affected her appetite or inventiveness. He returned to the *Al-Deira* with an hour to change and mentally prepare himself for the day ahead.

'I called your room just after midnight.' This was Paul's idea of a morning greeting.

'Did you? I'm quite a heavy sleeper. Was it urgent?'

'Well, I would have liked an answer. Are you sure we can rent clubs at the Creek?'

'No problem. I checked that when I booked.'

Mmm. Have you checked that our car is on its way? Oh Anthony, how are you on this fine morning. Did you sleep well?'

'Morning Sir Anthony.'

'Morning Paul. Morning Richard. Do you know where I can buy stamps?'

Richard felt humbled and honoured to witness these high level Company Executives using their razor sharp prowess to focus on the essential. Perhaps a lobotomy was mandatory when you reached their level in the corporate stratosphere.

Despite the heavy morning traffic over the Al-Maktoum Bridge and near the busy Clock Tower roundabout, they reached Shaikh Faruk's office in the business district with five minutes to spare.

'Good to see you again Paul and to meet you Sir

Anthony.' Faruk greeted the visitors warmly. 'How was your trip? …What do you think of our city…? Weather too hot?' Paul began to become visibly impatient as Faruk went through the ritual small talk before starting business.

'So tell us about the Air Defence requirement.' Paul cut through Faruk's description of his time in the UK.

'I am convinced you're in a strong position as long as you don't slow down your development or try and amortise too many of your start-up costs on this contract. Richard has done an excellent job with the Army. They trust him which means they trust *AGC* to provide what they want and on time.'

'But I believe the French have some very effective representatives here.'

'Paul, you must understand the politics here. The French have done well in competitions in the past but have not lived up to their promises. I think you'll find that their agents are no longer influential and that salesman of theirs, Henri Latour is a bad joke. He's unlikely to do business outside of France with his crass attitude and dreadful English.'

'I disagree Faruk. I think Latour is good value. He looks the part, is always well turned out, knows his subject, is confident; he's everything a salesman should be.'

'Yes Paul but it depends what you're selling.'

'Well, Faruk you're going to have to convince me you still have influence in the right circles as I'm doing a review of our representatives and looking carefully at their performance.'

'I have no concerns there Paul. If you can find a better partner, I will wish you good luck.'

'So when can you get us this contract?'

'It's in the Army's budget for eighteen months from now.'

'With all your influence you say you have, can't you get them to bring it forward?'

'I wouldn't be popular meddling in the government's budgets. The General has to work within his allocation and timescale. It is not within his culture to challenge the Shaikhs bidding. Be patient, Paul, you will win this.'

'Well, we shall see. But I'll be watching your performance very carefully.' Paul stood up and made it clear the meeting was over.

'I have prepared some lunch.' Faruk looked distressed by the visitor's rudeness.

'Another time Faruk. I need some time in private to make calls to the UK.'

'Thanks for the coffee. I hope to see you in London sometime.' Sir Anthony made his one and only contribution to the meeting.

On the way to the General's office, Richard tried to re-enforce the need to keep him on their side and not pressure him over timing of the contract. He explained that the budget was not within Ahmed's control and would only embarrass him – saving face was important to every Arab, especially those in command.

Predictably, and after only ten minutes into the meeting, Paul began bludgeoning the General over his tardy procurement procedures and how this requirement had drifted on for too long already. Strictly against Arab custom, he used his left hand to eat some titbits that had been provided with the Arabic tea and crossed his legs in such a way as to point the soles of his feet at their host.

Sir Anthony thought it was about time to say something and committed another local *faux pas* by asking Ahmed about the well-being of his wife.

As they reached the elevators, Richard made an excuse he had left his pen in the conference room and returned to give a brief apology to the General for the visitors and said he would make time to see him again before he returned to the UK to put the record straight.

'My friend,' replied Ahmed. 'I appreciate your concern and am not offended by those who are ignorant of our ways. Do come and see me whenever you wish.'

With immense relief, Richard joined his seniors to escort them to the hotel, and hopefully safely out of harm's way. Or so he thought.

Who should be seated in the Reception area of their hotel but none other than Latour and his two local henchmen, Hamad and Fahed.

'Paul,' he called out. 'Please come and meet my friends from Sharjah.'

'You two go along, I'll catch up with you later.' Paul dismissed Sir Anthony and Richard with the wave of his arm and bounded over to the unwholesome group. 'Fancy tea in the lounge?' Richard seized on the chance to try and convert Anthony to the real world.

'Yes. That would be nice.'

They settled in the lounge and Richard was careful to talk generalities before revealing his hand. Eventually, he raised the subject of the air defence requirements in both the UK and Dubai. He covered the opportunities for a new 3-D radar in other countries and their strong position in defence products. Anthony nodded a lot and said little. He did probe a little about the commercial radar market, which Richard was able to provide him with some meaningful facts and figures. When he gauged that he had progressed sufficiently, Richard steered the subject back to more general matters.

'I thought I'd find you here.' Paul had returned from his meeting. 'Ugh. Are you smoking Richard?'

'Yes Paul, it's OK here in the Lounge and Sir Anthony said he didn't mind.'

'Well I do. It's a disgusting habit.'

Richard took a long puff on his cigarette. 'Good meeting with Latour?'

'Yes, as a matter of fact it was. Hamad and Fahed

backed up everything that Henri had told us.'

'Well, they would, wouldn't they Paul? They're in *Elsa's* employment. I'd bet my bottom dollar that they'd deliberately positioned themselves there, lying in wait for your return.'

'Don't be so negative. I'll have you know they've offered us part of the action.'

'Paul, they don't have any action! They haven't won this competition. They're not in a position to make any deals. I suppose they said they would win in the UK as well.'

'As it happens, they did. The French government will make an agreement with our Secretary of State for Defence. And they'll help us into the civil market as well.'

'But they're not in the civil market, Paul. Anyway, our Board has already approved our plan. Nothing has changed. We are going to win.'

As if pre-programmed, on hearing the involvement of the Secretary of State, Anthony suddenly came to life. 'I'll ferret around in the corridors of power when we get back. See what I can find out.'

At the Consul General's dinner party, their hosts, Charles and Mary Wilkins, introduced them to his Commercial Director, Peter Black and his wife June, Mike Hargreaves, a Jersey banker and an attractive forty-something single lady called Marianne Charlton-Browne.

To Richard's relief, the gathering was purely social and after a short discussion on their itinerary and the purpose of their visit, they talked generalities. Topics included the Dubai racing scene, the impressive recent changes to the city, the Sharjah antique souq and suchlike. Richard was amazed at the change in Paul and Anthony. Once they had finished talking about business, Paul looked ill at ease and said only a handful of words. Anthony, on the other hand, spurred on by several whiskies and the convivial company, positively effervesced. He majored in racing, fine wines and antiques and gazed into Ms Charlton-Browne's grey-blue eyes whenever the opportunity arose. After coffee was served, he played Chopin and Debussy on their Yamaha Clavinola to an exceptionally high standard. By eleven, Paul had became more distanced and introverted and announced that they must leave as they had a long day ahead. Despite Anthony's muted protests, they left for their hotel.

It's an ill wind that blows no one any good, thought Richard, as he called Hanna to arrange some after dinner recreation.

Their visit to Abu Dhabi had been condensed due to Paul's refusal to meet with the Air Force Deputy Commander. The Ambassador had thoughtfully gathered a number of local businessmen and members of his staff for drinks ahead of a smaller party of ten at the lunch table. Sir Anthony was visibly delighted to see that Marianne C-Browne had travelled to Abu Dhabi and was one of the guests at lunch. The old goat repeated his star performance of the previous evening and positively gushed all over her. Richard's suspicions were further aroused when later that day, Anthony announced that he had to look up one of his old friends – some Minister – that evening.

Richard left his visitors during the drinks part of the reception and used the time to catch up on the local news and gossip. He managed a quick word with Zoë to explain that he was trapped by his visitors but would definitely see her on his next visit.

'I keep getting calls from Henri Latour inviting me out,' she taunted.

'Well, that's a waste of time, I'm sure.'

'But, Richard, he is quite good looking and has that, you know, *je ne sais quoi*.'

'Yes, *je ne sais quoi* either Zoë, but I think the man's a prat.'

'Just be sure to call me on your next visit. Sorry, I've to go back to the Comms Centre now. Take care sweetie.'

Richard was about to check on what his visitors were up to when their hostess, Helen Gray whispered in his ear, 'God, that Hamilton fellow's appalling.'

'Yes, he's my boss, Helen.'

'You poor soul. I hope they pay you well.'

'You have to be kidding Helen. Thanks anyway to you and Phillip for putting on such a splendid show for them. They really don't deserve it. What did I do to deserve a boss like him?'

'I guess you must have been just as naughty in a previous life, Richard. We all have our crosses to bear. Suppose I'd better circulate. I'll see you at the lunch. How's the girlie situation anyway? I guess you're still a hopeless case.'

During the lunch, Paul was at his worst. He lectured the Ambassador on Middle East business, berated the Defence Attaché for his limited commercial knowledge and complained bitterly to the Chairman of the British Business Group on the abysmal performance of the UK industry compared with the French and the Americans.

The remainder of their time was without incident. Richard was glad to lose them to the Creek Golf Club and euphoric to see them disappear through the Departure Lounge doors. He knew, however, his work would be cut out over the next few days to nullify the damage perpetrated by the presence of his incredibly stupid boss.

Chapter Seven

When Richard returned home on Tuesday evening, he found Becky sprawled on the settee in her bra and pants, sipping a glass of Chablis and reading David Lodge's *Nice Work*.

'Good book this. All about a woman who shows this guy how to sort out his business. He's got a boss like yours. Good trip?'

'Hi Bex. Dreadful trip. I'll tell you all. Did you wear those tiny thingies you're wearing to work today? You obviously haven't got to the point in the book where this wonderful woman causes the workers to strike.'

'Grab a glass, there's some dregs left in the bottle.'

'No need, I bought some plonk at the Duty Free.'

Richard dropped his case in the bedroom and returned carrying an open bottle of *Cuvée Napa* and two glasses. 'No the trip did not go at all well. Sir Anthony's a pudding and Hamilton turned out to be even worse than expected. He's an arch pain in the butt who should never be allowed to meet customers. In fact he should never be allowed out of his house. Have I missed anything whilst I was away? '

'Oh, not much really. The weather's been lousy. I had my highlights done on Tuesday, but I wouldn't expect you to notice that. And there's a rumour about that Kate Webber is preggers?'

'What? You're pulling my leg. How could you possibly know if she was anyway?'

'Simple. Jennifer Green saw her buying a DIY testing kit in Boots. Anyone we know Richard?'

'I certainly hope not but I'd have to say twix thee and me, it's not impossible.'

'Well, if you will go around as if your brain is three feet from your head.'

'Thanks Bex, what would I do without your sympathy and support?'

'So d'you think it really could be yours?

'Well it's not impossible Bex. But Marvin was with her a couple of months ago. I know what I'll do. I'll go to the lab tomorrow and innocently ask her how things are and see what she says.'

'Oh I'm really fine Richard. Didn't you know I get pregnant all the time? It's no problem at all. Life's a bunch of roses,' Bex mocked, aping Kate's voice.

'Perhaps I won't go to the lab tomorrow.'

'Well, don't let it spoil your evening. Pour the wine and flop down here with me. I got the video of *Three Men and a Baby* out today. Thought we could watch it together'.

It was some relief to Richard that when Bex started the video, it turned out to be *Notting Hill*. However, it didn't stop her making the odd jibe whenever the opportunity arose.

'Are you sure you should be drinking at this time Richard? And you really ought to cut out smoking altogether.'

It was over an hour before Bex admitted that the whole story had been a leg-pull but this did not stop her cackling away from time to time. 'You should have seen your face Richard. I wish I'd had a camera ready.'

'You witch. How could you? I've had the most dreadful week and you do that to me. Just you wait.' Richard picked up a cushion and playfully attempted to suffocate her. As she writhed beneath him, he felt a surge of excitement from the close contact with her half clad, gorgeous body. At one point, she stopped giggling and he saw a fleeting but unmistakable expression of pleasure and sexual desire captured in her pale blue eyes.

Becky quickly recovered her composure. 'Richard, I'm really feeling dog-tired. Must be the time of month. Still, I suppose I should feel happy and relieved about that. At least I won't have to go to Boots tomorrow. Do you mind if we watch the rest of the movie another time?'

'If you live that long! Sleep tight.' He gave her a brief hug and brotherly kiss, turned off the video and retired alone to his empty bed.

The following morning, Richard crossed to the Engineering Block to bring Clive up to date on the events of the past week.

'Oh, the weary traveller returns. How was your holiday? You don't look very tanned.'

'Nice to see you too Clive. Well, the main news is that the Board wants us to do a 'dog and pony' show around the Middle East. We'll be away for about a month.'

Clive's face was a picture as the thought of having to tell Annie the news struck home. 'A whole month?'

'Oh at least that and there's a rumour we may have to continue on to the Pacific Rim afterwards.'

'Well, I'll need to look at this carefully. We have to think of the development programme. That would be badly affected if I were to be away for…'

'No problem Clive, your deputy, Hugh Thomas can take care of that. You're always telling me how good he is and how he needs more responsibility.'

'Yes, but… well, I'll have to talk to the Technical Director about this. I'm not sure it is a good idea at all…'

'OK Clive. There really is no such trip. Just thought I'd have a bit of fun after your cheap jibes about my holiday's abroad.'

'You bastard.' Clive burst into laughter tinged with great relief. 'Good one though, you certainly had me going that time.'

Richard then told him about Becky winding him up over Kate's supposed pregnancy.

'Wish I'd been there for that one. How is Becky anyway? I hardly ever see her these days. She's a lovely girl. I thought by now you two would be a permanent entity. You're just made for each other and have the same crazy humour.'

'Stop matchmaking Clive. You know I'm not ready to settle down. Now I really came to tell you about a meeting between Paul Hamilton and the *Elsa Mafiosa*…'

Richard related the various problems of the week including the added complication that *Elsa* was likely to try and expand into the civil business.

'I don't think Paul understands the civil connection, but if O'Leary finds out *Elsa* is interested in an unholy alliance, he'll use this to beef up his diversification argument. Then we'll have double trouble.'

'It won't be easy to dispute on pure technical or development cost saving grounds Richard.'

'No I realise that; but I also know that *Elsa's* Management will have our Board for breakfast. They're not in the same league. It'll be as good as a takeover and guess which Company will suffer in job and revenue losses?'

'No doubts there. They'll have a field day.'

'So what are we to do Clive, just lie back and let it happen?'

'Need to think about it a lot more. You might want to sound out your mates in the Ministry, Richard. Won't they want to retain a purely national technology base?'

'Good idea Clive. The shock of spending a few weeks overseas works wonders for your imagination.'

Richard was about to leave the lab when a familiar voice called out to him. 'I was hoping to catch you today. Have you got a minute?' He turned to see Kate Webber, looking as striking as ever.'

'Of course Kate. How are you?'

'Oh, not so good lately. Must be one of these bugs going around. Not eating much but I've been sick five mornings on the trot.'

'Sorry to hear that Kate. Perhaps you should see the doc.' His eyes wandered to her waist. Was that a tiny bit of podge he could see?

'No, I'll be fine. You've been off on your travels again, I hear. Bet it was hot over there. You know, I do miss our little evening excursions, but I guess life goes on and there's Marvin... But what I really wanted to talk to you about today is an idea I had about the technical campaign for anti-diversification. Clive asked me to look at the technical factors. I've already run them past him, so I am now hoping you'll be able to use some of them to help you get your message to the Board.'

Richard went through her logical, well thought out and presented technical papers. 'These are excellent, Kate. I like your illustrations. If we added Mickey Mouse with a pointer, even the Board might understand them. No, seriously, this is good stuff and I can certainly use it all in our campaign.'

Kate looked delighted that her work had been so well received. Perhaps she still thought Richard was quite dishy, in a rakish, boyish sort of way. Not a bit like Marvin.

Richard returned to the office with the hint of a spring returning in his step.

'Mr Hamilton's been on the phone. Says to call him immediately please.' Liz greeted Richard with the dismal news as he passed her office.

'If I must,' he sighed and began dialling. 'Didn't you tell him I was off sick with disinterest? I'll give it another half hour. He'll probably forget why he rang by then.'

'Mr Hamilton's office.'

'Hi Pat. The old git asked me to phone. How was the misery when he came back from our trip?'

'Yes, it's terrible, isn't it? You couldn't possibly

believe how bad it was. No, I don't even think there's a cure for it. Well, not a legal one, anyway. Yes Mr Bryant, Mr Hamilton is right by me now. I'll put you through to his office.'

Speakerphone on. Light cigarette. Sit back in chair. Pause... one... two... three.

'Richard. Hello. Are you there? Hello!! Pat I thought you said the bloody man was on the line.'

'Oh hello Paul, I gather you wanted me to call you.'

'You need to get your phone checked. It's clearly on the blink.'

'Yes Paul. I'll get it checked as soon as we finish.'

'Right then. About *Aphrodite*. I'm not at all convinced that we're going in the right direction. I don't believe any of the rubbish I heard about timescales at either our Ministry or during the visit to Dubai. We need to give serious consideration to what the *Elsa* people said at my meeting with them.'

'You have the advantage Paul as I don't know what you discussed apart from them taking over our bit of the Air Defence market.'

'You're being negative again, Richard. *Elsa* gets a lot of French government funding and is offering us a share of the development and manufacture of a state of the art joint radar product if we agree to withdraw *Aphrodite* from the market.'

'What percentage share?'

'I don't know that yet because we haven't got into that level of detail. It would mean we could use the funds more beneficially for something else – such as a civil derivative.'

'Oh I see. They get us out of the military market, apart from some share of the action yet to be defined. We pool development and save, say, five million and lose a three-billion pound core market. We then enter a new market where we have no experience of the product or the customers. That doesn't seem a wonderful deal to me.'

'Well that's just what I expected from your small-minded attitude Richard. You can think what you like but I'm going to have further meetings with *Elsa* and make my recommendations to the Board. You're far too biased to be involved in these discussions.'

'You mean that I will not be allowed to attend any of the meetings on the subject?'

'I doubt it. You'll just have to wait and see.' *Click.*

'Up yours too.'

'I didn't catch that Richard. I'd finished. Did you say something?'

'No, I've finished too Paul, must have been someone talking on Liz's extension.' *Click.*

Richard sat glumly at his desk wondering if it was time to look for another job. It didn't seem fair that one man could negate so many people's hard work.

'Richard,' Liz called again. 'General Ahmed's holding for you.'

'Right Liz put him through.' 'Morning, General. How good to hear from you.'

'Richard, I hope you had a good trip back. Thank you for coming to see me after your visitors left Dubai, I much appreciated your concern. I've a favour to ask you.'

'Go-ahead, General. I'll do what I can.'

'Well, I have three of my staff in France with *Elsa* at the moment. They are due to fly out of *Charles de Gaulle* tomorrow. I know it's extremely short notice, but could you possibly provide them with two nights accommodation, preferably in London and take them around your site and the labs where you're carrying out the project development?'

'Delighted to look after them. We'll be able to show them the working prototype, which is more than they'll have seen in France. Would you please ask your staff officer to fax me the names, appointments and arrival details and I'll take it from there?'

'Thanks Richard, I'm sure you're right about the French. I'll fax you myself in the next hour. Thank you again for clearing up any possible misunderstandings over the visit last week.'

As Richard stood by the crowded exit of Heathrow Terminal One Arrivals, he reflected on the large number of hours each year he stood around waiting for passengers to arrive at airports. As usual, the exit pathway was blocked by excited friends and relatives together with what seemed to be hundreds of chauffeurs holding apologetically their hastily scrawled name boards.

Fortunately, his visitors were easy to pick out from the crowd as they came through the exit wheeling trolleys bursting with luggage and boxes with Paris labels. It took nearly ninety minutes for their chauffeur driven car to reach their hotel, the *Shoreham Towers,* in heavy evening traffic. He'd chosen the *Shoreham* because of its close proximity to Harrods. The senior of the group was Colonel Mohammed Al Hadi, the Head of Procurement. Major Suhail and Captain Salem were both Engineering Officers on his staff. Only the Colonel had ever been to England before. Richard told them about the programme and asked them how they would like to spend their spare time and what kind of food they preferred.

They were all keen to try a typically English restaurant that evening, so he took them to *Tiddy Dols* in Shepherd's Market. He recommended the speciality of the house, the Beef Wellington which they all ate heartily. Although Richard enjoyed the live *Gilbert and Sullivan* ditties performed by some talented students, he felt his guests might have missed the subtleties of this brand of British humour. As the visitors never drank alcohol, Richard was subjected to the rare experience of eating an excellent meal without the benefits of fine wine. The guests relaxed as the evening unfolded and began to speak about their French experience. They'd all enjoyed the *George-V* hotel and the Paris dining and shopping. Clearly, and as he'd have expected, Henri had also pulled out all the stops to ensure they stayed and ate at the best.

'They tell me that the French government has an agreement with your Ministry that they will share the production of the *Elsa's* new Radar.' Colonel Mohammed explained that he'd learned this from an Army Major who had been present throughout their visit to the *Elsa* site.

'That's certainly not my understanding Colonel. However, tomorrow I've planned to take you to our Ministry where you will meet senior people in our procurement chain. I'm sure this will allow you to be reassured that they still intend to run a real competition between *Elsa* and *AGC*. You see our Ministry believes, rightly or wrongly, the best way to get value for money is to compete all major procurements and being a British competitor counts for little unless you offer best value for money.'

'Of course Richard. I'm sure it will be most instructive to visit your Ministry and meet these people. The French Major of whom I spoke was not in uniform.' There was a slight glint in the Colonel's eye.

'I also know you'd like access to the mosque at prayer times and I've included it in your programme whenever possible.' Richard had been briefed that the Colonel was particularly dedicated and committed to his faith.

'Thank you, that is most important.'

'I also am sure that you still have some unfulfilled items on your shopping lists, so I've included some time in Harrods and Oxford Street before you leave.'

They all smiled and nodded their approval.

'Well, gentlemen, our driver's outside. If you're ready, we'll return to the hotel.'

They arrived at the *Shoreham* just ten minutes after leaving *Tiddy Dols*. The visitors thanked Richard profusely for the evening and agreed to meet at nine for breakfast. Richard went straight to his room, downed a gin and tonic from the mini bar, spoke with Becky to check if he'd received any mail or messages and fell asleep reading Alex Garden's *The Beach*. He slept soundly and dreamt of a happy encounter with the beautiful Thai girl on one of the romantic deserted islands.

When Colonel Mohammed met Richard at breakfast, it was immediately obvious that something was wrong.

'Morning Colonel. Hope you slept well.'

'No Richard, I had a bad night. I don't know how your Company could do such a thing.'

'Do what Mohammed?'

'I think you know. I'm talking about last night after I left you in the Reception.'

'Look, I'm sorry but I'm not following this. When I left you all last night, I went straight to my room, took a drink from the minibar, read a book and was asleep in half an hour.'

'It was what you arranged for me then.'

'Please, Mohammed, if there is something wrong, tell me. I think there's been a misunderstanding somehow'

'Yes Richard, there's been a misunderstanding all right. It's about your Company's special delivery last night. Are you telling me that you don't know anything about it?'

'Not a thing. What special delivery?'

'The two girls who knocked on my door and told me they'd been sent with the compliments of *AGC Electronics*. They even showed me your business card.'

'Ah, all is becoming clear now. This, I assure you is a set up. First of all, neither I nor anyone else in *AGC* would ever insult you in this way. We all have the greatest respect for your religious commitment and personal high standards. I assure you that this is the work of someone deliberately trying to upset our good relationship. And I've a pretty good idea who would do such a thing. There're very few people who knew you were coming to London. Even fewer could know where you were staying as it was only two days ago that I booked the *Shoreham* myself and faxed you the confirmation.'

'Richard, if you say so, of course I believe you'd nothing to do with it. I was shocked by the whole event and when the large blonde lady showed me your card...'

'I assure you; I've never arranged such a thing for anyone in my life. Even for a willing customer, let alone someone like yourself who I know would be terribly offended.'

'But it could well be someone in your Company. I need you to find out for me Richard. I really must know.'

'Of course, Mohammed, I'll do all I can to find out what happened.'

The others joined them at breakfast and the subject matter was dropped although he was a little worried that Captain Salem seemed to be smiling a lot that day. Surely he would have said something?

Half an hour later, they made their way across London to the Ministry of Defence Main Building.

Following a thorough check at the Main Entrance, the guests were shown to one of the secure briefing rooms. As coffee was being served, they were joined by Group Captain Ted Green, Wing Commander Ian Tucker and a civil servant, Nigel Eldridge. Although Ted Green led the proceedings, he frequently invited approval from Nigel Eldridge, called him Sir and eventually explained he was the Director General who approved all their budgets and procurements.

Unfortunately, Nigel was the archetypal civil servant but was not at all civil and certainly did not behave like a servant.

'Well you need to understand,' he began, 'these RAF chappies want everything and its up to me and my team to make sure they spend the taxpayers money wisely. I also make sure that we hang on to any technologies which are valuable to the UK's security.'

'Does that mean that the *Aphrodite* technology released to us is not the same as your country will buy?' Colonel Mohammed looked concerned.

'That we may buy old chap, may buy. We are running a competition you see. We always do and anyone can compete, not just the Brits. We invite bids from the Americans, the Germans, the French, of course, and even the Spanish sometimes. Our chaps have to fight for business along with the others.'

'You do not support the UK industries then?'

'Course we do sport, we just like to keep them mean and lean.'

'And release to us?'

'When you place a contract, we'll look at it in excruciating detail and then give the appropriate level of technology release. Case by case you see. Can't have MI6 breathing down our necks. But you needn't worry about it, old chap, I'm sure you're in our good books.'

'So you cannot guarantee release?'

'Well, not exactly old bean. No can do now. I'm just saying it shouldn't be a problem if you choose British.'

Richard listened uncomfortably to the damage being unwittingly perpetrated by this senior goon. By emphasising his power to control access to technology, he was raising grave doubts in the Colonel's mind. Richard realised it would take an immense amount of effort to obviate the harm exacted during, what should have been, a confidence-building meeting. He was beginning to wish that this visit had never happened.

Following the Ministry meeting, the visitors spent the afternoon shopping and were then taken to the London Mosque near Regents Park for evening prayer. They then joined Richard at *Caravan Serai*, an Afghani Restaurant in

Paddington Street. The guests clearly appreciated the gesture of the more traditional food after their European diet over the past week.

Following an early departure, Richard and his three visitors arrived at the *AGC Electronics'* site gate at ten. Richard had arranged for them to leave early to clear the heavy London traffic and breakfast on the way. Despite the three-hour journey, they were all in good spirits by the time they were taking coffee in the Main Briefing Room. Sir Anthony had left his Headquarters fortress to join the party as the Company Senior. Paul Hamilton had declined the honour on the grounds that he'd a previous engagement. By interrogating Pat, Richard had discovered Paul was in fact making a two-day trip to France. She'd only found out about his arrangements because a friend in the Travel Office had called to let her know his tickets were ready for collection. So Mr Hamilton was apparently on a highly important and confidential mission. Richard felt depressed at the thought of Paul running around France and making some deal with *Elsa* that would cause such long-term general damage to *AGC* in general, and the Radar business in particular. But there was absolutely nothing he could do about it for the time being.

Richard was pleasantly surprised at how differently Sir Anthony behaved when Paul was not around. His introduction was both welcoming and informative. He reeled off a number of figures about Company turnover, performance, profit and projects around the globe. His visual aids were professionally made and employed some slick animation. Perhaps the old stick wasn't past it after all.

Richard followed Sir Anthony with a short presentation about the Radar Division and the day's specific programme. He emphasised that they'd spend time viewing the development labs, production support areas and would have plenty of opportunity to operate the equipment. He assured them that any further presentations would be strictly limited to technical explanations by experts who'd also be available throughout the day to answer their questions.

The visitors appeared to appreciate the day's visit. They displayed an almost unlimited thirst for knowledge and asked several deep technical questions. The seeds of doubt that had been sown by the arrogant twerp in the Ministry meant they were still concerned over any differences between the UK version of *Aphrodite* and the one that would be released to them. Over the lunch in the Executive Dining Room, Sir Anthony was the perfect host and showed himself to be knowledgeable about the business and able to talk entertainingly on almost any subject. He also went to great lengths to try to put their minds at rest over the subject of technical release.

It was late evening by the time Richard had taken his visitors to Heathrow, watched them leave the check-in area and was able to return to the Farnham flat.

'Hi sweet, you look shagged out.'

'Hi, Bex, yes I have had a couple of rather crappy days. I'll tell you the interesting bits when I've had a noggin. Anyway, I must say that the literature and displays you did for their site visit went down really well.'

'My aim is to serve. You sit down, relax and I'll get you a drink and then you can tell auntie Bex all about it. I was just going to uncork a bottle of red. That OK or do you want something stronger?'

'The red will be perfect as long as it's not French.'

Richard related the highlights of the problems of the week and, in return, received a great deal of wine and sympathy.

'So what are you going to do about the hooker incident?' Bex thought it was funny when Richard first told her, but soon realised the seriousness of the problem. 'And you know, if Sir Anthony has got hidden depths and you seem to get on with him OK, perhaps he could become your ally at *Fawlty Towers*.'

'That's true Bex. Yes, I'll give that one some thought. Thanks, good thinking bat-person. Now let's get down to some serious drinking and you can tell me how your week has been.'

'Nothing as exciting as yours. But you know you told Clive about that little tiny prank I tried on you about Kate being preggers. Well the story of her being in the club seems to have spread around the site. Good job not many people know what you were doing to her not so long ago.'

'Oh that's great. That's all I need for that rumour to do the rounds. You know how they all enjoy a good scandal at work.'

'Well, you know how these tales get exaggerated. The story will soon get around that you also put me in the family way.'

'Oh I believe they already are Bex. They already are.'

Chapter Eight

Richard arrived early in the office that day to catch up on his mail. Amongst his faxes, was a hidden copy of Sir Anthony's notes on the Dubai visit, which was openly addressed to just Paul Hamilton. To his surprise, the report was extremely positive. It was also particularly complimentary about Richard's excellent relationships with the customers, their partners and Embassy staff. He believed that General Ahmed had been most encouraging on their prospects with *Aphrodite* and that the visit was well organised throughout.

His second surprise of the day was from Kate phoning to say that she'd like to meet him after work. She wouldn't give any details, as she said she could be easily overheard by others in the lab. Richard agreed to meet her in the *Welcome Stranger* at five-thirty.

When it seemed the day was shaping up well, Pat rang to say that Mr Hamilton would be visiting the site at noon. He wanted Richard to find him a suitable office in the site headquarters building for the day, book him a twelve-thirty lunch in the Executive Dining Room and be available to see him at two-thirty.

This was all too much. He thought he'd better check his stars and reached for *The Mail* and read the day's predictions for Aries. *As Mercury is in ascendance with Pluto and the moon is in its third quarter, expect an intriguing meeting later in the day, which is likely to have a far-reaching effect on your future. Handle tricky situations with care, tolerance and tact. Be sympathetic to other people's predicaments. Lucky number –3.*

Perhaps his three surprises would be lucky after all.

During the morning, Richard prepared for as many eventualities as possible. He reviewed business plans, order intake and forecast figures. He wrote up the hooker incident with the Colonel and completed his Travel Expense claims. Finally he re-read the latest three Project Reports from Clive. This done, he wished he could prepare in similar fashion for his rendezvous with Kate.

Richard arrived punctually for his two-thirty meeting to find Paul's two o'clock appointment sitting in the outer office. He recognised Michael Petty from his attendance at Company functions and exhibitions. Richard thought his family name well suited, although Michael Creep Upstart Petty would have been even more apt. At aged twenty-five, every important and influential member of the Company knew Petty. He had been a salesman for four years but was still yet to make his first sale. But somehow, his smart turnout, phoney accent, upwardly directed enthusiasm and total devotion to anyone above who could assist his career, masked this minor deficiency, as well as general incompetence.

'Afternoon Michael.'

'Hello. Richard isn't it? You here to see Paul?'

'Yes Michael, looking at his watch. 'Supposed to be two-thirty.'

'Hard cheese. I'm at two. Paul's interviewing for an Assistant.'

'Oh, that's why he has all these half hour appointments until six, is it? Now I understand.' Richard couldn't resist the taunt.

'I don't think so.' Petty looked worried nevertheless, 'No, it's a formality. I've really come today to agree the salary, company car and sign the new contract.'

'You might well be right Michael. I've probably been misinformed.' Richard enjoyed seeing Upstart squirm in

101

his chair.

'Yes you're definitely wrong, Paul said…'

'Hello, Michael. Good to see you,' Paul oozed, totally ignoring his two-thirty appointment. 'Come on in, I've sent for some coffee. How was your trip down from Birmin…'

The door was shut firmly behind them.

By the time Paul freed himself from Upstart and other distractions, it was four o'clock when he called for Richard.

'Ah Richard, come in. Fancy finding you on site. You must have exhausted your travel budget.'

'No, there's plenty left Paul. It might surprise you to know that travelling as much as I need to do my job effectively has little glitz. But it's just one of those crosses we international salesmen have to bear.'

'Yes, Richard, I didn't call you in to talk about your holidays in the sun. You're here because I need to remind you that I set the policy for this part of the Company and I want serious consideration given to prospective partnerships and civil diversification. Do you know Michael Petty?'

'Yes, very well Paul.' The phrase was delivered in a tone that could have meant that he wouldn't have peed in Upstart's mouth if his teeth were on fire. But Paul failed to notice.

'Yes he's a good man; always looks and behaves the part.'

'Yes he certainly does. A little bird told me he may be working in Company HQ.'

'Yes. I need a number two. Someone I can trust who gets on with it without challenging everything.'

'Yes Paul.' He would've liked to have pointed out that slavery had been abolished.

'So, what are you going to do about it?'

'About it?'

'Opposing my every attempt to move this Company

forward.'

'I'm not sure what you mean Paul. You employ me to sell military radars around the world. This I've done well and have exceeded my sales targets every year that I've been with the Company. As for my future, in order to continue winning orders, I must air my beliefs within the Company. We've agreed our short-term targets; we've an approved Business Plan and funding for the next major product. I'm following this strategy. How is this a threat to your policy setting?'

'As usual, you're just twisting things. You know damn well you oppose me at every opportunity on both working with *Elsa* or funding a civil derivative.'

'But isn't our top priorities to achieve this year's budget and build on that product for tomorrow's market. To do this I need to use the funds, which the Board approved to produce *Aphrodite*. Then it's my job to make sure we sell it.'

'Well, you need to understand this. I've had an excellent meeting with the Chairman of *Elsa* and am convinced that both companies would do better combining their efforts to produce the next military radar and developing a civil version. This would make the product cheaper and faster to the market.'

'I'm not against the principle of partnership, only your choice of collaborator. Firstly, their development is at least a year behind *Aphrodite* and, like us, they don't have a civil market. Also, *Elsa* is known to be devious in the way it wins orders and doesn't have a good reputation for integrity, quality or aftercare.'

'So you think you know better?'

'In as much as I'd seek a partner with a similar technology base, not a direct competitor but already well established in the civil radar market. The chosen partner should be well respected by its customers. I'd first look in the USA, as a partnership there could open up opportunities in their home military market which currently is unavailable to us.'

'As I said Richard, I set the policy and there's something else I need to talk to you about.'

'Yes Paul.'

'I am hearing some ugly rumours about you and one of the young ladies in Engineering.'

'Really, Paul?'

'Yes really, Richard. What's going on?'

'Going on? Can you be more specific please?'

'You heard me, is it true?'

'What true?'

'That you are having it off with one of the young ladies in Engineering.'

'I'm not sure what you are getting at but I'm a bachelor. My personal life is no concern of the Company unless I do something to damage or embarrass *AGC*.'

'So is it true then?'

'No, I would never do anything to damage or embarrass the Company.'

'But about this engineer?'

'Sorry Paul. Do you know of someone specific? Is this person married or something or is she not performing at work. Does she have a name? Perhaps we could get her to join our meeting.'

'There's no time to go into all that now. Just remember I have warned you. Just be careful, that's all. I'll be looking out for you.'

'Yes Paul, I'll be careful. Anything else?'

'No, you can go. But remember all I've said today.'

'Of course, Paul. I have one topic I'd like to raise with you.'

'Well, get on with it. I've got to drive back to Epsom tonight.'

Richard explained about the problem with Colonel Mohammed in London. Paul's reaction was predictable. He blamed Richard for not taking better care of the visitors and allowing their whereabouts to be made public to every Tom, Dick and Harry.

'Well, I'll do everything possible to placate the Colonel but I felt you ought to know about it.'

'As long as you remember it's your problem, not mine Richard.'

'Of course. I brought my travel expenses for your signature…'

'You'll just have to leave them with me. I'll get round to checking them when I've time. I must leave now. Remember all those things I said to you today Richard. I'm not putting up with any more nonsense.'

Richard knew now that he would have to wait several weeks for Paul to get around to approving his expenses. He returned to his office feeling as if he had just finished eight rounds with Mike Tyson. He hadn't made any progress on weaning Paul away from *Elsa* or protecting the *Aphrodite* development. And in just half an hour he would be meeting the stunning Kate in the pub. He wondered what surprise was awaiting him then.

The *Welcome Stranger* was almost deserted in the early evening. The pub was well off the beaten track and an unlikely calling house for any *AGC* staff making their way home. Richard ordered a pint of Speckled Hen and settled down at a corner table. On the stroke of six, Kate burst through the door looking as gorgeous as ever, but may have added a couple of pounds since Richard had last been able to take a close look at her. The impish smile, bobbed hair and green eyes were just as captivating as ever.

'Oh great, you're here. I wondered if you would come.'

'Hi, Kate. Of course I came. What's your poison?'

'Just an orange with ice please. I'm on the wagon.'

'Well that must be a first. Sit down, I'll refill mine and

get you an orange.'

Richard returned from the bar with the drinks and a bowl of nuts.

'Oh, that's a temptation but I'm trying to get back down to my fighting weight. Put a bit on in the last month you know.'

'Burning the candle at both ends?'

'No, since Marvin came back, we hardly went out at all. As you know, no one would eat enough of my cooking to get fat. So how are you Richard? What's new in your life?'

'Nothing changes with me. You know, same old thing every day – excitement. Still struggling daily to keep my job. No new love in my life, if that's what you mean. Just the odd ship passing in the night. So how have you been? How's Marvin?'

'I'm absolutely fine, now. I've had a few ups and downs lately with Marvin… sorry. I'd better rephrase that. We haven't been getting along lately, so now he's finally out of my life forever.'

'Oh, I see. So does that mean we can get together again sometimes?

'Yes, definitely, but I'd understand if you were cool about seeing me again.'

'Of course not Kate. I enjoyed our time and romps together too much. We always said it wouldn't be a permanent relationship. But there's something that I need to clear up with you though.'

'I'm all ears.'

'Paul Hamilton has got a bee in his bonnet that I'm having a fling with a colleague in Engineering. You know the Company frowns on such liaisons in the workplace, even in this day and age.'

'Well Richard, he can go jump in the lake as far as I am concerned. It's out of office time and not affecting our work – except for the better, that is.'

'That's basically what I told him but it's not quite as simple as that.'

'Go on.'

'You see, to all intents and purposes I'm not married. I told you that my wife Maggie ran off with a Diego hotel owner on our honeymoon. The truth is, I have never bothered to divorce her and she's never asked me either. This is despite having had two of his bambinos. I'm sorry I didn't mention it before but...'

'There was absolutely no reason why you should have. Look, I knew you weren't famed for your monogamy when I met you. What we had was brilliant. If nothing else ever came of it, I will always have fond memories of our time together.'

'That's really good to hear. I've never tried to fool you, or anyone else for that matter. The marriage was as dead as a dodo so the legality of a divorce didn't seem to be important. You know what I'm like. What you see is what you get.'

'That's one of the attractions Richard. Now then, that sorted, let's drink up, go to my place and celebrate amidst the sheets.'

'If only you would be a little more assertive Kate.'

'Well I've had a hell of a month, what with bloody Marvin. Then I thought I might be pregnant. I missed one, started throwing up every morning and had a yen for strange foods.'

'No obvious symptoms there, then.'

'Anyway, Marvin left five days ago and nature returned to normal. Always fancied having a *Little Richard* too.'

'Oh, really. I'm not quite attuned to that just yet, thanks. Right then, last one at your flat is a sissy.'

Richard was on his way to the airport again, when his car phone rang.

'Hello, Richard Bryant.'

'Gee there Ritchie, long time since we spoke.'

'I'd know that deep American drawl anywhere. How are you Chuck? And more to the point, where are you? It must be four in the morning in Atlanta.'

'I'm in *Win-chester*. Over here for a bit of business and a few day's pleasure. Brought Trish with me; she says Hi. Was hoping to catch up with you.'

'Yes Chuck, that would be great, but I'm just on my way to Munich for two days. Back on Friday. Can we meet then?'

'That'll be fine Ritchie. Come on up on Saturday. We're in *The George and Dragon*. In fact, join us for lunch. They do a wonderful buffet here. Stay over in fact. We'll do a bit of hiking on Sunday'

'Look forward to it. Mind if I bring Bex?'

'We'd be cross if ye didn't. By the way, how ya doing with the girlies these days. Piss poor as ever?'

'As always Chuck, I'm still on the defensive. See you Saturday.'

As Richard made slow progress through the morning M25 traffic, he looked forward to meeting Chuck and Trish again. The couple had always been so hospitable during his visits to Atlanta. Chuck (Charles Hammond Jnr) was Vice President of Marketing at the *Georgia Radar Systems Corporation*. Now in his late fifties, he had been with *GRSC* all of his working life. He liked the street fighting, a term he used to describe winning orders. He'd therefore turned down promotion on at least three occasions, as he was unwilling to be chained to the corporate desk. Chuck was an outgoing, *huntin' and fishin'* man who sported a large tangled beard and was rarely seen in a 'matching jacket and pants'. He married Trish, some twenty years his junior, after a three-day romance in Vegas. Yes, he thought, it'll be good to see Chuck and Trish again.

As he entered the airport complex, he also reflected on the return of Kate into his life and the pleasures of the night before. Certainly, if her feelings were mirrored in her enthusiastic gymnastics, she obviously still liked him a lot.

From the recently opened new Munchen airport, Richard caught the U-Bahn to Mairianaplatz. His hotel was only a few minutes' walk away, so he checked into his room before taking a taxi to their German prime contractor, *Stern Gmbh*. Once there, he was greeted by the Air Radar Project Director, Manfred Gunter.

'Thank you for coming at short notice Richard. The coffee is on its way up. Make yourself comfortable.'

They talked for a while about generalities, the difficult radar market and the knock-on effects of the Americans cutting back on their defence budget.

After coffee was poured, Manfred became more serious.

'Well Richard, my plan is for you to see our joint airborne prototype radar under test, followed by various meetings with our project staff tomorrow. However, I have to tell you that although we are generally pleased with the quality of your subcontract work, you are running about four months late on some of the software, including the anti-clutter and second time around algorithms. I also gather your antenna elements require some modification and the power unit ripple level needs to be reduced.'

'Yes, I was warned there have been some problems, Manfred. Clive told me that some of these matters were raised at the last progress meeting and asked me to reassure you that the team is doing everything possible to catch up.'

'But you see there's another factor Richard. My boss has been approached by the French. They're saying that you've some more general technical problems with all your new developments. *Elsa*, with government backing, is trying to persuade us to give some of our joint contract to them. Personally, I think the 70% for *Stern* and 30% for *AGC* is a sound and workable partnership and I don't wish to complicate things by involving *Elsa*. I don't trust them but they do have some keen supporters at various levels within our Company. If you continue to miss deadlines, I'll be under mounting pressure to involve them in some workshare.'

'Of course. I understand your concerns and will carry the message back. I do believe we're doing all we can to put matters right.'

'OK Richard, enough about that. On to other matters; you know we need some help to market our new product in the Asian Pacific Region?'

'That I can do something about, Manfred. I'm off to Singapore for the Asian Aerospace Exhibition in a couple of weeks. If you can sort out the publicity material and arrange for a model to be shipped out in time, we'll include it on our Exhibition booth.'

From that point on, Richard's host did everything possible to ensure his remaining time in Munich was businesslike, pleasant and comfortable. Part of their hospitality included Richard consuming a number of steins of Bavarian beer. Not being a seasoned beer drinker, he was content to let Manfred down two litres to his one.

Richard endured two long days and late nights, some difficult meetings and a surfeit of food and Pilsner. He knew that *AGC* would have problems in meeting the demanding specification and tight timescales required by *Stern*. That was the result of the pressures of fierce competitive defence contracting. To help see *AGC* through this difficult period, he was committed to doing his utmost to maintain the best possible relationships and communications with Manfred and the other *Stern* key players. As long as these connections remained strong, he believed *Elsa* would have their work cut out to seize part of their contract.

By the time he arrived home late that evening, Bex was already asleep. She left a note: *Waited up. Drank too much. Your dinner's in the cat. Welcome back. See you tomorrow.*

When Richard and Becky arrived at the *George and Dragon,* they found Chuck and Trish enjoying a late but large English breakfast. They were greeted loudly enough to attract the attention of the other diners. That was the way of Chuck and Trish. *Inhibited* was not in their vocabulary. It was doubtful if Chuck, in his personal life, had matured mentally much past the age of twelve. Yet a more honest, jolly, thoughtful and generous friend, it would be hard to find. In business, Chuck was a force to be reckoned with. He was knowledgeable, forthright and tough. He knew instinctively how to strike the best deal and yet had customers quickly eating out of his hand.

Most of the weekend was spent touring the sights of Winchester and walking the Hampshire countryside. Chuck had already planned the routes to ensure there were ample watering holes along the way. He loved the English country pubs. In the markets, he sought out objects that were little over twenty years old, which he fondly referred to as antiques. Trish was the perfect partner for Chuck. Despite his seniority in age, she mothered him constantly and was clearly besotted by his idiosyncrasies.

They talked little business over the weekend, except Chuck used the opportunity to test the water on how *AGC* would react to an approach from *GRSC* to strike up a transatlantic partnership. Richard counselled that the matter needed to be handled with extreme care, as the *AGC* Board was hooked on being good Europeans and was therefore seeking partnerships within the EU. He suggested that an approach at the highest level would be most likely to succeed, rather than running the gauntlet through the many unimaginative and incompetent Luddites below (although he toned down this criticism a little). He suggested that Chuck needed to concentrate on the complementary nature of such a liaison, highlighting the *GRSC's* strength in the civil radar products worldwide and their ambitions to expand into their military home market.

On Saturday night, Richard found himself again sharing a bed with Bex.

'Look Richard, why pay for two rooms?' she had decreed. 'We can easily manage in one like we did in Amsterdam.'

But it was much easier when they were in Amsterdam, as he'd fallen asleep quickly after their long day of sightseeing and drinking. What was more, the bed was much larger. Chuck and Trish always had dinner at six-thirty and retired at ten. Whilst Richard lay awake close to the lovely Bex, she seemed oblivious to the slow torture she was inflicting on him by just being there and looking so desirable. By morning, Richard appeared as if he had not slept for a week; whilst Bex looked as if she had just returned from the beauty salon.

They returned to Farnham late on Sunday afternoon having both enjoyed a relaxing weekend with the genial and agreeable Americans.

Early Monday morning, Richard visited Clive and discussed the visit to *Stern*. Clive said the main problem was simply lack of sufficient experienced engineers assigned to the contract. He readily agreed to take the matter up with the Technical Director again. However, Clive didn't hold out much hope of obtaining a speedy response. He was happy that Richard should send out his Visit Report, without pulling punches, on what he'd described as the risks of failing to perform on time and to specification on the subcontract. They also agreed that the Report should have a wide distribution in the hope it might exert enough pressure to secure the much-needed technical resources.

Whilst in the Engineering Department, Richard managed to have a fleeting word with Kate. He knew he needed to catch up on his sleep, rest his liver and have a light dinner so delayed meeting her until the following evening.

As things turned out, it was as well he had not invited Kate to dinner that evening. Just after five, his office phone rang.

'Security here, Sir. We've a lady to see you at Reception. Says she must see you 'cos it's urgent. Didn't get her name.'

'I guess I'd better come over then. Say I'll be there in five minutes.'

Richard put away his files, locked the cabinet and, with his mind racing, made his way quickly to the Main Gate. As he entered the Reception area, it took him several seconds to recover from the surprise that awaited him.

'Good Heavens! Maggie. What on earth…'

'Hello, Richard. This is Paolo and this is Monica.'

'Err… hello children… Can we go somewhere else to talk?'

'Of course. I have hired a car. I'll follow you. Where do you suggest?'

'I think a pub will be difficult with the kids. There's a *Little Chef* about a mile from here. Will that be OK?'

'Fine, Richard.'

'I'll get the car.'

'Nice kids you've got there. So well behaved,' the security guard complimented Richard as they were leaving the Reception area.

Throughout the short drive Richard could feel his head spinning in the aftershock of seeing Maggie after nearly five years. And she'd even brought kids. Once settled at a table, Maggie selected something from the

113

Children's Menu for the bambinos and ordered just coffee for the adults.

'Well this is a bit of a surprise Maggie.'

'Yes I know. Sorry to come to your work but I didn't know your latest address and I guessed you'd still be with *AGC* or someone would know where you were.'

'So what's this all about?'

'Well, I began to miss the UK and running the hotel means long days over an eight month season. To tell you the truth, Georgio and I were beginning to get on each other's nerves. So he suggested I took a month off in England to see if that will make a difference.'

'Where are you staying?'

'Don't worry, Richard. My folks have moved to Woking so I'm staying with them. I just thought it would be good to see you again and perhaps you could come over for the weekend.'

'Look. This is all a bit of a shock. I need to take all this in, but certainly we could have dinner together on Friday evening.'

'Anyone in your life these days or did you go back to collecting flags of the world?'

'No one in particular, I think you cured me of that. So how's Sorrento?'

'It's a lovely place. Running the hotel is hard work but we've been pretty successful. The weather's good for most of the year and I don't think I could live in England again. I speeka zee lingo and the kids are just as happy chattering in English or Italian. I guess I wasn't very nice to you, so I thought the least I could do was to look you up and say I'm sorry for the way I treated you. You didn't deserve it.'

'OK. Look I'm still a bit shell shocked by all this. If you write down the address and directions, I'll definitely meet you on Friday. Do your folks know I may be coming over?'

'Yes, that won't be a problem. They regret they didn't

have chance to meet you the first time.'

Richard drove home slowly that evening, wondering what on earth Maggie was really up to. Why had she been so keen to search him out after all this time? What was her real motive for wanting to meet him at the weekend?

That evening he confided in Becky and told her everything he could remember about Maggie, their whirlwind romance, marriage and lightning separation.

'So what d'ya make of it all?' he asked.

'Tricky one this. Maybe Georgio's on his way out. Perhaps she's looking for reconciliation and someone to be a father to the kids. Perhaps she thinks you're some kind of soft touch.'

'Whatever she's up to, why should she look me up after all this time? She said it was to say she was sorry for the way she treated me. It's probably because she doesn't know anyone around here and is feeling a bit lonely.'

'Yes, and I'm the tooth fairy. I told you, she's probably looking for a new meal ticket. In a nutshell Richard, you weren't designed to have a normal relationship with the opposite sex. Basically, you bring out the worst in us all.'

'Even you Bex?'

'Shut up and open the wine Richard.'

Although Richard was having a stressful time, it wasn't obvious in his pattern of behaviour. He still displayed a cheery youthfulness and went about work in his own particular way. The night with Kate should have provided a welcome respite from his problems, had he not made what turned out to be, with hindsight, a stupid error of judgement. He had suggested Kate came to Farnham on Tuesday evening, so she could sample the local pubs and restaurants.

All went well until they returned from an enjoyable meal at the restaurant and surprised Becky sipping a glass of red in front of the television.

'Hi Bex, I think you know Kate.'

Becky looked as if a bomb had dropped on the house.

'Yes… of course… hello Kate. What's happened?'

'Nothing's happened, we just decided on a change in venue.'

'Oh. Well it's OK. I'm going to bed now anyway. Sorry, I didn't know.'

'Bex, relax. Sit down. Have a glass with us. We've got all night.'

'Yes, of course you have. No, sorry, I feel really bushed. I'm off to bed.'

Becky's reaction may well have gone unnoticed to Kate; but it was so out of character that Richard knew that something was wrong. He decided that there was nothing he could do to help that evening but would tackle her about it the next day.

So Kate and Richard finished a bottle of Cava Grande Reserve and retired to Richard's bed to exercise their rekindled attraction. However, he suggested they should do it quietly, so as not to disturb Becky in the next room. In the morning, when Richard went to make the coffee, he found that Bex had already left for work.

He and Kate drove in their separate cars to the site so as not to attract any gossip or unwanted attention. This was fortuitous as he nearly collided with Paul Hamilton in his Jag as he drove through the Main Gate. Richard noticed, as he narrowly missed the front wing, that Paul's passenger was none other than Michael Petty. That definitely spelt trouble Richard reflected as he parked his car and walked through the drizzle to his office.

'Raise the drawbridge Liz; we're about to be invaded. I saw Paul Hamilton at the gate.'

'Well, I don't think he'll come all the way over here Richard. Particularly in this weather.'

'You're right Liz. And of course, I would have been somewhere else today, if only he'd warned me.

Unfortunately he's seen me now as I attempted to remodel his Jag as I drove through the gate.'

'Yes. You don't seem to get on with him very well, do you, Richard?'

'No. He's not exactly top of my *people worth saving on the Titanic* list.'

'Takes all sorts I s'pose. My gran said there's some good in everyone.' Liz saw the best in everybody. From what Richard knew of Liz, it was her one and only, but extremely serious fault.

It was eleven before Paul summoned Richard.

'Come in Richard. Was hoping to find you on site. Have you got any brakes on that car of yours? You obviously drive without much care anyway. Do you realise the Company would have had to pay for two damaged cars if you hadn't just missed me by less than an inch.'

'But we were in a one way system Paul and, you were going the wrong way.'

'That's no excuse for dangerous driving Richard. I believe you've met Michael Petty?'

'Yes, many times.'

'Well, we're doing a tour of the sites together. Michael has been appointed as my *Number Two* and will take much of the great admin load from me.'

'Does that include processing expenses?'

'Yes, of course. In fact, he'll be the main contact for you on a daily basis. This will allow me to concentrate on more important tasks such as future planning and strategy.'

'And Michael will process the Product Plans?'

'Yes, Richard. Are you dense? I said admin tasks.'

'Sorry, but I thought Product Plans came under the future planning category.'

'Don't be smart Richard. I'll decide who does what. Suffice for you to know that Michael will be handling the day-to-day management of things. He'll also be my representative at the Asian Aerospace Exhibition.'

'Yes, I'll be calling a planning meeting on that later this week?' Michael interjected clearly enjoying Paul's treatment of Richard.

'Bit late for that Mike. It's in two weeks time. The exhibits and publicity material has been shipped. The invites have gone out and Becky Martin seems to have everything well under control.'

'No Richard.' Petty looked embarrassed. 'I'm talking about the Sales team. I've noticed that many of the exhibitions do not run smoothly. There's either too many or too few people on the stand at various times. We need to coordinate things properly this time.'

How unreasonable for customers to arrive at inconvenient times, pondered Richard as he decided not to pursue the topic further at this time. He'd wait to draw some blood at Petty's meeting. Much more entertaining.

'So tell me more about the visit to *Stern*.' Paul attempted to take back control of the meeting.

'I took the flak on the Engineering problems. *Stern's* well advanced with their prototypes so I believe we're really holding up their development. The French have tried to make some capital out of our problems and want a share in the work. And Manfred wants us to front some of the marketing activities, especially in the Pacific Rim.'

'Well. I'm sure Michael can help you with the latter. On the delays, I think it would make good sense to share the work out further. Your Divisional engineers aren't performing well, so I think we should actively encourage *Elsa's* participation.' Paul seemed to be enjoying himself in front of his Upstart.

'But Paul, we spent a lot of time, effort and money to win this contract. Why give it all away? It's not as if orders grow on trees and we all have budgets to achieve.'

'I must agree with Paul,' Petty intervened. 'We should be sharing our development costs and getting more into Europe.'

'Fine words Mike, but we're being paid for this development. All I've ever asked is that we capitalise on our technology lead with *Aphrodite* and win some contracts. We can then negotiate any partnerships from a position of strength and objectively. Why collaborate with Europeans when we could get a share of the US market by seeking a partner there?'

'Richard, we've been over all this before and you appear to be well out on a limb. You can see Michael has already picked up the importance of the European partnerships and keeping costs down. Dave O'Leary also understands and is being constructive. Why are you so stubborn?'

'Just following my beliefs Paul. As my boss, what do you prefer me to be – a nodding donkey or speak my mind?'

'I expect you to tell me the truth, of course.'

'Exactly. That's what I'm trying to do,' Richard replied with a sly grin at the nodding donkey by Paul's side.

It was Friday when Petty called his disastrous pre-Asian Aerospace meeting. Those summoned included all sales staff attending the Show and selected publicity staff, including Becky. As Richard drove Becky to the venue of the ill-conceived meeting, he decided to tackle her about Kate.

'Bex, I want to ask you something.'

'Go on.'

'Well, the other night. You know, when I brought Kate back. You didn't seem to approve.'

'Oh, it was obvious, was it?'

'Yes, to me. I'm not sure if Kate saw the difference in you, but I certainly did.'

'Ah, I see. If you really want to know, I'm annoyed at the way Kate is treating you. She's all over you until her boyfriend arrives; then she dumps you like a toy she no longer needs. Then behold, her boyfriend gets fed up and leaves and it's Hello Richard again.'

'Oh is that all.'

'That all! I think it's a terrible way to treat people. And you don't deserve it.'

'I probably do Bex. Anyway, I'm under no illusions about Kate. In the meantime, she's good company and extremely active between…'

'Yes, I heard Richard. I had to put cotton wool in my ears last night.'

'Anyway, needs must and all that. Perhaps we're just using each other until the real thing comes along. So I don't think there's any harm being done.'

'Just be careful. I don't want you to get hurt. And by the way, if that's not enough, you now tell me you're off to Woking to have dinner with your ex on Friday!'

'Look, I appreciate your concern. I really do. But don't worry about me getting hurt. I see the pitfalls.'

'But you're so naive at times.'

'I know and I'll be careful. Thanks though Bex. I don't know how I'd manage without you.'

'Now don't get soppy with me. I've got to look my best for this damn meeting.'

Richard was glad he raised the subject when he did. He knew that Bex would not be in such a good mood after the meeting.

In fact, it didn't take long for the coltish upstart to tread heavily on Becky's toes. He began discussing actions that she, as Exhibition Manager, had necessarily completed several months before. He even wanted to review the Booth design and the choice of equipment which had, of course, already been shipped. Finally he tried to cut numbers of sales people attending. Therefore, by the end of the hour-long meeting he had managed to alienate all those present. Definitely a man carefully selected by Paul Hamilton and superbly qualified to follow his master's clumsy footsteps.

Bex was furious. She fumed all the way back to the Farnham flat and again for much of the evening.

'He'd better not start this bloody nonsense when we're in Singapore or his goolies will end up on a spit in Newton Market.' Bex was not known to be one who suffered fools gladly.

As Richard drew into the *El Paso* Mexican restaurant in Woking, he was somewhat apprehensive about spending an evening with Maggie. He took some comfort that she'd agreed to meet at the restaurant rather than her parents' house. Maggie had graciously declined his rather mischievous suggestion to dine in the *Casa Luna.* However, he'd have felt much more comfortable if he knew exactly what she was up to. Still, he'd only known her for a few days both before and after they had married.

Maggie arrived about five minutes after Richard wearing a short white dress which contrasted admirably with her auburn hair and golden tan. He could still see why he'd been swept of his feet five years ago. He gave her a brotherly peck on the cheek and ordered a drink from the bar.

'Kids OK?'

'Yeh, they're fine. Being spoilt rotten by my mother but it's given me a well earned rest.'

'You look as fit as a flea.'

'Yes, I just needed a change of scene and chance to think things out.'

'That bad?'

'No, not really. You've probably realised I'm prone to occasional impulsiveness and…'

'Impulsiveness? You? Surely not.'

'Fair do's. Well, I think I told you the other day, it's been a long hard summer and we're not getting along that well, so I decided to take a two-month's break. Of course

Georgio is very Italian and not used to the idea of women going off on their own. So he's licking his wounds and sulking a bit.'

'So how d'you feel now?'

'Too early to say. Truly, I've nothing really concrete to complain about. I think it's just the way I am. And I do miss England from time to time.'

'Sorrento's a nice place.'

'I don't really get out that much to get the benefit of it. Anyway Richard, that's enough about me. Let's talk about you. What do *you* think of my situation?'

'Still got your sense of humour then. Come on let's eat.'

They talked through the meal. Maggie asked about the women in his life and about his work and his interests. They both relaxed but the conversation brought home to Richard just how little they knew about each other. They must have been crazy to rush off and get married like that. But when she smiled and looked straight into his eyes, he could see how easily it could happen.

At the end of the evening, Richard was none the wiser. It was rather like going out on the first date with a stranger. They were clearly still physically attracted to each other but the situation lacked reality. It was almost as if he was an observer rather than being one of the key players in this soap opera. The evening was enjoyable enough, but slightly disturbing. They agreed to meet from time to time whilst Maggie was in the area. As he watched Maggie drive off, Richard wondered how he continually managed to get himself into such bizarre situations.

Chapter Nine

Richard was delighted to be back in Singapore, his lucky city, again. He had always admired the well-ordered society, the modern attractive buildings, the absence of graffiti or litter and the large landscaped parklands. When he checked into the Orchard Road Hotel, he could be sure that the local standards of hospitality and efficiency were second to none. From the minute he stepped through the swing doors, everything would be done to make his stay as enjoyable and stress-free as possible.

'Welcome back, Mr Bryant. You're here for the Aerospace Show?'

'Yes, I'll be checking out on the fifth.'

'Fine, that's in our computer. Here's your Welcome Letter from our General Manager, your key card, and a message left for you earlier today by Miss Martin. By the way, we've changed the entry code to our Club Lounge since your last stay. It's now 7771.'

As soon as he arrived in his room he opened Bex's note.

Hi Sweet

Nearly finished setting up our Booth. All looking good, Mike Petty arrived last night. What a pain! If he gets any further up my nose, I'll call him Vic. Hope you can join Emma and me tonight. She's French, lives in UK and works for the American 'Defense Now' magazine. You'll really like her. She's 31, blonde of course, about my height and very attractive. Make sure that Petty doesn't join us!!
Love Bexxxxx room 913

PS This is a no smoking, no bubblegum island!! You'll be pleased to know that drinking and the other thing you do are still legal!! xx

By the time Richard had lunched, sunbathed, completed twenty lengths of the pool and unpacked, Becky was champing at the bit.

'Come on, Sunshine. We gals are ready for a night on the town. How was the flight?'

'Hi Bex. Flight was fine but they kindly upgraded me to First again. Sickening, isn't it? I'll be down in five.'

'Drinks are on you then. Our Exhibition Booth's finished so we all have a free day tomorrow. That means there's no holding back tonight.'

Richard began to worry. Bex was a party animal at the best of times. But off the lead, she was positively dangerous. He hoped Emma wouldn't be of similar ilk and could help him see Bex safely to bed. The thought of two unmanageable females was scary for even the most ardent womanising reveller.

When Richard met Emma, his heart went a flutter. She looked as if she'd popped out of the cover of Vogue. Not only did Emma look good but also had a personality to match.

'Oh, so you're the Richard I've heard so much about,' she purred.

'Not too horrible I hope.'

'Only from Becky. Others, such as Kate Webber and Zoë Clark speak highly of you.'

'You know them?'

'I know Kate from riding; we use the same stables in Godalming. Zoë, of course, I know from my visits to Abu Dhabi. I also know your friend Henri Latour.'

'Oh, you seem to have the advantage. Don't believe everything that Latour tells you. I had my horns and forked tail removed two years ago. Anyway, I've brought a couple of bottles of *Don Melchor*. Not French I'm afraid Emma,

Chilean.'

'Oh, don't worry, I haven't lived in France since I was fifteen and I love Chilean Cabernet.'

'And know your wines, I see. Latour thinks that winemaking stops at the French border.'

Bex soon joined in the rapport and, after they had finished the two bottles of Cabernet, they thought they'd better eat something.

'D'you fancy Newton Market girls? It's a sort of vast outdoor food hall with hundreds of stalls, tarot card and palm readers, street artists and performing monkeys. It shouldn't be missed. The atmosphere is electric but the wine's a bit naff. Suggest you try the Tiger beer; it only contains ninety-three known poisons, they tell me.'

Bex and Emma soon agreed with Richard's description of the market. The clientele comprised some locals mingling with a mass of tourists of every possible nationality. The trio walked each bustling passageway. All three had their palms read. Bex was supposed to be in an ideal relationship, would get married within two years and have a boy and a girl. She was going to live abroad in a hot climate. Emma was about to have a passionate romance whilst in Singapore but it was not destined to last. Her career was going to be meteoric and she was destined to marry a rich Texan. When it became Richard's turn, the Palmist looked perplexed. After several minutes of trivia, the gypsy-like soothsayer reached the bits that they were all waiting to hear:

'I see a rough passage in your work and it will last for many months. There are three devils; you need to be alert and vigilant. They are out to harm you. Your love line is like a maze of cracks and crevices. You don't seem to have much fortune there do you? Oh, now I see a special lady… no I think it's a scar from your childhood. But you are a Dragon and therefore strong and resilient. Your health is good and I think you will have a happy life anyway, with much travel.'

'Well, I don't know what you think ladies, but I don't believe a word of it.'

'We do,' they both chorused.

When Richard awoke at midday, he concentrated his thoughts, trying hard to remember the previous evening. He remembered Newton Market, the Karaoke Bar, singing *Uptown Girl* with Emma, two bars in Boogie Street, an affectionate tall girl with an Adam's apple and Bex throwing up in the street. He had a vague recollection of going into the Hard Rock Café, dancing with Bex and Emma but then things got a little cloudy.

As he forced open his eyes, he noticed that the gorilla had been in his room during the night, throwing his clothes around and stealing his money. Anyway, there was much to be thankful for. They hadn't been arrested. He was safely in his own bed and was a proud owner of a Hard Rock Café tee shirt and a toy monkey on a stick. He waited until one and called Bex.

'Hi Bex. You awake?'

'Well I am now Richard. Charged your mobile up yet?'

'What?'

'After you rang all those people. You know – It may be four here but it's only nine in the evening in the UK! Now do you remember?

'Oh god, who did I ring?'

'No one much really. Just Kate, someone called Zoë to tell her you met Emma. Someone else called Hanna-Sweetie or something like that. You tried to get hold of Paul Hamilton to see if he had signed your expenses but fortunately his phone…'

'Stop. I don't want to hear any more.'

'Not even about your offer to take Emma to America on holiday?'

'Oh no.'

'And the horse and trap…'

'Stop, stop. I promise never to touch another drop. Ever again.'

'That's a pity Ritchie, there's a Reception at *Raffles* tonight and I've got three tickets.'

'OK, I'll stop drinking the day after tomorrow. See you by the pool in about an hour.'

At four-thirty Sir Anthony appeared by the poolside. 'Just looked for someone with the two prettiest girls and I knew I'd find you, Richard.'

Richard introduced Bex and Emma.

Sir Anthony seemed concerned. 'I think you've probably heard that I was clobbered to be the Show Director at the last minute. Paul had to drop out. Now, I know nothing about the Region and need to find out what's on our Stand and what I need to do during the week.'

'Not a problem,' Richard assured him. ' If you come to the Exhibition Hall about eight tomorrow, we can take you through it all. Becky knows her way around the exhibits and publicity material. I can show you the customer list and we can get the Stand Manners to give you a rundown on their pitch. The official opening is not until eleven so we've plenty of time.'

'Well that sounds simple enough. Thank you. I'll also get young Petty to join us; he's still a bit wet behind the ears so it'll do him no harm to listen.'

Richard's view of Sir Anthony improved with every meeting.

'I left an invitation to the *Welcome Reception* at Raffles tonight for your check-in,' Bex interjected.

'Oh yes. I'm jolly well not going to miss Raffles. I have a chauffeur driven stretched Mercedes at my disposal, so you're all very welcome to come with me.'

The trio nodded their thanks and arranged to meet in the Bar at six.

The Grande Ballroom of the Raffles hotel was enormous. About a thousand guests stood around a buffet table which ran the full length of the hall. The display was bursting with a vast variety of local and international dishes, elaborate ice carvings and bunches of sweet smelling orchids. Soft music from a small orchestra added to the finishing touches to this truly magnificent scene.

Champagne flowed like water. An army of waiters supported giant trays filled with drinks of every description. Richard noted the look of self-destruction in Becky's eyes. 'Steady Bex, it'll be a long night.'

Despite the large number of guests, the majority of them would be likely to know at least a hundred other attendees. About twenty Defence Exhibitions are held annually around the world and company representatives are drawn from much the same cast of sales and PR staff. Becky was receiving a lot of male attention and seemed to be enjoying herself. Her admirers included the thick-skinned Petty who clearly could not read her body language or even take a broad hint.

Richard spotted several friends and competitors but preferred to spend time with the effervescent Emma. There'd be plenty of opportunities to catch up with them during the Show. After about an hour, Latour, obviously drawn by Emma, joined them balancing three fresh glasses of champagne.

'Mes Amie. Emma, Richard, good to zee you both. I 'av brought you zome goodwill for ze Show.'

He handed them the champagne. 'I give you a toast. A profitable week.'

Perhaps it was because Emma was present that Henri was at his most pleasant ever. They talked about the Singapore social scene, where best to go and old friends they had seen at the Reception.

'It 'as been good talking to you both. I 'ope to zee you in zee week.' Henri bade them a cheery *Au Revior*.

'Well, that was quite painless,' Emma remarked, 'I usually avoid him but he's a sort of customer of mine, I suppose, so I have to make some effort.'

'Yes, he was unusually pleasant. Wonder what he's up to?'

Fifteen minutes later Richard became all too aware of Latour's mischief. He began to feel light headed and started sweating profusely. It became difficult to focus and he could now see two Emmas through a mist.'

'Richard. You look awful. Are you all right ?' Emma took Richard by the arm at the moment he crashed to the floor, taking part of the buffet and an ice carving of a swan loudly with him. The orchestra stopped playing. People stopped talking in mid-sentence. The vast hall became eerily silent as everyone turned to see the source of the loud crash. Richard felt dizzy but was immediately regaining consciousness and trying unsuccessfully to climb back onto his feet.

By now three nearby guests had rushed to his help and one loosened his tie. 'Take it easy old chap. Don't get up just yet.'

Emma found a waiter and returned with a glass of water.

Richard gazed up at the sea of faces as the background burble of voices gradually returned to normal. He was vaguely aware of being helped into a taxi and seeing a perplexed Sir Anthony, a worried Bex and an extremely concerned Emma. He also recalled hearing a jubilant Latour loudly proclaiming to all around him 'I theenk Mr Bryant should take more water with it zee next time.'

Two colleagues, together with Bex and Emma saw Richard safely to his hotel room. The girls said they'd stay with him until they were sure he was all right.

By midnight, Richard had gained much of his composure, taken two Aspirin and drank several cups of tea the girls had ordered from room service.

'Becky, you have to be up early in the morning. You go on to bed. I'll keep an eye on Richard for a while until I'm sure he's OK.'

'Only if you're sure it's not a problem Em.' Richard thought he caught Bex giving her a knowing look. 'I do have to go through all the Show Daily magazines before the Company meeting in the morning.'

'No problem at all. No one will know if I don't go in until after lunch.'

Becky pecked Richard on the cheek. 'Don't worry, chicken. We'll get our own back on that dreadful man. Just you see.'

Soon after Bex left, Emma placed her hand on Richard's forehead. 'How are you feeling now?

'Much better. Whatever it was, it seemed to go straight to my head. It just aches a bit now, but I feel much like my normal self.'

'Good. That's very good indeed,' said Emma, slipping out of her clothes and climbing into bed beside him. 'I've always enjoyed playing doctors and nurses.'

Richard felt her arm fall across his chest as she cuddled her soft body close to his.

'There. Doesn't that feel better?' she enquired, placing her mouth close to his face and gently stroking his torso.

'Much. Very much better,' he gasped. 'I'm not too ill to respond you know.'

'That's good,' she cooed, gently stroking his body and increasing her concentration on his upper thighs.

Unable to stand her soft teasing any more, he turned to face her and pulled her towards him in a passionate embrace. They made love with slow deliberation, as Richard savoured the newness of her touch, sweet scent and the swaying rhythm.

At six o'clock, they made love again. Half an hour later, as Emma was about to leave, she met Becky in the doorway.

'Florence Nightingale, I presume,' grinned Bex. 'I trust the patient's feeling fine and his blood pressure's normal again.'

'Well, you know how it goes Bex. A champagne reception, soft lighting, a warm bed and a virile young man...'

'Not exactly Em. But I'm sure you both look and feel much better for it.'

After a few more choice comments, they left together, giggling like a pair of schoolgirls. Neither had showed the slightest sign of embarrassment, nor Bex resentment. What a pity, Richard thought to himself, that they both hadn't stayed in his room that night. Emma might have made a lasting impression on Bex. Not that Richard was complaining. Emma's nursing had well compensated for the incredibly embarrassing situation at *Raffles*.

Richard's rapid recovery meant that he was able go to the Exhibition in time for the morning briefings. Sir Anthony leant heavily on Richard's experience and seemed quite content to follow his advice. In fact, as the delegations arrived, Sir Anthony was happy to greet them and leave the detailed tour to Richard, as he shepherded them around the *AGC* Stand. The system worked well, and Richard was able to feed him with enough information to customise Sir Anthony's welcome script. Anthony proved to be an extremely able host and completely at ease with important customers. Thank goodness he took Paul's place, thought Richard. What would it have been like with Hamilton snarling and snapping around the place?

Of course, Michael Petty couldn't wait to raise the matter of the *Raffles* cabaret with Richard. 'Oh. You've recovered then,' he taunted. 'How's your hangover? Any chance of you giving us a repeat performance tonight?'

Before Richard could say a word, Bex stepped between them. 'Now you listen to me sunshine. Richard was ill, not drunk last night and we've a strong suspicion that someone, possibly one of your cronies, put something into his drink. So, stop making stupid, infantile comments. Should I find out you've said a word about this when you return, I'll tell them all about when you tried to hit on me yesterday.'

'But Becky, That's not true. I never tried to hit on you.'

'And who do you think they'll believe, Moron, you or me? Just be more careful what you say about your colleagues in the future, especially any friend of mine.'

When Upstart retired hurt, tail truly between his legs, Richard told Bex that he was truly amazed and impressed by her performance.

'Just remind me never to get on the wrong side of you Madam.'

'I know, I probably went a bit over the top. I just can't stand people who behave like he does. He thinks that he's so perfect and loves to gloat on other's misfortunes.'

'No, don't apologise. You were great Bex. Just great. And you certainly got me off the hook. But I guess someone else will carry the gossip back anyway.'

It was soon after Becky's verbal assault on Upstart that Richard felt he should have a quiet word with Sir Anthony over the *Raffles'* fiasco.

'Now, Sir Anthony, I know I've a bit of a reputation for wine and women but the incident at last night's reception was due to neither. I am convinced a devious French salesman slipped something into the drink that he brought me less than half an hour before I collapsed. I can't prove it, but ask anyone who has seriously partied with me and they'll tell you I never even got started last night.'

'I'm pleased that you brought the matter up Richard. Of course, the whole incident was most unfortunate for the Company as well as yourself. I believe you, and have seen for myself that a few glasses of bubbly wouldn't have that sort of effect. I intend to head off any rumours when I get back. I'll merely say that one of the salesmen became ill at a Reception due to a combination of jet lag and a local stomach bug.'

'That's very good of you. Thanks. I believe that's the fourth attempt Latour has made to fix me in a month but I can't prove a thing.'

Throughout the week, the Show was packed with foreign visitors and delegations. Most of the salesmen, unused to standing around for eight hours at a time, began to suffer pains and cramps in their legs and feet. To ease the problem, many would practice standing in bars and nightclubs during the evenings. There was plenty of time to catch up with friends and colleagues from other companies. For Richard, this included Chuck, who had also managed to bring Trish along to top up her tan and enjoy the sites and shopping. They spoke again about the advantages of partnership and Richard suggested Chuck might like to raise the matter on the quiet with Sir Anthony.

'It would be worth sounding him out on it. If he thinks there's some mileage in it, I'm sure he'd test the water with the Chairman. That way, we'll know what we're up against before your Company raises the matter formally.'

Richard arranged for them to meet in Sir Anthony's suite at seven.

Chuck handled the discussion superbly. It was a soft sell but well thought out and presented. He knew the market and had all the necessary figures at his fingertips. An entrée into the US market sounded appealing. Chuck sold the concept as incremental business, arguing that *AGC* would be unlikely to win orders in America whilst they were a wholly UK company. He talked about the synergy of their technology, respective leads in the civil and military markets, as well as their complementary geographical customer base.

Sir Anthony listened intently and without interruption until Chuck had completely finished.

'Well that was most informative and your case is well thought out. Thank you Chuck for that. From a first look, what you say sounds logical and advantageous to both our companies. I'm more than willing to have a quiet word in the Chairman's ear. Before you leave Singapore, can you please write down some key points, including the facts and figures on the market? I'd like to include those in my little chat.'

Richard decided to buy Chuck and Trish an expensive dinner in celebration of Chuck's star performance.

The rest of the exhibition week was relatively uneventful. Richard did notice that Upstart was in Latour's company frequently throughout the week. This didn't bother him until he cornered Richard one day and asked if it was true that he had an embarrassing incident with a married Lebanese girl in Dubai. It didn't take a degree in sociology to work out from where Upstart gleaned that titbit of gossip.

'Mike, you really shouldn't listen to stupid stories put about by jealous competitors. Anyway, the Company didn't fly you all this way to hobnob all week with the opposition.'

'Not the opposition Richard, they're potential partners.'

'No Mike, at the moment *Elsa* is our key competitor. Latour will pick up all sorts of useful information from what you think is just harmless chat. And if *Elsa* is a potential partner, all the more reason to keep them at arm's length until *Due Diligence* has been carried out. You should know that the Company would take a very dim view of any information being passed to *Elsa* at such a critical time. It could hamper any negotiations.'

'But Paul…' Upstart looked worried.

'No Paul couldn't protect you from any formal enquiry should you have said anything untoward. Anyway, he'd have naturally expected you to use due discretion in any dealings with competitors or would-be partners. I'm sure he'd throw a fit if he thought anyone was being indiscreet.'

Richard could see by the look on Petty's now ashen face that he had rattled him. He couldn't resist a final twist of the knife.

'I'm not the only one that has noticed what has been going on this week. I wouldn't be surprised if Sir Anthony wasn't a bit suspicious by now. And you know how close he is to the Chairman.'

Game, set and match, thought Richard as Upstart skulked away.

Bex watched from a distance. As soon as Upstart left, she edged across to where Richard was standing. 'Nice one. Wish I had a video camera. So what's the plan for our last night Richard? I mean, before you slip between the sheets with Emma.'

'Well the prat deserved it. I think he'll be a bit more circumspect in the future. As for tonight, I thought we'd eat in the hotel, have just one drink at the bar and then go to our separate rooms for a good night's sleep.'

'Yes, and this is me, Becky Martin who knows you better than anyone.'

'OK. You win. We'll get trashed in some bar. Grab something to eat and then go out for a drinking binge. We'll then sup some more. Get totally plastered. Stay up until we're absolutely exhausted. Then I'll take Emma to bed and be totally useless at it and won't remember a thing in the morning.'

'OK then. That's better. What time are we meeting up?'

On this occasion, Richard truly had the gift of prophesy. All his predictions came true except that he and Emma made love before they went out and again when they awoke the following day. Richard's flight to Bangkok didn't leave until two. Emma was tearful when Richard kissed her goodbye but delighted that he said they'd meet up that weekend, following his return from Thailand.

This was Richard's first visit to Thailand and the city of Bangkok. One of the Air Force Colonels had asked him to make a presentation to his staff on *Aphrodite*. His hosts had arranged for him to stay near the City Centre, as they wanted him to get the true flavour of the capital. Up to the point when he arrived at the hotel, the only flavour he had experienced was that of traffic fumes in the hot, humid, early evening air.

As he approached the Reception desk he was greeted by a beautiful Thai girl in bright silks, holding ice-cold towels and a welcome drink.

'*Sawatdee ka*. I am Kiad. Welcome to Thailand,' she said, bowing with her hands pressed in a greeting that was to become a familiar sight throughout his short stay.

He gave his name and she collected a wallet from another beautiful girl behind the desk.

'Come this way. You may leave luggage. Porter will bring.'

He followed her through the plush foyer and they took the elevator to the eighteenth floor.

'This Executive Floor. Special guests,' she practically sang the words in her soft happy voice.

Once in the room she took some details from his passport and completed his arrival form. Kiad then showed him how to operate the lighting, conditioning and explained the various hotel facilities including 'Special Thai massage.'

Whilst Kiad was talking, Richard found it hard to concentrate on anything except her beautiful dark brown eyes, her smooth dusky skin and flowing body movements. She looked about sixteen, but that seemed to be true of every girl he had seen in Thailand.

After they chatted for a while, he said she looked so

young to be working.

'I am twenty-nine,' she replied, no doubt well used to Westerners thinking that she looked so much younger. 'I work in Guest Relations for more than two years now.'

'So what you recommend I do tonight?'

'You like beautiful Thai girls?'

'Yes, if they are all like you.'

'Then you should meet one.'

'How?'

'Just ask.'

'OK. What time do you finish work?'

'Nine o'clock. You go downstairs at nine and ask for Noonie the taxi driver. He will look after you.'

What had started as light-hearted banter had now blossomed into a fully-fledged date with a gorgeous Thai girl, who seemed quite unabashed by Richard's cheeky advance.

Promptly at nine Richard went to the lobby to seek out Noonie.

The driver was waiting for him and they headed out into the stop-go traffic. As they approached the tourist area, the taxi drew up in a side street.

'The lady wait in the *Phuket Island* bar.' Noonie pulled into a small piece of wasteland and a barrier was soon moved so he could park in the congested area. He gave the attendant ten Baht. He then nodded in the direction of a small bar. 'You go, take your time. I wait here for you.'

As he entered, he saw that Kiad had changed into a small black dress and long leather boots. Her long black hair was now allowed to frame her pretty face with her expressive eyes and pert nose. She greeted him warmly.

'Good you come, Mr Richard. We have drink here, then I show you sights of Bangkok.'

They both drank *Singha* beer, the strong local brew. Kiad told him that she'd been married to a Thai for four years, but then he'd left her for an American girl. She had a daughter of two who was being cared for by her parents who lived in *Nakhon*. After two beers, they returned to find Noonie sitting in the cab eating some kind of meatball on a stick.

'Let's go sightseeing.' Kiad flopped into the back seat of the Mercedes and snuggled up to Richard.

They drove for about twenty minutes whilst Kiad pointed out various landmarks, temples and shops including several that would make two bespoke suits, three shirts and two ties, all for about two hundred dollars and within twenty-four hours. They then returned to *Patpong*.

Kiad dismissed Noonie and suggested Richard should give him fifty Baht which he calculated was less than ten pounds.

Kiad led him down the long, crowded street lined with an assortment of stalls vending silks, jeans, CDs, rattan, jewellery as well as a host of souvenirs. He let Kiad bargain for a number of small gifts which he bought for Bex, Emma, Kate and Zoë.

'Here Elvis Presley Bar.' Kiad pointed excitedly at one of the hundred look-alike shop fronts blasting out music in the hope of attracting punters. They took a table near the stage where Elvis, Tom Jones, Mick Jagger and Michael Jackson all performed over the next hour and a half. They then tried two more noisy and crowded bars.

It was well after midnight when Kiad left the table and spoke to a middle-aged woman in black who Richard judged to be the owner's wife. When she returned, she beckoned to Richard saying, 'Come with me, I show you another part of Bangkok.'

Richard followed her along a narrow corridor and up one flight of stairs. They crossed the landing and Kiad unlocked and pushed open a door on which an elephant was engraved on a small pewter plate.

'Come,' she called locking the door behind them. In the dimly lit room was a bath, double bed, tape player and several towels draped across a chair. Kiad started to run the bath, chose a tape and started to play soothing Thai music.

'Now you experience Thai massage.' Returning to him she held him close to her. They hugged and after a few minutes she unbuttoned his shirt and continued her caresses whilst removing all his clothes. She then tested the bath, slipped out of her clothes and invited him to join her.

'Just relax. Enjoy.' Kiad began to soap Richard's body from head to toe. She then unhooked a hand shower, again testing the water and rinsed everywhere she had soaped. Richard was self-conscious at first over the whole procedure but her winning smile, soothing hands and easy manner soon relaxed him completely. She soaped herself and rubbed her small brown body against his. Kiad then used the shower to rinse them both and used two towels to ceremoniously dry his body. She then invited him to lay face downward on the bed whilst she quickly dried her tiny body.

Soon he felt some warm oil being poured onto his back followed by her kneading and gently pummelling his joints and muscles. Occasionally, she would change to light and gentle sweeping movements, which he especially enjoyed on his thighs. Every now and again she would rub her body against his in slow writhing movements. After about twenty minutes, she asked him to turn *sunny side up*. Kiad then began the same treatment starting on his chest, then to his toes working upwards. By the time she reached his thighs, Richard was visibly and demonstratively excited. She gave a little squeal of delight and concentrated the rest of the massage to light, teasing strokes around his groin. Such was her expertise that she was able to continue this treatment for more than an hour before Richard succumbed to her expert touch in a burning, powerful, shuddering climax.

They bathed together again, dressed and left the room. Kiad placed a five Baht note on the chair, which she explained was for the cleaner. Downstairs, Richard settled the bill for the drinks and the hire of the room which came to the equivalent of twenty dollars.

'Now we take Tuk-Tuk.' Kiad hailed a brightly painted converted scooter, resembling an oversized psychedelic Reliant Robin, which raced them through the side streets to where Kiad lived.

'I see you in hotel tomorrow. Thank you for wonderful evening.'

'The pleasure was all mine,' replied Richard, meaning every word of it.

The strange vehicle was manoeuvred through the side streets to deposit Richard safely back at his hotel. He was surprised that Kiad had not asked for any money for herself and decided he would buy her a gold bracelet. He reasoned that, should she need money, she could sell the gift.

After only four hours sleep, Richard made his way again to Reception, this time to meet Colonel Hang.

'Richard, good to see you again. I trust the hotel made you most welcome. I asked them to take special care of my important guest.'

Oh, they did, Colonel. You could say they went out of their way to make my stay memorable.'

Richard spent the morning with the Air Force officers who listened to his briefing attentively and asked a lot of searching questions. They then lunched together and Richard was thanked emphatically before being returned to his hotel in the Colonel's staff car. He found a shopping centre close to the hotel and chose a classic design of a twenty-two carat gold bracelet which he had gift-wrapped. He obtained the assistant's help to write his thank you message in Thai. As he returned to the hotel, he asked Kiad to walk with him to the patio where he presented the gift.

'But Richard, I just hope you will come back to my country again and soon. Next time, I will do my best to make your stay even more enjoyable.'

Richard wished he didn't have to fly out that night. It meant leaving the hotel at five. But hopefully, there'd be a next time.

After the long flight home, the week's excesses were beginning to take their toll. The last thing he needed now was to be greeted by a cheerful, wicked Bex.

'Hi Richard. How was Thailand? Stayed in, went to bed early and thought of Emma did we? Or was it Kate? Or Hanna maybe? Or even Zoë? Perhaps you visited the museums and temples. Or perhaps you spent your time out and about trying hard to integrate with the locals? Ah, but you're seeing Emma tomorrow, aren't you? I'll suggest that she puts you in a bath full of water and checks if anything floats that shouldn't. Then she'll know for sure what you've been up to.'

'Hi Bex. I'll tell you all about it, I promise, but later. Right now, I'm whacked. I'm going to bed.'

Chapter Ten

When Richard awoke on Saturday morning, he was still suffering from the excesses of the past week, with the added effects of jet lag. He could hear Bex bustling about in the flat, singing quietly to herself. He dragged himself from the bed, donned a pair of boxers and made his way to the kitchen.

'Is that the morning nightingale I hear?'

'Oh. It's arisen, has it? No I'm the Richard Bryant message service. Emma, Kate and Maggie all want you to call back. Paul Hamilton wants to see you first thing on Monday morning in his office. Sir Anthony also wants to see you sometime next week when you have a moment. So who's Mr Popular then? You're bank statement arrived so I guess the manger wants to know whose banking with whom. There's coffee on the hob and yoghurt and croissants in the fridge. I've put your washing on and... god Richard, what's that all over your back and chest?'

'What do you mean on my... Bex. What on earth is it?'

'Don't know. Let's have a gander. Mmm... Looks to me as if you've been in a fight with a Portuguese man of war and lost. Been anywhere you shouldn't have lately Richard? Apart from Thailand that is.'

'What can I do Bex. I can't go to the doctor on a Saturday morning with a rash. Can I?'

'Looks a bit more than a rash, hun. Maybe you've got the pox or some strange tropical and highly contagious and life threatening disease. Perhaps I shouldn't be this near you. Perhaps it's even too late already. God Richard, we're going to die, we're going…'

'Enough Bex. Why is it you're such a pain in the butt at times of adversity? Be sensible, advice please.'

'Advice Richard. Don't visit Thailand and don't speak to strange foreign ladies and keep your…'

'Bex!'

'Sorry. But you can't help seeing the funny side of things, can you?'

'Oh really.'

'Well, how about if I drive you down to the local chemist. Pharmacists are highly trained people, you know, although I have to admit, I'm not sure about their experience in Tropical Dis…'

'Bex!'

'Seriously then. We'll go see the pharmacist. You show the nice man your rash. By the way is it all over your body?'

'I don't know but it looks like it.'

'Then you'd better just show him your chest and get his advice. He'll either give you some calamine lotion, suggest you call the doctor without delay or spray you with strong antiseptic and put us out into the street.'

'Good idea. Amongst all the crap that is. I'll go and shower. Give me ten minutes.'

'Scrub everything down afterwards with some bleach, won't you?'

'Bex, shut up.'

'Do you want me to tell the girls that you're out of action?'

'No thanks Bex, I'll call them afterwards.'

As expected on Saturday mornings, the Pharmacy was crowded. Richard waited his turn whilst Bex continued to make smart comments in his ear.

'D'ya think these people know what a risk they're taking just being here today?'

'Shut up Bex.'

'I knew it was a mistake, you going to Bangkok like that on your own.'

'Bex, enough. Someone will hear you.'

'Next please.' The young female assistant nodded at Richard.

'Err, well… I err need to speak to the Pharmacist please.'

'Mr Thomas. Customer wants to see you,' she called loudly. By now, everyone in the shop was alerted.

'Yes young man. How can I help you?' Mr Thomas looked searchingly at Richard through his pince-nez.

'Well, I need your advice.' Richard was conscious that several people had interrupted their browsing and edged towards the counter.

'Yes. What is wrong?'

'I have *rash,*' he whispered, barely enunciating the last word.

'You have a what, young man?'

'A *rash.*'

'Where's the rash?' By now his secret was out.

'On my chest.'

'Well you better show me. Come into the back room.'

As he made his way beyond the counter, he could hear the shoppers mumbling to each other, no doubt speculating about the cause of the dreaded rash.

'So, let's have a look at this little problem.'

Richard unbuttoned his shirt.

'Mmm. Yes, that looks a bit nasty. Not at all pleasant, is it? Any idea where you got it?'

'I've been abroad.'

'Anywhere specific?'

'The Far East.'

'That's a big area.'

'Singapore.'

'Yes, I see, Singapore. Anywhere else?'

'A couple of days in Thailand.'

'Ah, I see. Really. Bangkok. Mmm. Maybe we're getting somewhere now. OK, you can button up your shirt. Is it anywhere else on your body?'

'Yes, everywhere from my shoulders to my knees.'

'I'll give you something to tide you over for the weekend. You need to see a doctor first thing on Monday morning, though.'

'Is it serious?'

'Not if you're careful. I'll give you some tablets and some cream. You've had a strong allergic reaction to either food or some of the exotic oils they use in the sort of places you've been.' He gave Richard a knowing look.

'Oh, will it last for long?'

'About a week to ten days, I should say. Avoid fish, pork, bananas, soft cheeses, no wine of any colour and stay away from exotic oils and things like that.'

Richard left the shop with Bex nudging his side. 'What did he say Richard?'

'He said you're going to die Bex. He said in fact that it'll probably be today.'

When they returned to the flat, Richard decided it best to call the girls and tell them he was indisposed.'

'Hi Kate. Yes I got back yesterday. Picked up a bit of a bug though. I'm taking some medicine but will have to see the doc on Monday morning. Ya' know what these hot places are like for tummy bugs and things.'

'Yes, Richard, I hear Bangkok is particularly bad for that sort of thing. One just can't be too careful. By the way, I spoke with Emma on Thursday. She seemed to enjoy Singapore. And she thought you were good fun.'

'Yes, it's a nice place. Did she say anything in particular?'

'Not much. She said she liked the social life there and thought you and Bex were absolute sweeties.'

145

'Oh. I liked Emma a lot. I promised to see her again.'

'Don't blame you Richard. She's quite a catch. Did she tell you her father's a multi-millionaire in the Paris couture business?'

'No, but you know that wouldn't make a jot of difference anyway. If anything it's a turnoff.'

'I know you well enough to appreciate that Richard. I just felt you ought to know.'

'Thanks Kate, I'll get in touch when I'm mobile again.'

He turned to Bex. 'That was a funny call. She seemed OK but I detected an edge in her voice.'

'Maybe she's ever so slightly pissed off that you're bonking one of her friends as soon as you're out of her sight for five minutes. Maybe she's just a jealous old cow.'

'I knew you'd see the good in the situation Bex. After all, Kate did say she didn't want a relationship.'

'Richard. You're hopeless. You don't know the first thing about women. Don't you know by now we never say what we mean and hide everything under some protective shell? Any wonder your love life's such a mess.'

'Bit deep for me Bex. I always treated girls as such honest, shallow creatures. Now I'd better ring Maggie.'

'Hello Maggie, how are you?'

'Not bad Richard, how was your trip?'

'OK, but I've picked up some dreaded tummy bug so I'll not be out and about for a few days.'

'Oh, that's a pity Ritchie. I really need to see you. Can I come round?'

'I just want to rest up over the weekend. I'm seeing the doctor on Monday. I'll know better what's happening then. After all, I don't want to pass on some bug to you that the kids might catch.'

'OK Richard. Please call me on Monday.'

Richard went into the kitchen where Bex was mixing a sauce.

'Don't worry. Haven't put any wine or bananas in the

sauce.'

'That was a strange call Bex. Maggie seems to be a bit low.'

'Really Richard, is this the same Maggie that you're concerned about that ditched you on your honeymoon?'

'Yes, but I guess she's nobody to turn to in the UK except me. After all, she hardly wants to involve her parents and worry them.'

'Course not Richard. Not when she's still got you. Sometimes I wish you were tougher.'

'Really?'

'Well not too tough.'

'I'll go and ring Emma and then Paul at home.'

Emma was extremely sympathetic and understanding. 'Oh, you poor thing. Shall I come round and look after you?'

Richard politely declined and said he would just spend the weekend in bed and call her on Monday.

Fortunately Paul was not at home so Richard was able to leave a message on his answer machine regretting that he couldn't see him until he'd been to the doctor.

Bex had had her fun but was a perfect nurse over the weekend. It didn't stop the teasing comments but she was even more attentive than usual and insisted Richard should take things easy whilst she waited on him hand and foot.

'Bex, I'm not an invalid. I can still help around the house.'

'No, you take it easy. You've had a strenuous week and Auntie Bex wants to know every little tiny intricate detail. So start talking. Right now. Or I'll cover you in itching powder.'

Richard was much relieved when the doctor confirmed the Pharmacist's diagnosis and told him to continue taking the tablets and using the cream and that he could return to work. But having arrived on site, he soon began to wish that the doctor had confined him to bed for a month.

Liz popped out of her office as soon as she heard him arrive. 'Richard, there's lots of urgent messages for you. Clive wants to speak with you as soon as possible, Mr Hamilton says you're to call him the minute you walk through the door. Sir Anthony asks you to call when you can. Michael Petty has sent you a request for a business plan. He's also called a meeting on Wednesday at two to explain what is needed. Oh, and that Dave O'Leary has been over twice now asking when you're coming back.'

'Well that's great, Liz. Nice to know I've been missed. Is there some coffee in the jug?'

'Now I'm sure that you are missed Richard. I miss your joking around the place, especially when people are trying and make your life difficult and you're still the same as ever. I'll make you a fresh pot. You don't look very well at all though. I think you travel far too much. It's such a strain. I know. When me and my Ernest go to Mablethorpe, it takes us a few days to recover when we get back. You settle down to your calls. I've left the mail on your desk.'

'I'm back Clive. What's up? It sounded urgent.'

'It is Richard, and serious. I don't want to talk here. Can I come over?'

'Sure, come over now Clive.'

It seemed that Clive must have sprinted the two hundred yards to Richard's office, as it was less than a minute before he appeared out of breath at the door.

'Gosh Clive, you look like I feel.'

'Oh just wait until you hear what I've got to say.'

'Well, come on in sit down, have a coffee, close the door and tell me about it.'

Clive started to relate his meandering story. He explained that whilst Richard was in Thailand, Paul Hamilton called and told him he had to go to France the next day.

'Just like that. Drop everything and go with him the next day. And Annie was supposed to have the car as there was a big golf match on and we were supposed to be going to see her parents that evening.'

'So what happened?'

'Her brother in law took…'

'No Clive. What happened about the trip?'

'I met Paul at the airport. He told me to bring all the technical stuff on *Aphrodite* and give *Elsa* a full-blown presentation. Apparently he'd cleared everything with my boss.'

'Go on.'

'Well, we went to the *Elsa* site and met with several of their high-ups. Also, Henri Latour was there. He'd just got back from Singapore, but I didn't recognise anyone else.'

'So how many people?'

'About ten in the room, excluding us.'

'So what happened?'

'Well they gave an *Elsa* Overview Presentation of the Company, which was little more than a drawn out wiring diagram. Then they ran through their products; there was nothing new there. Then Paul did a pretty poor job of doing the same for *AGC*.'

'So where was this leading to?'

'Well, they wanted to talk about how we could combine our 3D radar development into a common programme with them.'

'So how did you tackle that without giving our trade secrets away?'

'With a lot of difficulty actually. Paul kept pressing me to tell more and, as you'd expect, they told us precious little about their new design.'

'So how did it go?'

'There was just a lot of talking around the issues so not much progress was made at all. Of course Paul blamed me afterwards for stifling the discussion.'

'Well he would, wouldn't he? So is that the problem you came to talk about?'

'Gosh no. It's much more serious than that.'

Clive went on to tell Richard that Paul had insisted on his taking several technical documents; some of which were Confidential. Paul wouldn't listen to any of his protests and during the day at *Elsa* he was parted from his briefcase at lunchtime. Latour had said not to worry, he'd lock it in a safe place.

'Anyway Richard, it wasn't until I returned to my office here and opened my briefcase that I found one of the documents missing. What was worse, before I had time to unpack my bag fully and check all the documents, Security rang to say that a confidential document had been found at Heathrow. Their Airport Security had handed it in to the Police and then of course all hell broke loose.'

'So you're carrying the can as it were?'

'Yes, of course. Paul was the first to remind me that the safe custody of the documents was entirely my problem. What makes matters worse is that, because I'd no notice of the meeting, I was unable to follow the normal Company procedures and obtain the correct authority to take classified documents abroad.'

'Hardly your fault Clive.'

'Oh yes. Everyone now tells me I should have refused.'

'Twix devil and deep blue sea then? What happens next?'

'In a nutshell. I'm told there's going to be a lot of form filling and then a full enquiry. The Ministry might well get involved.'

'You'll just have to tell the truth Clive.'

'It won't make any difference, Richard. The docs are on my slop chit. The buck stops with me.'

'Is there anything I can do?'

'Was hoping you'd have a bright idea or two. You're pretty used to getting out of the mire.'

'Thanks Clive. Tricky one this. I'll give it some thought. I guess you believe the document was stolen from your bag at lunch time and then taken to Heathrow and left lying around knowing it would be traced back to you.'

'It must have been, I didn't open my bag at all on the way home. It was kept locked from when I left the *Elsa* site until I got to work the next day.'

'How good is the lock?'

'Not too good. It wasn't a proper security bag. Just my normal briefcase with a very basic lock. Anyone who wanted to get into it over the lunchtime wouldn't have had much of a problem. I reckon it could be opened with a bent pin.'

'Particularly by the dishonest gits in *Elsa*. OK Clive, let me think about it and I'll try and come up with something to help. Not easy, mind.'

'No, I know. Thanks anyway Richard. I'll wait to hear then.'

As Clive made his exit, Dave O'Leary arrived at Richard's door.

'Mixing with criminals I see Richard.'

'You didn't come all the way over here to gloat over Clive's problem I hope Dave.'

'Na. I've got far more important things to do than that.'

'So what can I do for you?'

'Quite simple really. I need ya to stop this silly campaign of yours to prevent the company progressing in line with the proposal to develop civil products.'

'That's one way of putting it. On the other hand, I'd say what you are proposing is more likely to prevent the Company from achieving its core business.'

'You need to move with the times, Richard. The market's changing.'

'It won't be any easier fishing in somebody else's

pond, you know. Change is fine but don't throw the baby out with the bath water. We need *Aphrodite*. It's our business. And more importantly, it's my business.'

'Well, Richard, I can see ya won't listen to reason. I was told to come and talk to ya but I told them I'd just be wasting my time. At least I tried.'

'Who told you to come?'

'I'm not prepared to tell you that.'

'OK Dave, you can tell Paul, I'm just as stubborn as ever.'

'You'll regret this Richard. You're making too many waves for your own good.'

With that, O'Leary turned on his heels and slouched out of the office.

Liz brought another coffee. 'I thought you might be needing this. Don't forget Mr Hamilton is waiting for your call.'

'Thanks Liz. How could I forget? Suppose I'd better.'

When Richard called, Pat gave the good news that Paul was out for the rest of the day. Then followed the bad news. 'He insists on seeing you first thing tomorrow though Richard.'

'His first thing or mine?'

'I think he wants you at eight.'

'Thanks Pat. Could you do me a favour and try and get me a meeting with Sir Anthony afterwards, whenever that will be?'

'Sure Richard, leave it with me. You must tell me all about your travels whilst you're waiting for him. I'm sure you've got some stories to tell.'

'Pretty boring really Pat. Same old routine you know. See you tomorrow.'

During the morning, Richard gave more thought to poor Clive's predicament. He was particularly concerned that it had become a reported security breech. He knew that once the Security Department got their teeth into

152

things, they never wanted to let go. If Clive were found to be culpable, it would probably result in a Formal Warning and the breech of security would stay on his personal documents forever. Mid-afternoon, he made his way to Clive's office. 'Just need a few bits of information about your problem Clive.'

'Ask away, whatever you need to know.'

'Now I need exact details, including times and dates of when and how you were told about the meeting, what you were instructed to take and suchlike.'

'OK. The visit was on the fifth and the flight left Heathrow at eight that evening. I had a call from Paul's secretary at about three o'clock on the fifth when she told me about the meeting and said she was sending a fax on what was required. That arrived at three-fifteen. I'll give you a copy before you leave. Pat arranged for me to collect my ticket at the airport.'

'What next?'

'We arrived near the *Elsa* site just before ten that evening and checked into a small hotel nearby. The meeting started at nine-thirty the following morning in their main conference room. We stopped for lunch between one and two, left the site at five and arrived back at Heathrow just before eight.'

'You didn't have much notice at all then. I wonder how long Paul had known about it before he suddenly realised he needed a technical presence?'

'I don't know the answer to that one.'

Richard rang his friend in the Travel Office and asked her when the request was made for their flights. As expected, Paul's was made on the first of the month and Clive's rushed through at three o'clock on the fifth.

'No surprises there then Clive. Now, I see from the fax that he required a technical presentation on *Aphrodite* in Power Point with full backup documentation to be taken with you to France.'

153

'That's correct. I rang him to tell him I shouldn't take the technical stuff without the necessary approvals but he just told me that was my problem, not his and just to damn well get on with it.'

'Fine Clive. As well as the copy of the fax I need you to jot down as accurately as possible a diary of times and events and who said what to whom. I'll try and come up with a cunning plan.'

'Thanks *Baldrick*. Any help would be appreciated.'

Richard's final task of a fairly miserable day was to look over the nonsense requested by Petty for his Business Plan. As expected, this required him to give a host of meaningless figures in excruciating detail about the cost to produce, quantities and phasing of a product that would take a further eighteen months to complete the development. He was also asked to give the same on the competitors including products for the civil market.

Richard was beginning to think he was in the wrong job, or in the wrong company, or both. Yet, he reflected, he'd always been successful in exceeding his sales targets. He had excellent relationships with customers and with his colleagues in most departments on site. He enjoyed the variety and opportunity to travel to new places. He liked the cut and thrust of the job, especially *the kill*, the final stages of winning a competitive tender. Why was his life made so difficult by these Muppets? He seemed to be at a major crossroads. He'd become utterly frustrated with the many diversions from his real work, his incompetent boss and meddling amateurs. Even his love life, which at first sight was vigorous, interesting and exciting, had become complicated and unfulfilling. As he drove back to Farnham that evening, he began to contemplate what changes could redirect his life and maybe his fortune.

However, some of the pressure began to dissipate as he opened the front door to the flat.

'Goodness Richard, you look as if the bottom's just

dropped out of your world.'

'Hi Bex, I think it has.'

'What's up Chicken, had a bad day?'

'Yes – one of those when I wish I'd stayed in bed.'

'Anyone in particular?'

'No, alone.'

'No, Richard, I meant did anyone in particular upset you?'

'Only the usual ones. And tomorrow I get to spend the day with Hamilton and Petty to add insult to injury.'

'Someone told me today that Clive's in a bit of trouble.'

'Yes, it's pretty serious too. I'm sure he's been set up by the French. I just don't know how to prove it. He's also having problems with his projects as they won't give him enough engineering resources to do the job.'

'And are you having problems from your fan club as well?'

'Not particularly. I know I've some really nice girlfriends but I can't see any of the current relationships going anywhere.'

'I thought that's what you wanted.'

'Well yes, most of the time. But it's not normal, is it? Anyway, I can't see any of them until this rash disappears. It's no better today. Just glad it's not on my face or they'd think I was elephant man.'

'So you won't be having wine with me tonight then?'

'Just the odd bottle. If I was seriously allergic to wine, I'd have been dead years ago. It must be one of the other things. Shellfish, I hope. I've never liked eating the rubbery little beggars anyway.'

As expected, when Richard arrived promptly at eight at Paul's office, Paul was nowhere to be seen.

'Sorry Richard, I knew he wouldn't be here for eight.' Pat offered to make him a pot of coffee.

155

'No, I'm actually quite pleased we're alone Pat, I wanted to ask you a favour anyway.'

'Of course. What is it?'

'Well you've probably heard about Clive Deacon supposedly losing a confidential document at Heathrow.'

'Yes, I did hear Paul on the phone ranting on about it.'

'Well frankly Pat, it's a set up and Clive could be in big trouble unless he gets some help.'

'But what can I do Richard? I don't really know much about this sort of thing.'

'I just want you to be a super PA and protect your boss.'

'Must I? OK go on.'

'Well the gist of it is that firstly, Clive shouldn't have taken those documents from the site in the way he did. Secondly, they weren't carried in a proper security bag. Thirdly, he didn't have the proper authorisation to take them overseas.'

'Go on. I still don't see how I can help.'

'Well you see, neither Paul nor Michael Petty will take any notice of what I say, but they will take notice if you make an effort to protect Paul.'

'So what do I have to do?'

'Really simple. This is a copy of the fax you sent from Paul telling Clive he's to go to France at short notice and to take the classified documents. I want you to show it to Michael Upstart, sorry I mean Petty, and say you're really worried that Paul will get into big trouble.'

'How will that help?'

'You're showing it to Petty so he can protect Paul and gain him brownie points. So he'll be on to Paul as quick as a flash. Say you've heard through the secretary Mafiosi that the fax is likely to be used in evidence by Clive to show that he was merely carrying out an instruction by a very Senior Company Director. Say Clive is also likely to argue that his ticket was issued several days after Paul's, showing that Paul knew about the trip well in advance. This is all true of course. Clive will use this stuff in evidence if it comes to a full-blown enquiry. We just make Paul realise that he's in the firing line. Once he realises that he's in trouble, all sorts of pressure will be brought to bear.'

'Are you sure Clive would use the faxes?'

'Course he wouldn't. He's far too nice and loyal to the Company but Paul doesn't know that.'

'Well it all seems fine to me. But how does that help the fact that Clive lost the document?'

'Petty will rush to Paul saying he's found out something that could have harmed him. He'll relate the story and show him the fax. It'll scare the living daylights out of the good Mr Hamilton in that he'll be seen as culpable of forcing Clive to ignore the usual company precautions to properly protect the documents. Can you imagine what he'd do if he thought the Chairman might hear about that? If my guess is right, Paul will use his power to crush the enquiry and stop things there and then.'

'Well, I'll try Richard.'

'That's super of you Pat. I wouldn't ask for myself but it's really in a good cause and they can only accuse you of looking after the interests of your boss.'

'Well, I hope the other PAs don't find out about that bit. They'd rather see him hang. They can't stand the sight of Paul either.'

It was nearly another hour before Paul strolled into the office.

'Ah Richard, got you at last. Recovered from your excesses of the Far East yet?'

'Almost Paul. I still get terrible nightmares about sitting on sunny, sandy beaches with topless waitresses wearing Hawaiian skirts bringing me champagne and oysters and...'

'That'll do Richard. I brought you here to talk about

serious matters.'

Pat brought in some fresh coffees and told Paul she would be out of the office for ten minutes whilst she took some of his internal letters around the Headquarters.

'Well, put the phone through to one of the other secretaries Pat, I don't want it ringing in here, jumping up and down all the time when I'm trying to have a meeting.'

'I've already switched it through to Betty. Won't be long.' She gave Richard a knowing look.

'Right Richard, let's get down to it. Haven't got much time.'

'Yes Paul.'

'I brought you here to tell you that you and I are on a collision course Richard.'

'Collision course?'

'Yes. Not only are you being an absolute pain over *Elsa* and developing a civil product but also you're never in the country when I need you, your personal life's a shambles and your expense claims are a work of fiction.'

'Really Paul?'

'Yes. Let's start with your behaviour when away on Company business. What's this I hear about you and a major incident with some married Lebanese tart?'

'I don't know any Lebanese tarts.'

'You know exactly what I mean. Something about taking her to hospital in the middle of the night.'

'Oh, that problem. Someone had an accident. I was just doing my Boy Scout bit and drove her to hospital. What could possibly be wrong with that?'

'The woman's married and it was the middle of the night.'

'So are you accusing me of some impropriety?'

'Well you must admit, it's all a bit suspicious.'

'I'm not sure what you are suggesting Paul. Can you be quite specific?' Richard reached for a pen and paper. 'Do you mind if I make some notes?'

'I can't be any more specific than I've already been. You need to be far more careful. And then there's the incident at the Raffles Reception.'

'Incident Paul?'

'Richard, you know exactly what I'm on about. When you drank too much, and collapsed.'

'Who told you that Gallic fairy story Paul? I had hardly anything to drink and I fainted at the Raffles.'

'Look I know you've a reputation for knocking back the drink and partying until the last guest goes home.'

'I don't quite see the connection Paul. So is there another incident you are talking about? Perhaps one when someone thought I may have drunk too much?'

'Why do you have to twist everything Rich...'

Paul stopped speaking as Petty appeared at the door. 'Sorry to interrupt you Paul but your phone is through to someone else and I must speak with you urgently.'

'That's all right Michael. Go ahead.'

'Well... err... I need to speak to you in private.'

'OK. That's all for the time being. I'm sure you've got lots of work to do. Just take this silly expense claim with you. It looks as if you had two breakfasts one morning in Singapore.'

'I did Paul; I had a breakfast meeting in the hotel with Major Sang before we went to the show. I made a note in the remarks column.'

'Well take it with you and make sure it's clear. Just remember all I said today.'

'Of course, Paul. Goodbye.'

'Shut the door behind you and tell Pat to hurry back if she's not sitting outside.'

Richard met Pat in the corridor. 'The old git is pining for you Pat. Said he wants you back chained to the desk *ASAP*. And thanks a bunch for what you did.'

'Any time Richard. You've always helped me.'

'Oh would you please put this expense claim back in

the top hundred documents in the misery's In-tray. Perhaps he'll read it properly this time.'

Richard made his way to Sir Anthony's suite of offices.

'Go right in, Sir Anthony's expecting you Richard. Coffee?'

'Yes please Jane. Milk and extra sugar please. I need the energy.'

'I'm sure you do, if all what I hear about you is true.' Jane grinned, 'I'll bring it in to you. You need to take it easy.'

'Morning Sir Anthony.'

'Hello Richard. Come in. Take a pew.' Sir Anthony waved to a pair of easy chairs in the corner of his office. 'How are you feeling now? Fully recovered, I hope?'

'Yes, I'm still a bit bushed but on the mend. Thanks for your help, by the way.'

'Not a problem. I appreciated all the help you gave me in Singapore. I called for you to let you know I had a word with the Chairman about Chuck's proposal.'

'How did he take it?'

'Well good and bad really. He thought the venture made good sound business sense. He liked the logic of the complimentary business argument. He knew the President of the Company and had actually visited their site once and liked what he saw.'

'That's good.'

'Yes, but that's not the end of it. He's under a lot of pressure from within *AGC* and the Government to get closer to European companies. So that seems to be his priority for the next year at least. There's already been a lot of discussion with prospective European partners. As you know, we've even bought four European companies in the last year to merge with our various Businesses, including the Communications, Components, Marine and Combat Divisions so far.'

'And they're all now worth a lot less than we paid, partly due to the falling Euro, but mainly because their governments have ceased funding them as they did before. I'm surprised the penny didn't drop.'

'Well, that's as maybe, but unfortunately, the view at the top is that it is merely a temporary setback.'

'And the European Businesses you mentioned only really ever served their own home markets.'

'True Richard, I'm certainly not defending the decisions. I was much against the acquisitions at the Board Meetings but I'm only one voice in many.'

'So how strong is the no?'

'Pretty strong, unless we can muster support from the managers within your Division. And with Paul, Michael Petty and Dave O'Leary all running around Europe, we'll have our work cut out. The only other possibility is if you could get Chuck to get his Company to invest some money in the business – set up a joint venture, for example. That could change things dramatically.'

'But surely the Board aren't too keen on that normally. They feel they lose control.'

'Times change Richard. I don't think the Board can be that arrogant any more.'

'Thanks, Sir Anthony. I appreciate your efforts and will certainly have another word with Chuck.'

'As I said, I'll help when I can. How's that lovely girl that came to Singapore with us by the way? You know, Rebecca Martin. She did such an excellent job and she's charming and attractive as well as efficient.'

'She's fine. She enjoyed the challenge of Singapore. I'm sure you'll see her at most of the big Exhibitions in future.'

'That's good Richard. We could do with a few more willing hands like her in the Company.'

'Yes indeed, we certainly could do with recruiting a few more like Becky.'

Chapter Eleven

When Clive arrived at Richard's office on Wednesday morning, he looked even more miserable and dejected than before.

'Morning Clive. How are things?'

'Worse than ever Richard. Annie's got a bout of flu and is feeling very depressed. *Stern* has made a formal complaint to Head Office about the slippage in the programme and our failure to meet specification on certain sub-systems. I'm still waiting for the formal enquiry on the loss of the document and my best engineer has been poached by a telecomms company.'

'What've you done about the *Stern* complaint?'

'Nothing as yet. All I have is an information copy of the letter they sent to the Chairman.'

Clive showed Richard the letter that described their great disappointment with *AGC's* performance, their embarrassment with the German customer. They asked for assurance that the matter was being taken seriously and that *AGC* would provide the necessary resources and expertise to redress the situation. In the final paragraph there was a reference that they were giving consideration to *Elsa's* interest in assisting with the programme.

'My view, Clive, is that you shouldn't wait for the crap to come down from above. Attack is the best form of defence. I'll draft you a letter to send to the Technical Director that will hopefully send him running for cover. Let's face it; if you do nothing, you'll be the fall guy. Give me an hour, I'll bring it over.'

It took less than an hour for Richard to produce the letter to the Technical Director. In the draft, he referred to the letter from *Stern* to the Chairman and attached a copy for reference. He drew attention to the last two Progress Meeting Minutes that had clearly stated all of the problems and emphasised the need for adequate resources. He left spaces for dates when Clive had notified the Technical Director of the problems and drawn his attention to the inadequate numbers and skills allocated to the programme. The final paragraph requested an urgent meeting to discuss the Division's response to the Chairman.

'Are you sure about this Richard? You're basically telling my technical Director it's his fault.'

'But subtly Clive.'

'He won't like it.'

'That's just tough. Is what I've put in the letter true?'

'Well yes but it's not entirely my boss's fault. He has to work with the resources he's given as well.'

'Tough, it's still his problem, not yours and his pay packet compensates him for the added responsibility. We'll copy it to Lady Penelope in Human Resources as well and add a paragraph about their inability to fulfil recruiting and retention targets. That'll send HR into a spin as well. At least it will take some of the heat off you and it's not your fault anyway. What have you got to lose?'

'Nothing apart from my job and my pension.'

'Over things that are clearly not your fault. They wouldn't dare. They need your experience. Who else from the current Engineering Department could take over your job? Anyway, with your length of service with the company, it would cost an arm and a leg to get rid of you.'

'Well, I suppose so. If you're sure.'

On leaving Clive's office, Richard stopped off for a word with Kate.

'Oh. Hi Richard. How are you feeling now?'

'Still a bit rough but should be all right by the end of

the week.'

'Yes, you still look a bit peaky.'

'So what's new with you Kate?'

'Nothing much. I've been working quite a lot of overtime lately and it looks as if that's going to include some weekends soon.'

'Guess you'll welcome the extra money.'

'Sure, as long as it doesn't go over the top. I do like a social life as well.'

'I'll give you a call later in the week to see if they'll let you out. I also promised to see Emma sometime.'

'Yes Richard, I know, she told me. You seem to have an ardent admirer there.'

'Now you know me better than most and that I'm not interested in any serious relationships.'

'That's what they all say, Richard. You really don't understand women, do you? If Emma decides she wants you, believe me, you'll be putty.'

That afternoon, Petty took over one of the spare offices to run through his innovative Business Plan requirements. Richard wasn't the only one to challenge the logic of the new format or the demand for unavailable or non-existent information. But Upstart was adamant. He was determined to have a myriad of inaccurate facts and figures to weave into his work of fiction. The situation would be aggravated by Paul believing anything shown to him on a computer printout as being gospel. Paul was also utterly deceived into thinking that Upstart had the slightest idea what he was doing in the first place.

After some token protests, Richard decided to take the line of least resistance. If they wanted daft facts and figures, they could have facts and figures. He decided that the overall trend of his input would be to show a five point five per cent improvement in sales each year for five years. He'd adapt the source figures to make sure it gave the desired result. He knew from several years experience of drafting meaningless plans that the management would not accept less than five or believe more than seven. If pressed really hard, he could bump up some of the figures to show a further one or two percent growth without arousing suspicion.

Even by Wednesday, Richard's rash had not subsided enough for him to risk close contact with either Kate or Emma. However, he did feel he could risk an evening with Maggie, who was phoning him daily to arrange a meeting. Maggie suggested they should meet near Farnham to save Richard the trouble of driving to Woking. This time, Richard pre-warned Bex that Maggie would come to the flat, although he intended to take her into the town to dine.

'Oh that'll be interesting Richard'. Bex seemed quite pleased that she was going to meet Maggie. 'I've always wanted to meet the girl who got you to the altar. I look forward to interrogating her on her secret technique.'

'Just try it Bex. But a word of caution. Just remember that you have to sleep sometimes and you might wake up with a very different hair style.'

'You too Richard, need to sleep. I can imagine you with green spiky curls. And then I'd think of something else to do with the hair on your head.'

Richard was still in the bedroom dabbing cream on his rash when Maggie arrived. He could hear their muffled voices but couldn't quite make out what Bex was actually saying. He struggled to finish dressing as quickly as possible.

'Hi Maggie, sorry I am running a bit late. Had a slow journey back from work. The traffic's terrible around here lately. You've already met Becky I see.'

'Hi Richard.' Maggie gave him a peck on the cheek. 'Gosh what's that smell? Reminds me of being around horses.'

'Probably my new aftershave. It's a bit strong when I first put it on.'

165

'Well, bring back *Brut* I say, in that case.'

'You go finish getting ready, Richard. I'll keep Maggie amused and get her a drink. Don't worry about us.' Bex, the little minx, was clearly enjoying winding him up.

'OK, I'll only be a very few more minutes.' When safely out of Maggie's view, Richard waved his finger threateningly at Becky and then swept his hand as if to cut his throat. 'Why don't you tell Maggie about your avid interest in Neo-Gothic art whilst I'm out of the room?'

'I thought my trip to Singapore and the tropical research programme might be more interesting to Maggie.'

Richard quickly finished dressing, wondering what mischief Bex might be perpetrating. Not that she'd ever do anything intentionally to hurt him; it was just that she sometimes became carried away with her overactive sense of fun. Not everyone had the same amount of self-confidence as Bex to allow them to accept others at face value. If only everyone in his life could be as straightforward and uncomplicated as Bex.

'Ready Maggie.' Richard lost no time in ushering Maggie out the door.

'She's a very nice girl,' Maggie commented as soon as they were halfway down the drive. 'Are you and Becky … err… you know… an entity?'

'Goodness me no Maggie. She's a lodger, helping to pay my extortionate mortgage.'

'Well she treats you like you're her boyfriend.'

'That's Bex. That's just the way she is.'

'Well be careful. You're a good catch Richard, and someone will take advantage of you. You never seem to see what girls are really like until it's too late. Just be very careful.'

'Yes Maggie, I'll be careful.' Richard couldn't believe that Maggie, of all people, could say such things. In any case, he knew he was extremely intuitive about the fairer sex and was truly one of the few men he knew who really understood them. He was merely a bit unlucky sometimes, that was all.

Following a drink at the bar of *The Plough*, they were seated at a table in the small restaurant area.

'This is extremely cosy,' Maggie remarked when the waitress had left them with the menus.

'Yes, and the food is plain country cooking but I think you'll like it.'

'Sounds perfect. I love English country cooking.'

Richard thought that she was much more relaxed than the last time he'd seen her. She had looked strained before, the stress had shown in her eyes and in the tautness of her face muscles. Now she looked like the Maggie he once knew. Even after seven years and two children, she'd hardly aged at all and was still extremely attractive.

'So how are things going with you now, Mags?'

'Oh, the last few weeks have been good for the children and me. They're spoilt rotten by my parents who love them to bits. The kids have been well behaved and don't seem to miss their dad at all. Which is not really surprising as he spends hardly any time with them.'

'And you?'

'I've had lots of time to think things out and I don't intend to go back to Italy.'

'Really?'

'No. What I didn't tell you before was that I left because I found that Georgio had been unfaithful to me with one of his old girlfriends. I knew she was still carrying the torch but I didn't know that he still had a thing about her.'

'You're absolutely sure about it?'

'Fairly sure, as I caught them in bed together in one of the guest rooms. I went in to leave some clean towels and there they were, humping away.'

'That must have been quite a shock.'

'Richard, you really are the master of the

understatement at times. I was bloody furious. I went mad, chased her out and gave him hell. The next day, I packed, took the children and left.'

'I see.'

'Well it's not that simple as the children have Italian nationality, Georgio could make me take them back to Sorrento where he'd undoubtedly get custody.'

'Is that likely?'

'Not from our last phone call. I think he'll move in his girlfriend and start all over again.'

'What a shambles.'

'Yes, you could say that. And you could say that I deserve it.'

'No Maggie. It's not the same at all. When there are kids involved and you've been together for seven years, it's different.'

'Thanks for saying that. I'm quite touched. That's enough about me. Tell me all that has happened to you since we last met.'

Over the remainder of the meal, they chatted over generalities, travel, good wine and Maggie's intention to return to her career as a teacher. They then walked back to the flat where Maggie had left her car, pecked goodnight and promised to meet up again sometime in the not too distant future. As she drove off, Richard began to wonder why he was getting involved with Maggie again. It really didn't make any sense at all.

'Hi Bex. All quiet?'

'Like a morgue. How was the meal?'

'Fine. We ate at *The Plough*.'

'I had a pizza delivered. How was she?'

'Oh, OK considering she found her husband knocking off one of his ex-girlfriends in one of their guest rooms.'

'One could say what goes around, comes around.'

'If one were being uncharitable.'

'Rubbish Richard. You be careful. You've been down

this road once before. Remember. You're such a clot at times. It's not your problem anymore.'

'Yes Bex but she has got the kids and hasn't lived...'

'Richard stop. Don't be a chump. You have your choice of beautiful birds at the moment. Leave the hen alone. Anyway, go open a bottle. I need your company.'

Late that Friday afternoon, everyone was told to congregate in the site Dining Hall. The only reason given was that the Divisional General Manager, Tony Brooks had something important to say. As there was no public address system, it took nearly half an hour to gather up everyone who worked at the site. Small groups of people stood around speculating on what it was all about. Richard managed to find Becky amongst the milling throng.

'Hi Bex. What's happening?'

'Search me. I was just about to pack up and go home.'

'Well, you can bet your bottom dollar that as the announcement's on a Friday afternoon, it's bound to be bad news. That way, everybody has the whole weekend to get over it. So when the news incenses them and they are ready for a fight, by Monday morning they've got used to the idea and they're like pussycats again.'

With that, Tony Brooks arrived with a posse of Directors, including Lady Penelope.

'It must be bad news if HR has left *Fawlty Tower*s for the occasion,' Richard whispered to Bex.

'I'm sure she's changing sex, Richard. Look at the body hair.'

The gathering was called to order and after the usual preamble, the General Manager announced that he was the bearer of bad tidings. As the level of the overall company business was down by more than twenty percent, some austerity measures would need to be introduced immediately. These would include an across the board fifteen percent reduction in staff whose time is not being

169

charged directly to contracts. There would also be a moratorium on hiring temporary labour, works services, new equipment purchases and of all but essential travel. All air travel must be booked in Economy Class. He went on to talk about other economy measures regarding telephones, electricity and stationery.

'Finally ladies and gentlemen, many of those affected can expect to receive *At Risk* letters during the next week. This is a measure we must take to satisfy the requirement of employment laws on selection for redundancy. Getting such a letter doesn't mean that you'll be given redundancy. It simply means you are being considered in competition with your colleagues; a process that will take several weeks to complete. The Union representatives have been pre-notified of our intentions and will be consulted on our future actions. I'll not be taking any questions today. I'll leave this in the hands of your line managers who'll discuss matters with you in more detail as we implement the measures I have outlined today. Thank you.'

At this point, Tony Brooks and the team turned on their heels, made a rapid exit and left immediately in the chauffeur driven cars. Instantly, there was a noisy background din, as everyone seemed to start talking at once.

'What does it all mean Richard?' Bex looked concerned

'It means that when we go to work for the next few months it will be a bigger pain in the butt than it was last week, Bex. Everyone will be looking over their shoulders. We'll probably have to return used biros to get new ones. Humour will be rationed along with anything that makes coming to work seem in the least bit pleasant. But don't worry; you'll be all right. I'll tell you more about it when we get home.'

A number of the worried employees made their way to the local pub to speculate on the outcome of their future and the austerity measures. Richard and Becky decided this would be a pointless exercise, preferring to open a bottle or two of red and put the world to rights in the comfort of their home.

'So tell me about this *At Risk* thing Richard.'

'Don't worry about it Bex, it's a formality that the Company has to indulge in to protect itself from people like me who would love to take them to court or an industrial tribunal. You see, where there's more than one employee doing a certain job, they have to consider the merits of each individual to decide who goes and who stays.'

'How do they do that?'

'Usually with reference to their manager's assessments, Annual Reports and sick records. They then draw up a scoring matrix. The idea is to show that the decision is arrived at objectively. Then they give people numbers and throw darts at a board, to see who should go.'

'So does it really work?'

'It works as well as the Company and the managers want it to. The good thing about signing one's Annual Report is that the Company can't suddenly change all the assessments because it's redundancy time. However, if they want to, they can usually find reasons to get rid of people they particularly want to lose.'

'Not really sure that I'm a lot wiser on how it affects us.'

'No and we wont be until we see which way the cookie crumbles. I'm positive that you'll be all right. They'd be daft to get rid of you and if they did you'd be snapped up by someone else within the week, But if you're worried, dust off your CV anyway and put it around. At least then you'll know how marketable you are.'

'What about you Richard?'

'Well that's a bit different. If Paul wants to use this opportunity to get rid of a thorn in his side, he has a superb opportunity. And frankly, I wouldn't blame him. He hates people who won't suck up to him. Nevertheless, if I were a betting man, I think he'll take the easier route and get rid of a couple of the new salesmen without a track record. That way he'd be less likely to be challenged. And you know how he hates accounting for his actions.'

'I hope so. I think they'd be absolutely stupid to lose you.'

'Thanks Bex. But if the Directors were really that smart, we wouldn't be facing these problems now. In fact, I believe that Neanderthal man is not extinct at all. There's at least a dozen or so of them working at our Headquarters.'

Fortunately, Kate was scheduled to be working that weekend, so Richard was able to ask Emma out with a clear conscience. His rash was little evident now except in bright sunlight.

It was mid afternoon when Richard arrived at Emma's bijou cottage near Woking.

'It might be small but it's all mine and the Abbey National's,' Emma called from an upstairs window as Richard eyed up the building and admired the well kept garden.

'Hi Emma. Nice place.'

'Thanks, I'm on my way down.'

Richard handed her a rose bush he had bought at the local nursery. 'I heard you're a keen gardener. I must say it all looks very professional. Do it all on your own?'

'I do everything here: gardening, cleaning, plumbing, painting; cooking, you name it, Come on in.' She gave him a lingering welcome kiss.

'Most impressive. This all looks very *Homes and Gardens*. Is this all due to the French influence?'

'Probably, I grew up in a small village near Bordeaux. My father died when I was quite young so my mother, younger sister and I looked after the house and garden. I actually enjoy it. It's such a change from my working life. My mother married the owner of a Parisian fashion house about the time I left home. He seems fine and they're happy but I only tend to see them a couple of times a year.'

'Well you certainly show a talent for design.' Everything complemented the house: the stripped pine kitchen and dining area, the cottage style furnishings and rugs, the plump scatter cushions and a small Welsh dresser.

'I'm pleased you like it. Let's have a coffee before we go.'

'How long have you lived here?'

'Nearly five years. I had one serious partner from when I was eighteen. We married when I was twenty and I was dragged around the country for the next six years as he moved from job to job. Then things went pear-shaped and we split up. So I started working for *Defense Now*, got a mortgage, bought the cottage and five years later, I'm still here.'

'And you seem very happy with things.'

'Yes. I enjoy the stability and the control over my own life but long term... Who knows?'

'You mean babies and things?'

'That depends. Maybe. Step at a time, I think. Gosh, this is awfully philosophical. Come and see the upstairs.'

The two bedrooms and small bathroom were furnished and decorated in keeping with the rest of the house.

'The bed's a small double, I'm afraid. Not quite like the one we tested in Singapore. Perhaps we'd better make sure we can fit in before it gets dark.' Emma moved slowly towards Richard, kissed him seductively, then took his hand and pulled him gently onto the bed.

After they had made love, they lay quietly together for nearly an hour.

'Richard, I've something to tell you.'

'What's that Emma?'

'I've been offered a job in the Washington office.'

'That's great, you're really lucky Em. Wish I had the chance to work there.'

'I haven't actually said yes or no yet.'

'Why? What's holding you back?'

'Oh, I don't know. The house. England. Friends. You.'

'But Emma, we only met a couple of weeks ago. How can I be part of your decision process?'

'Because, although it's a short time, I feel completely happy and natural with you.'

'And I feel the same Emma. Look, I rushed headlong into things once before and it turned into a total disaster.'

'It doesn't mean that we'd go the same way Richard.'

'I believe you should take this opportunity of a lifetime. We can still see each other. I travel through DC about four times each year on business and there's always holidays.'

'I know. I guess I'm being silly but I really do like you Richard.'

'And I you Emma, but I'm a terrible catch. I don't know what I want and I could be out of a job in a couple of month's time if this redundancy scheme goes through.'

'Oh I saw something in this morning's Telegraph about that but I never thought it would affect you.'

'Quite possibly might. I don't get on with my boss for a start. What did the paper say about it?'

'Not much. Just that *AGC* had experienced a downturn in business and they were taking corrective action to protect the end-of-year profits. Oh, and that there would be some small job losses and they were in full consultation with the Unions.'

'Mmm. Is that what they said? Anyway, what would you like to do this evening?'

They decided to have dinner in the local Italian restaurant and then have a few drinks back at the cottage.

Richard found Emma more subdued than usual and put it down to her disappointment that he'd not tried to dissuade her from taking the job in Washington. Although they made love again that night, Emma was much more passive than usual.

The following day was pleasant but uneventful. They visited Wisley Gardens, had a pub lunch and Richard returned to Farnham late afternoon.

'You're back early. Got another date this evening or something?'

'No, just came back to be with you Bex. How's your weekend been?'

'Oh bit of shopping. Went out last night with a couple of the girls. Usual thing, drank to excess, went to the disco, remember dancing, and drank some more. Don't remember coming home and woke up on the bathroom floor.'

'Average Saturday night out then.'

'Yep. How was Emma?'

'She's thinking of taking a job in Washington and I believe she expected me to try and talk her out of it.'

'Guess she doesn't know you very well then Richard.'

'I like her a lot, but I'm certainly not ready for a serious relationship. I've only known her a few weeks.'

'Some people have been known to get married in less time than that.'

'Exactly Bex. Are you surprised I'm wary? Frankly, I know Emma is not Miss Right. There's not enough rapport there for the rest of my life.'

'You mean she doesn't go in for the banter enough then, Richard?'

'Probably Bex and I'd miss the verbal chess. I need that more than anything else in a partner.'

'God, who's being an analytical bunny today. Go open a bottle of red. I've got the video of *War of the Roses*. That'll give you something to think about.'

Bex returned in a tight tee shirt, brief silk shorts and football socks. Richard was sure she dressed like that just to drive him mad.

The mood at *AGC* on Monday morning was decidedly grim. Not much work was being done as everyone sat around in groups predicting who'd stay and who'd be for the chop. Richard went across to Engineering, where the mood was fairly normal, as they were all booking their time to existing contracts and therefore safe from the current round of cuts.

Clive however, was still depressed about his future. He'd still heard nothing further from his Director or the Security Officer. Annie had worked herself into a state of abject annoyance, compounding his troubles. She told Clive that she'd a good mind to go and tell his boss what's what and how much they undervalued him. This meant an additional worry for Clive that Annie may have a sudden rush of blood to the head and carry out her threat. He'd tried to reason with her that any such action would be counterproductive. But he could never be quite sure with Annie. Clive also said he was concerned about Kate as her work hadn't been up to her usual high standard lately.

'Has she said anything to you Clive?'

'Not a thing. She just seems to have been preoccupied over the last couple of weeks. Perhaps it's man trouble.'

'Often is Clive. I'll have a chat with her on my way out.'

As he approached Kate's bench, he could see that she looked a little under the weather.

'Hi Kate, you OK?'

'Oh, hello Richard; yes I'm fine.'

'Just thought you were looking a little down.'

'Well I have been working a lot of hours lately. How was your weekend?

'Not bad. I saw Emma on Saturday and we had dinner.

She may be taking a job in the States.'

'Yes, she rang me last week. Sounded a bit unsure. Can't think why. I'd jump at a chance like that.'

'Me too, especially as things are at the moment.'

'I'm sure you'll survive the cuts. They'd be daft to get rid of you.'

'Thanks Kate but unfortunately prats are making the decisions. Anything could happen. Let me know when you get some time off. I'll buy you slap up dinner and cheer you up.'

'I certainly will Richard. Hopefully this coming weekend I'll be free.'

Soon after Richard returned to his office Liz called to him. 'Wing Commander Tucker's on your line.'

'Hello Ian. I was going to call you and suggest we had lunch.'

'Well, you'll forget that when you hear what I've got to say.'

'Problem Ian?'

'Only for you. I've just heard from Procurement. We've brought forward the Radar procurement by about six months. They've cancelled some Army Field Communications requirement and allocated the funds to us. Seems that Air Defence is being taken seriously at long last. The tender document for the new Radar is ready for collection. You've got thirty days to respond. That's ten o'clock on the morning of the twenty-seventh.'

'Well I guess that cancels my social life for a month. I'll get Liz to pick it up mid afternoon and crank things up here immediately. Any surprises in the spec?'

'Not that I can see. Hopefully it's close to what you're developing on your own funds. But you know that it's the cheapest compliant solution that will be selected, Richard. Our masters are hell bent on competition at any price. They'll willingly spend Francs if *Elsa's* price is less than yours. UK jobs don't seem to count any more.'

'I'll press the message home Ian.'

'There's one other thing Richard. General Ahmed has been in contact with both the French and our Defence Export Organisation regarding his Radar requirement. He now wants to procure the same system as the UK and will then buy government to government. He's decided this for two reasons. The first is to ensure he gets the same standard of equipment as we do and secondly that we'll both benefit financially from the larger production run.'

'That's terrific news Ian. I'm sure I'll be able to use that to get our prices down. I guess I'd better close the loop with the General later.'

'OK Richard. I'll have to keep my distance now until after the tender submission. Good luck. I'm sure a month away from the girlies will be very therapeutic for you.'

Richard called Clive to give him the news. 'I'm sure you need another distraction to add to your workload, but we've got thirty days to put in our Proposal to the Ministry with fixed prices.'

'Yes, I need another task like a hole in the head but I guess this is the big one. We've got to win it.'

'It'll be virtually impossible to sell *Aphrodite* to Dubai, or anyone else for that matter, if our own Government selects a competitor; that's for sure. Liz is on her way to pick up the tender now. I'm calling a meeting for all those involved in the bid tomorrow morning.'

'OK, I'll see you when the tender arrives.'

That evening, Clive and Richard sat in the Conference room going through the tender document line by line. Clive was somewhat relieved that *Aphrodite* was ninety-five percent compliant with the specification and therefore much of the Technical Proposal wouldn't have to be amended. Richard prepared a Progress Chart showing when everyone's inputs were required to ensure everything would be ready for the due date. He allowed a full week following the Division's sign-off to obtain Headquarters' approval on the prices.

That night, Richard slept fitfully, dreaming of proof reading thousands of pages of the Proposal, the heated arguments with Contracts over prices, spurious diversions from Paul and Michael Petty, Clive collapsing under the strain and missing the tender deadline.

Although Richard had conducted many tender preparations before, none had been as important to the Business, jobs and his own career as this one. In addition to three attendees from Engineering, many other departments were represented at the *kick-off* meeting including Purchasing, Quality, Manufacturing, Estimating, Support and Finance. Dave O'Leary did not attend, preferring to send the most junior of his minions instead. However, Richard knew that all contractual aspects of the response would be dictated by O'Leary, who would do everything in his power to ensure that *Aphrodite* was damned forever.

Richard ran through the main points of the tender, win strategy, deadlines for individual inputs and suchlike. He knew most of the team well and had few worries that most would do their utmost to provide the best Proposal and costs estimates. He also knew that his most challenging task would be to convince the Board to take a sensible view on risk and contingencies and trust his judgement on the winning response. At best, the Board was risk averse, timid and profit greedy. But after the downturn in business, they would be particularly cautious and attempt to recover the end of year figures to appease the shareholders.

It was late on Thursday morning when a jubilant Clive burst into Richard's office.

'I don't know how it happened but I've just been to see the Technical Director and he tells me that they're not going to pursue the formal enquiry over the document found at Heathrow. They said they'd reassessed the document and that it had no national security implications; only commercial confidences which can be dealt with within the Company.'

'That's great Clive. Must be quite a relief to you.'

'Well, I did get quite a ticking off but his heart didn't seem to be in it. So I used the opportunity to ask for more engineering resources again.'

'Good on you Clive. What did he say?'

'He said he'd look at it.'

'What d'you think he really meant?'

'That I'd be lucky. But he did appear to have grasped the importance of the programmes on our Business this time and acknowledged that something must be done. He said that we keep losing engineers as soon as they get two or three year's experience. They know they can then move to a new company and get a lot more money. So the Company spends a lot of time, money and effort recruiting graduates only to lose them when they've learnt to put their theory into practice. He said we then go and pay over the odds for some guy with similar experience from another company. Trouble is, when someone arrives from a different industry, it still takes a while for him to understand our particular business. Anyway, he promised to have another go at Human Resources about it. In the meantime, he assigned me three more software engineers from the industrial programme.'

'Sounds as if all's well that ends well Clive.'

'Yes. Believe me, it's quite a relief. And the last few weeks have taken their toll on Annie. She hasn't been sleeping either. Anyway, better get back to the coal face. Just thought you'd like to hear my good news.'

As Richard watched him leave, Clive looked as if the weight of the world had been lifted from his shoulders. Richard immediately called Pat to tell her the good news and thank her again for helping to save Clive's bacon.

Chapter Twelve

Richard was so busy working on the Tender, that he forgot all about the pending redundancy letters. That was until one of the HR juniors delivered a blue envelope and asked him to sign for its receipt.

'I always thought such matters were delivered in a brown envelope,' he commented, scrawling his signature in the mail book.

'Oh, no expense spared at *AGC,* you know. I'm really sorry Richard, but I'm sure you'll be OK. All of the salesmen are getting an *at risk* letter.

'Sure, I know. But thanks for saying so anyway.'

Richard read the brief letter which told him that, because of market pressures, Company performance had not met expectation and measures were being taken to correct the situation. This meant that he was being reviewed, along with others, as a candidate for redundancy and that he'd be kept informed of progress. He refolded the letter, placed it back in the envelope and rang Becky.

'Becky, have you had anything from Personnel today?'

'Just received the *at risk* thingy. Was about to call you.'

'Well, don't worry. Me too. This bit's just routine.'

'OK, you warned me to expect one anyway. We'll have a small celebration tonight. Just the two of us.'

'Good idea. I hope to get away by seven.'

Richard dialled Sir Anthony's office.

'Hello Richard. How's life at the sharp end?'

'In fact, the sharp end's just received their *at risk*

letters. Actually, pretty busy with the Proposal at the moment. You've probably heard by now that the Ministry has come out to tender for the Air Defence requirement. I'm really phoning to ask your help. We need some lobbying with the MPs about British jobs versus work going to France. Also, I'd appreciate it if you could visit our friend, the senior civil servant, Nigel Eldridge, to see if you can convince him to give UK industry some consideration. He's so arrogant.'

'Yes I know, Richard. A difficult man, but I'll make the rounds and do what I can.'

'Thanks very much. I'll fax you a four-page brief on *Aphrodite* covering everything you'll need. Whilst you're on the line, I want to ask another favour, if that's all right?'

'Ask away.'

'Well you know you told me that you were very impressed with Rebecca Martin's performance at Asian Aerospace?'

'Yes, she was super.'

'Would you be willing to put a note to that effect to her line management. You see, she's one of the candidates in the current redundancy review.'

'Already done it old chap. And I sent a similar one to Paul Hamilton with regard to your excellent performance. He didn't think to mention it then?'

'No, not exactly. I guess he'd other things on his mind.'

'Anyway, don't worry Richard. I'm sure you'll both survive these cuts.'

Richard thanked him, replaced the receiver and faxed the brief. He worked hard until six-thirty, when the print started to become blurred and he began to miss errors during his proof reading.

On arrival at the flat, he told Bex about Sir Anthony's letter to her boss.

'Funny thing, she never said anything to me. I believe Mary thinks that she's being weak if she praises anyone.'

'There's a lot about like that, Bex. So what's the plot for tonight?'

'The bottle's already open. The casserole's in the oven and I've rented the video of *Evita*.'

'Sounds good, I'll take off this hair shirt and go slip into something more comfortable.'

'Fine, grub up in fifteen minutes.'

Bex seemed unusually relaxed considering the prospects of losing her job. They dined by candlelight and settled down to watch *Evita*. They spoke very little during the musical and Richard couldn't help noticing Becky looked a little tearful when Madonna sang, 'Don't cry for me Argentina.'

'I really enjoyed that,' Bex gently rubbed her eyes, snuggling up to Richard. 'But it's so sad. To think she did all that and died at age thirty-three.'

'Yes, she certainly had a full life. I guess she knew what she wanted and just went for it.'

'Must be nice to know what you really want Richard. The letter today made me think a lot about what I want to do with my life.'

'So do you know what it is?'

'If only. I guess most girls would be looking at settling down having a family and finding a way to keep their career going at the same time.'

'Have you never wanted that?'

'If only I could get my head round that problem. You know I've this block over relationships with men. I guess it must leave some sort of unnatural gap in my life.'

'I don't know about your block really, Bex. Do you know why you have the problem?'

'No. I didn't have any frightening or awful experiences as a child. I had boyfriends when I was in my late teens but things never worked out. When they started to get affectionate, I'd freeze. Then they'd dump me. It's biological, I think. It happened so often that I decided the best way was to avoid the problem altogether.'

'And girls.'

'Well, it was logical for me to try that I suppose but that was never really satisfactory either. And then there's all the petty jealousies and disputes. So you see, I think they just missed something out when they made me.'

'I don't believe it's as simple as that. Have you ever seen a doctor about it?'

'A shrink, you mean? No. It just didn't seem important.'

'No I mean a doctor. You can see a shrink afterwards to sort out your other problems! It wouldn't do any harm, you know. They know so much more about these things nowadays.'

'Yes, I might give it a try. Anyway, enough about me. Let's finish the bottle off and forget about work and sex.'

***

For the next fortnight, Richard did little else but work and sleep. His long days were spent chasing narratives, circuit diagrams, illustrations and cost inputs. He began to get weary of the unending task of proof reading and editing the many lengthy volumes of the Proposal. As he began to receive the various cost estimates, he became more and more concerned over the escalating cost of the fixed price tender. Purchasing had added a twelve per cent contingency on all materials. Engineering had increased the cost to complete development by fifteen per cent. Operations had added over seven and a half million pounds for new special to type test equipment. Finance had taken a large contingency for any dollar content on materials. The final straw was Mr O'Leary recommending an overall risk factor of the contract at twenty five per cent. Thus, a bid that had been estimated at one hundred and sixty million two months ago, had risen to a staggering three hundred and ten million pounds. Richard knew that if this figure were submitted, they'd be simply handing the contract to *Elsa* on a plate.

He spent the rest of the day visiting each Department in turn and using every one of his powers of persuasion to get them to reconsider their inputs before they were made public. By the end of that day, he had managed to reduce the price by sixty-five million. He knew this wasn't enough, but there was still some time left and his final ploy would be to pressure the Board to take a low profit margin to launch the new product.

Richard decided it wasn't yet time to tackle Dave O'Leary. He knew that O'Leary would do everything possible to scupper the bid. He deduced therefore that the longer O'Leary believed he was getting his own way, the better. Richard therefore decided to leave this battle until the formal tender meeting, when he hoped to surprise O'Leary and convince the management that the risk figure was stupid, ill founded and unrealistic. He knew this would need a carefully constructed logical argument and that O'Leary would have already prepared some suitable work of fiction to justify his risk assessment.

Richard shared his concerns with Clive.

'What we need ready for the tender meeting, Clive, is a detailed risk assessment of every work package. You'll need to demonstrate that you don't have any concerns about achieving any of the module and system specifications. Show whenever possible that the development is an extension of proven work you've carried out before. In a nutshell, we need to convince the weak and the feeble that their pensions are in safe hands and they can look forward to a hefty bonus when we win this competition.'

'That shouldn't be too difficult. After all, most of the modules have been prototyped. Our biggest problem will be demonstrating to the Board that the software risk is manageable. The Company's had many problems in that area on past contracts and it's cost them a vast amount of money putting things right.'

'Can't help you on that one Clive. It's all magic to me, this software stuff. Have you thought of subcontracting some of this work to a specialist company? Pass the risk to them, as it were. At least you could get some quotes from them as a backup to your costs.'

'Yes, we could try that. We've a detailed enough statement of work and spec now. There's time enough, so why not? Anything to shoot O'Leary in the foot.'

'Aim higher Clive. The foot would be too good for him. Let's hit him where it hurts.'

The on-site cost review took place the following Thursday, a few days ahead of the need to send the figures to *Fawlty Towers* for approval. All departments were represented, but again Dave O'Leary had delegated attendance to one of his most inexperienced minions. Richard knew that there was still a need to reduce the current estimates by another forty million and then challenge O'Leary's risk factor. He could live with ten per cent, but certainly not twenty-five.

As each input was discussed and challenged, Tony Brooks, the General Manager, would adjudicate and rule on the figure to be submitted to HQ. As each package was debated, Purchasing was told to renegotiate all component costs by five per cent. Manufacturing was tasked to reduce specialist test equipment by three million. Engineering was directed to trim man-hours by five percent and so on. As the GM passed glibly over the Contracts input, Richard spoke out.

'Err... Tony. Can we discuss the risk factor? I believe Contracts have included twenty-five per cent.'

'Yes, that's correct. But Dave O'Leary is unable to attend this meeting, so he's given me a memo justifying the figure. Moving on...'

'But Tony, don't you agree that the figure is unrealistic and will kill our prospects? Just about every project we've ever bid is pitched at a ten per cent risk. How can we go to twenty-five on this one? As you're aware, *AGC* has lost a lot of tenders to our Ministry since they introduced their policy of competitive tendering. We can't add risk factors like this and hope to win.'

'Well, I can't possibly discuss this now when David isn't here to defend his corner. But he's a lot of experience in contracting with our Ministry, so I normally accept his judgement. He must have good reasons for including the higher figure this time.'

'Then can we have a meeting when he's available and discuss this properly? If we don't, we may as well throw in the towel now.'

'All right. Let's finish everything else and I'll address risk at a smaller gathering first thing tomorrow. From what we've discussed this afternoon, the price stands at two hundred and five million. Assuming, as you suggested, we ask the Board to take five per cent less profit than normal, that will give us an all up price of about one hundred and ninety five million.'

Richard decided to risk banging the message home once more, 'I'm convinced that, from evaluating the price of *Elsa's* recent contract in Greece and the Ministry's budget, to win, we must be less than one hundred and seventy. We must get this ridiculous risk assessment reduced if we're to have a prayer.'

'OK Richard, You've made your point. I said we'll look at that tomorrow.'

'May I take a copy of Dave's memo to look at how he justified the risk packages?'

'OK, but I want this matter resolved as quickly and painlessly as possible in the morning. The Board must receive all the paperwork by early afternoon tomorrow if we're going to get their approval in time. You know how long it takes to move things through HQ. They're bound to ask some questions and want changes.'

Richard took the copy of the memo to his office. As expected O'Leary had painted a picture of doom and gloom. He referred to the problems on the *Stern* contract as a recent example of Engineering failure to achieve what they had promised to do. Because of the more general financial problems at *AGC*, the memo highlighted the need to ensure that realistic returns were guaranteed on all future contracts. O'Leary also quoted the severe terms of the contract conditions and the justification to offset any penalties and damages for failure. As Richard absorbed the contents, he knew that O'Leary's tack was to appeal to the timid and the indecisive. Knowing he was up against the odds, he set about preparing the case for the following morning's skirmish.

It was late evening when he arrived at the flat.

'Hi Richard. You look drawn and aged.'

'Gee thanks Bex. The bastards are wearing me down. It seems that I'm the only one trying to win this bid sometimes Well, there's Clive of course, but he worries about job security too much sometimes.'

'I guess a lot of them just see winning as more aggro. If you don't win the contract, they can enjoy a quiet life.'

'Yeh, and in the meantime we go out of business. I sometimes wonder if it's all worth it.'

'So if you weren't doing your present job, what else would you like to do? You know you like the freedom and the challenge the job gives you. You'd not be happy in a boring desk job. And wouldn't life be dull if you didn't have Paul Hamilton to spar with daily? Come on Richard, what do you really want?'

'Don't know really. It's just frustrating. I just wish the team were playing on the same pitch, let alone the same side, sometimes.'

'Let's have one relaxing glass of vino. Then you can get an early night and be a sharper than average bunny in the morning.'

'OK Bex, just one.'

Richard should've known better than to think he could have one glass of wine with Becky. He was therefore still suffering a mild hangover when he joined Clive and Dave O'Leary at the GM's meeting.

O'Leary took the floor first and laboured his way through the points on his memo, whilst not missing the opportunity to remind Tony Brooks that they needed funds for the civil derivative. Clive went next and gave a logical and convincing account of the technical risk. He countered the criticisms over the *Stern* contract, arguing that inadequate resources had been the real cause of the delays and problems. He'd pressured the Technical Director to give his written assurance that this wouldn't happen should they win this contract. The quotation from the specialist software company was twenty five per cent below their own engineering quotation. Clive argued strongly that they should therefore subcontract this work. Richard was surprised and delighted at Clive's newly acquired confidence and forthright manner.

Richard made the final presentation, pulling no punches and making it clear that if they wanted the huge Air Defence market over the next five years, they must first win at home. He said that if they were to bid over one hundred and seventy million, he could guarantee that they would lose. He reminded them that Dubains now intended buying the UK winning system on a government-to-government basis. On this basis, Richard proposed that *AGC* could steal a lead by adding an option in the UK bid for a further ten systems. He suggested offering this option for around one year on an eight per cent reduction on all production prices. He argued that the UK and Dubai would jump at such an option and *AGC* would reduce component and start-up costs.

The debate continued for over an hour before Tony Brooks decided to call the discussion to a halt. 'Well, I've heard all the arguments and I've decided to take the middle road. I'll put the figure of one hundred and eighty seven million to the Board but suggesting that they should take less than normal profit margins. If they agree, this should take it to around one seven nine million and we'll include Richard's suggestion to reduce production prices if the Dubai systems are added to the contract within eighteen months.'

O'Leary left in a huff. Richard felt that the decision gave them an about evens chance of winning. Richard sent copies of his justification brief to Paul and Sir Anthony; the former because he had little choice, the latter in the hope he'd get his message to the Chairman.

Two hours later Pat called. 'Paul's asked me to track you down. He wants to ask you questions about the Tender. The Chairman wants him to discuss it at two today.'

'Has he seen my memo on the subject?'

'Well, I took it in to him about an hour ago and told him what it was about… but you know…'

'OK Pat, put me through and we'll no doubt play Twenty Questions.'

For once, Paul came on the line immediately. 'Richard, I need some more details on the *Aphrodite* bid.'

'What in particular Paul?'

'Well everything of course. I have to brief the Chairman in an hour.'

'Have you seen the figures from the GM and my memo on the subject?'

'Yes, I have them in front of me now.'

'So what isn't clear?'

'Well risk for a start. The GM appears to have ignored

David O'Leary's recommendation entirely. I received a copy of his memo several days ago.'

'Yes. Tony Brooks called an extraordinary meeting on the subject this morning. It was all discussed at length and, on balance, he disagreed with O'Leary's assessment. He believes we should take the usual risk factor on this bid.'

'With a little help from you no doubt.'

'Well of course. But Clive Deacon also provided a detailed analysis which Dave O'Leary was at a loss to successfully counter. There's nothing in this bid to justify setting the risk at a ridiculous twenty five per cent. Anyone who understood our business wouldn't give it a second thought.'

'Quite. But that's not all. What can I tell the Chairman to convince him that we should take five per cent less profit than usual in these difficult times?'

'Why not tell him that ten per cent of one hundred and seventy million is better that zero percent of two hundred million?'

'I can't tell him that.'

'Well that's the truth of the matter, Paul. I'm sure, with your long experience in dealing with these senior people, you'll be able to put it to him convincingly.'

'Well, yes of course I can. I just need to check all the facts.'

'Of course Paul. Is there anything else that is not clear?'

'There's bound to be but I can't see anything else just at the moment. I'll carry on going through it but you'd better be right in what you've told me. I'm going out on a limb on this one you know.'

'Thank you Paul. I'll be in the office all afternoon if you need anything…'

Click. The phone went dead.

It took several days for everything to be finalised and signed off. When he saw the outcome, Richard was delighted to see that they'd approved the Tender at one hundred and seventy million on condition that the option to purchase the Dubai systems was taken up within the year. He believed at this figure, they were in with a chance.

On the day before the tender was due to be delivered, Liz received a phone call to say that the due date had been delayed by one week to ten o'clock on the third.

'Who gave you the message Liz?'

'It was a Sergeant Tomma from the Ministry, Richard.'

'Did he leave a number or say he was going to fax us?'

'No, he just said, not to worry, it was not required until the third.'

Richard rang the Ministry and, as he suspected, no such instruction had been issued. He then sent a fax to Henri:

'With reference to the message from the good Sergeant from our Ministry, I thought you should know that in English we actually pronounce the ass in Thomas. Better luck next time. I trust Eurostar will be OK for you on the 3rd. I've heard there may a strike that day.'

Richard decided it was time to catch up with Kate, Emma and Maggie. That evening he took Kate out to dinner near her flat in Guildford. As the evening progressed, he noticed that she seemed slightly cooler than he remembered. He waited until they returned to her flat and decided to broach the subject.

'You don't seem your usual self tonight Kate.'

'Well, I've got a lot on my mind at the moment.'

'Want to talk about it?'

'It's just that everything is a bit pointless. Look at us for instance. Our relationship doesn't seem to be going anywhere at all.'

'But you said you didn't want a relationship.'

'That was then. This is now.'

'So is that what you do want, a relationship, I mean?'

'No. Well, I don't know. Possibly.'

'I don't get it then Kate.'

'It's simple. I know you well enough to know that, for you, this is not the real thing. It's almost as if you've someone else on your mind. I want something more permanent. It's the way I am. Marvin's started calling me again, you know.'

'I'm sorry Kate. I thought you were happy with the way things are.'

'Well I was. But now I'm not.'

'Do you want me to go?'

'No stay the night. I haven't taken any vows. I'm just saying things can't go on as they are now. Let's go to bed. It's been several weeks now and I need you badly.'

'I thought you'd never ask Kate. I've lived the life of a monk for several weeks you know.'

Chapter Thirteen

Just one week after the Tender had been submitted to the Ministry, Richard was on BA 073 flight to Abu Dhabi. During the climb, Richard was browsing through his copy of the *Times*. As he reached the business pages, he was surprised to see the headline news: *AGC Company Disappoints Market. 20% Wiped off Shares within Hours.* The article went on to say how turnover was down thirty per cent, profit down forty per cent, the order book by over forty per cent. The analyst believed that this was not the end of the bad news. He thought that large provisions would be needed to cover their unwise European acquisitions that *AGC* had paid well over the odds for in the first place and were now also hit by the falling Euro. He slated the management for gross misjudgement, taking their eye off the ball and, more particularly, for failing to warn the city. He expected shares would fall much more in the coming weeks.

Richard began to wonder if his journey would be in vain. How much of the company would survive and what the effect would be on the current round of job cuts? He decided that it would be sensible to put his CV on the market as soon as he returned. Perhaps there might even be opportunities in the Emirates or America. He'd like that.

Soon after Richard checked in at the *Sheraton*, he called Zoë on her mobile. After two rings it was switched to her voice mail and was invited to leave a message.

'Hi Zoë. Surprise trip came up. It's now nearly nine o'clock. If you get my message soon, please call my

mobile. If not, I'll call you tomorrow. I'm just going down to La Mammas for a snack.'

As Richard arrived in the brightly lit trattoria, he asked for a smoking table.

'This way Mr Richard, good to see you back.'

'Thanks, Marie,' he acknowledged to the smiling Filipina waitress.

As they crossed the restaurant to the smoking area, Richard was astonished to see Zoë, sitting at a window table with none other than Henri Latour. He knew they'd be bound to spot his arrival sooner or later. So he ordered a drink, left his phone and open menu on the table and crossed the short distance to where the couple were sitting.

'Good evening Zoë, Henri. How are you both?'

Henri was first to recover his composure. 'Ah Richard. Zis eez a big surprise. You should be back in England. I 'ear your Company eez in zee big problems.'

'News travels fast, Henri. But I'm sure we'll survive to give *Elsa* a run for their money. So how's Zoë?'

'Oh… err… fine Richard. You didn't let me know you were coming.'

'No Zoë. It was meant to be a surprise. Well, enjoy your meal. I'm sure I'll see you both around the city.' With that, Richard returned to his table and seated himself so the couple were out of his view. When he left the restaurant, they were still dallying over coffee and liqueurs

The following morning, Richard called on the Embassy where he'd arranged to see Colonel Bob.

He checked in at the consulate reception desk. 'I've a meeting with the DA and then the Ambassador.'

'Colonel Archer's expecting you Mr Bryant. You can go through.'

The electronic lock was released and Richard made his way the few steps to the office.

He tapped on the open door. 'Morning Bob.'

'Richard, come on in. Long time, eh? If you stay away

this long, these dollies will find somebody else, you know.'

'So I believe Bob. One already has. They're just fickle, that's all.'

Bob's assistant brought them a pot of coffee whilst they settled down to catch up on the latest gossip and news. Bob explained that General Ahmed had approached the Ambassador about three weeks earlier about his proposal to follow the selection of the UK competition.

'Well Richard, as you can guess, the Ambo gave it his utmost support, and of course, when he told the Defence Export Organisation, they were keen to jump on the bandwagon and make an overseas sale. They saw it as a feather in their cap and will argue it was beneficial to both industry and the customer. Of course, if *Elsa* were to win the UK competition, the General might purchase their system through the French government. But I don't think that will happen, do you?'

'Anything could happen, Bob. The rules change to suit the occasion. The UK will treat *AGC* and *Elsa* as if they're on a level playing field In the end, they'll take the lowest priced bid.'

'But what about UK jobs and buying in pounds sterling and all that?'

'Times have changed Bob. Unlike the French and the USA, our government doesn't fund development anymore. Yet we still have to submit the lowest price to win. It actually means we start at a disadvantage.'

'Mmm, see what you mean. I also noticed that the French have been taking the advantage of our Comms Officer lately too.'

'Yes, I saw Zoë out with Latour last night. To tell you the truth, I didn't even think she liked him.'

'Richard, when are you going to stop applying logic to the gentle sex?'

They spent nearly an hour with the Ambassador, which gave Richard another forum to air his views about the UK competition. He knew that, if convinced, Phillip Gray would be likely to feed the message to the many visiting Ministers. Before leaving the building, Richard knocked on Zoë's office door.

'Morning Zoë. Are you busy?'

'Not at all, I hoped you'd drop in. I would have returned your call later anyway. Coffee?'

'No more thanks. I've had two with Colonel Bob and another two with the Ambo. So how're things? What's new?'

'Oh same old thing Richard. I'm posted in a couple of weeks time. Paris.'

'Well that's convenient I'm sure.'

'Not what you think Richard. I was merely picking Henri's brains last evening.'

'Well that couldn't have taken more than ten seconds. Was it productive?'

'Quite. I wanted to know about accommodation, buying a car, shopping, that sort of thing.'

'I don't envy you living in France and especially driving in Paris.'

'No that bit frightens me.'

'How's your French?'

'Not bad, but they're going to send me on one of those cramming courses where you come out speaking fluent French after a month. So where are you taking me tonight then Richard?'

'Dinner at the Jazz Club at eight?'

'Look forward to it. By the way, Latour did say that he thought Paul Hamilton was all for getting rid of you.'

'Wishful thinking, I'm sure, but he's probably quite right anyway.'

Richard spent the afternoon relaxing at the *Sheraton's* beach and drafting covering letters to send off with his CV. The evening with Zoë was predictably pleasant and passionate. He need not have worried. She said she still thought Henri was a boring fart.

The next day, Richard took a taxi to Dubai and called on General Ahmed. He gave him an updated copy of the Technical Proposal and the revised specification. He explained that *AGC* had offered reduced prices to both parties if the Dubai contract was added within the year. Ahmed seemed delighted with this news but was naively convinced that the UK Ministry would, as a matter of course, choose the British system.

'Well, Sir, I'm sure if you make your preference known to our Ambassador and Ministry, they'll take account of it. But they're not in the business of feather-bedding British industry.'

'I will do that Richard. I just hope it will help.'

Whilst in Dubai, he called Hanna who told him she couldn't say much at the moment but to meet her in the *Crowne Plaza* coffee shop at six. When she arrived, Hanna explained that Tom was in town on one of his rare visits. She thought he'd heard the story about her collapsing in the middle of the night and was suspicious that something was 'going on' as he put it. Richard was slightly surprised when Hanna still suggested they went to Richard's hotel room. On this occasion, he decided for once that prudence was the order of the day.

Richard also took the opportunity to meet with Shaikh Faruk to update him on the bid and ask if he knew of any jobs in the Emirates for surplus to requirement Brits. Faruk felt he could help and said he'd ask around and let Richard know.

The following day, Richard flew back to Heathrow, arriving home at eight that evening. Bex was in her scanty garb, feet up, watching *The Weakest Link*.

'How's the trip Richard? How was Zoë, Hanna, the Dubai Ladies' Pipe Band and the entire female population of…'

'Hi Bex. Just routine. Work, work, work and all that.

Gather the Company's gone to the dogs while I've been away.'

'Yes, you're not kidding. The newspaper's full of it and we've made the *News at Ten* three nights in succession. Apparently the shareholders are livid that *AGC* held back the bad news for so long. The shares are now worth less than half what they were a week ago.'

'I'll never risk leaving the country ever again Bex.'

'Seriously though, they're now threatening massive job cuts and the Union is threatening a strike.'

'On second thoughts, perhaps I'll just take the next flight back to Dubai.'

'Oh, by the way, Maggie's been calling you again.'

'OK, I'll call her tomorrow. Did she say what she wanted?'

'Not exactly. Probably you I guess, Richard.'

'Ha. Come on Bex, I'm not that stupid.'

'Mmm, Richard, really?'

'Really Bex. The next time I see Maggie I'm going to make it clear there is no future in our relationship. I'll never go back with her. I'm happy to stay in contact but just as friends.'

'OK. We'll see. I just hope you do, for everyone's sake.'

'Heard any more about your work situation Bex?'

'Not yet, I'm expecting an interview with my manager in the next couple of days.'

'Yes, I believe I have to have one with Paul this week. That should be fun.'

'I'd like to be a fly on the wall at that one, Richard. Anyway, have you taken the pledge or are we going to have a glass of duty free vino tonight?'

When Richard returned to work, Pat rang to say that Paul wanted to interview him at two that afternoon.

'Has anyone else been interviewed by Mr Personality

yet, Pat?'

'Yes, lots of them. About fifteen I should say from the five Divisions. In fact you must be one of the last.'

'Any feedback?'

'Most of them looked pretty glum when they left. Their main complaint is that they are no wiser about their future after the meeting. I suppose you know that Michael Petty will be there during the interviews?'

'Surely not. Why? That's really out of order, you know. He's still wet behind the ears and will do whatever he thinks will impress Paul.'

'Apparently, he's there to record the discussion in case there's any dispute afterwards but has been known to ask the odd irritating question.'

'That's all I need. May as well pack my bags now.'

'Oh, I'm sure you'll be fine. Paul doesn't really like yes-men, you know.'

'Then why does he surround himself with toadies?'

'I think it gives him confidence,'

'OK Pat, so I'll see you at two and catch up on the rest of the news whilst I await Paul's pleasure.'

Before leaving for Headquarters, Richard arranged a meeting with Sir Anthony and then spent an hour with Clive to get his perspective on the situation.

'So how are things going with *Stern*, Clive?'

'Much better since I've been given the extra resources. We're not out of the woods yet but they should be much happier at next week's Progress Meeting.'

'Any rumours on the bid?'

'No, they've asked a few technical questions about our proposal which have to be submitted at the end of the week, but nothing that will cause us any problems. I believe they've also sent Contracts quite a few questions over our response.'

'That doesn't surprise me. I'm sure Dave O'Leary would've said no to just about every clause. I just hope it doesn't disqualify us. I'll try and see Ian Tucker this week to find out if he's happy with things.'

Richard was flabbergasted to find that Paul was ready promptly at two, to start the interview. Having been pre-warned by Pat, he was not surprised to find Upstart sitting there, trying to look important. Paul seemed nervous and was unusually polite.

'Good afternoon, Richard. Thank you for coming at short notice but all interviews have to completed and written up by cease work today.'

He went on to say that the Company required this formal interview for all *at risk* candidates and that Michael would make a formal record of the meeting including any questions, answers and discussions.

'Now, the first thing I'll do Richard is to run through your assessments. As you know, each personal quality is assessed on a five-point scale: one being well below average and five excellent.'

Paul then read out the scores – Effort – 2, Tenacity – 5, Judgement – 1, Written work – 3, Presentation skills – 3, Oral communication – 2, Accuracy – 2, Teamwork – 2, Overall personal qualities – 2. Performance in post – 3. He then read the narrative which slated Richard's lack of cooperation; his laid back approach to his work and his failure to grasp new ideas which would benefit the business. Paul then grudgingly admitted that Richard had consistently met his sales targets.

'So that's my assessment which will go forward along with other candidates for the business to decide who goes and who stays. Have you any comments or questions so far?'

'Yes, a couple. Why do you rate my judgement and effort so poorly when I've consistently exceeded my sales targets? If everyone had met their targets, the Company wouldn't be in this situation and need to get rid of people.'

'Because that's my assessment of you Richard. Your judgement over our attempts to cooperate with European partners has been poor, even downright contrary at times and you never appear to be working at your full capacity.'

'If the business hadn't squandered its cash on European companies, we wouldn't be having this meeting today. I also believe that however you think I *appear* to work, it's the results that matter. Do I miss deadlines or fail to produce quality work?'

'Well the Business Plan you recently submitted to me was superficial. And you rarely work past six.' This time it was Upstart who decided to join the discussion.

'I'm sorry Paul, but this is going too far. I'll not answer to Mike Petty on matters of performance, timekeeping or my work. For the record, whilst preparing this bid, I've put in sixteen hours days, seven days a week. You are entitled to write what you wish about me; I can do nothing about that, except ask you to reconsider certain aspects. I'm not willing to put up with any criticism from your administrative assistant here, who has yet to win one single order for the business. Unless you require me further, I further suggest that continuing this discussion will achieve nothing but bad feelings on your part and frustration on mine. I suggest that in the event I am selected for redundancy, such discussions would be more aptly held at an Industrial Tribunal, where we can examine all facets of our working relationship. I therefore bid you both good afternoon.'

Paul was speechless. Upstart looked shell-shocked. Richard slowly rose from his chair, reached forward, grabbed hold of Paul's limp hand, shook it, then turned and walked purposefully from the room.

'That was quick.' Pat greeted him with some surprise. 'Go all right?'

'It went extremely satisfyingly, Pat. I wouldn't have missed it for the world.'

By the time Richard arrived at Sir Anthony's office, his annoyance had given way to resignation but some satisfaction in the way that he'd handled the situation. If that was what the Company wanted, he felt he'd be better out of it altogether. He was actually smiling again by the time he bid Sir Anthony good afternoon.

'Come in Richard. I'm glad you're here today. There are some things I wish to discuss with you urgently. Would you close the door please, I don't want anyone to overhear what I have to say.'

Richard closed the door wondering what on earth was coming next.

'Before I get on to the interesting part of our meeting, let me tell you about my lobbying efforts on *Aphrodite*. As we anticipated, Nigel Eldridge was his usual nauseating self. He listened, occasionally, between lecturing me on his ideas about competition and value for money. This he punctuated with a xenophobic discourse on not letting lesser mortals have our technology and his well-known preoccupation with reds under the bed.'

'Well we both knew he'd be a difficult nut to crack.'

'Anyway, all is not lost. After that I saw a couple of Ministers and various MPs. Do you know, it hadn't occurred to most of them that if they kept awarding contracts to non-UK companies, we would lose our research and technology base. I also hammered home the cost in lost jobs, the uneven playing field whilst other governments were funding development and all that stuff. Actually, I believe most of them went away convinced that there was more to this competitive tendering lark than first meets the eye.'

'Well, that's encouraging. I hope they do something about it and quickly.'

'Now for the other thing I wanted to talk about, Richard. I said a while ago that the Company would be more interested in co-operation if partners were willing to inject some cash. So the next bit is not to be discussed with anyone outside of this room.'

'Of course. I won't say a word.'

'Good, well frankly the Company is in an even worse state than reported in the Press in recent weeks. So anything that will recover some cash is top priority. If we sell the European acquisitions, we'll lose a mountain of money. You know that everyone thinks we paid far too much for them. So this is where you come in.'

'But what can I do?'

'Go to America and trade on your excellent relationship with Chuck and see if you can get the *Georgia Radar Systems* to invest in our Radar business.'

'But how can I do that without arousing suspicion? Paul for one would know where I was.'

'Not necessarily Richard, and if Paul found out, the plot would go tits up anyway. He'd be on to *Elsa* in a shot and we'd have another European disaster on our hands. No, I've spoken with the Chairman and you take a week's leave. We'll pay your fare to Atlanta and all expenses. We'll also provide one of the corporate accountants to support you and leave it to your judgement to persuade *GRSC* to offer the best deal they can.'

'Sounds interesting. I'm sure they'll take it seriously.'

'Now the whole thing must be played low key. We don't want the City to think we're desperate, so try and have meetings away from the *GRSC* site.'

'What if Paul won't sign my leave chit?'

'We'll get Human Resources to say you must be granted some because of the redundancy threat. I've had a pack of Company information made up for you; high level stuff but should be useful to Chuck.'

'So how soon do you want me to go?'

'As soon as possible and within the next week.'

'Fine, I'll drop a leave pass in to Pat as soon as I leave here. Paul's bound to think it's because I'm sulking after the redundancy interview.'

'That bad?'

'Worse.'

'Mmm, well, try and put that out of your mind for the time being.'

'I'll leave as soon as I can. Can you ask the bean counter to contact me as soon as possible so we can coordinate flights and suchlike?'

'Yes, he can stay on after you've done your bit to provide them all the financial data they'll need to make their assessment. Good luck Richard. I'm sure you can handle it.'

'OK, Sir Anthony. Thanks for your confidence. I appreciate it.'

A happier Richard left Headquarters with a signed leave pass in his bag. It seemed that Paul was only too pleased to have him out of his hair for a while. Or probably forever.

When Richard arrived home that evening, he called Chuck and asked if they could meet on Sunday in Atlanta.'

'Great to meet you Richard, but it will have to be in Washington DC as Trish and I will be at the *Sheraton* there until Wednesday next week. I'll be at the *Old Crows* Annual get together and Trish will be doing the sights and checking out the bargains at *Tyson's Corner Mall*.'

'Even better. I'll fax you the details at home as soon as I've booked the flights.'

'Look forward to seeing you. Are you bringing Bex along?'

'That's a thought Chuck, I'll let you know.'

'The *Sheraton* will be full of *Crows* but there's bound to be some last minute cancellations. I'll try and make a booking as soon as we get there.'

'So d'you fancy a holiday in Washington, Bex? You mustn't tell anyone but my fare and the hotel will be paid for. So I'll pay for your rat-class flight.'

'When?'

'This Sunday?'

'If I can get leave, I'd love to. But wouldn't you rather take Kate? Or Emma? Or Maggie? The Scottish All-woman's Pipers?'

'No Bex. I'd rather take you. The cut and thrust of our rapport keeps my brain active. I'm also trying to disengage from all those other relationships which aren't really going anywhere. Except the pipers that is.'

'But I thought you really liked Emma.'

'I do, but it's not the real thing.'

'And Kate?'

'Kate's cooling off anyway, but that's not the right ingredient either.'

'And you're going to sort things out with Maggie next time you see her?'

'Yes. Definitely '

'So that just leaves me and the Scottish pipers?'

'Yes Bex. On second thoughts I'll take the pipers.'

Chapter Fourteen

When Richard and Becky checked into the Washington *Sheraton,* the place was swarming with delegates from the *Association of Old Crows* who were holding their annual gathering of members in the Electronic Warfare business. As they left the desk, they met up with Chuck.

'So, caught you sleeping with the enemy then, Chuck. I thought these *Crow's* purpose in life was to blot out your Radars.'

'Sure thing Richard, but it's a great way to get up to date on the latest countermeasures. So how are you both? Good journey?'

'Oh, Richard was fine riding up in Club whilst I was stuck down the back.'

'Really, Richard. How could you?'

'Don't listen to her Chuck. They gave her a seat next to me. Last time I ask for an upgrade for Miss Ungrateful here.'

'Trish is still out shopping. Why don't you two get settled in and we can meet up in the bar for business chat at six and the girls can join us at seven. Will that give us enough time for our first meeting?'

'Plenty. That'll be fine Chuck.'

Whilst Richard unpacked, showered and changed, Bex fiddled with the fifty odd channels on the television. This was her first trip to America and she'd behaved like an excited teenager ever since they arrived at Dulles airport.

Chuck was already sitting in a quiet corner of the bar when Richard arrived. A pitcher of beer and two glasses were placed strategically on the table.

Chuck raised his glass. 'Good Health, Richard. Put me out of my misery. Tell me what gives with all this cloak and dagger stuff?'

'Cheers Chuck. I've come to make you an offer you can't refuse.'

Chuck was already aware of *AGC's* problems as they're quoted daily on the New York Stock Exchange. The bad news had been given some prominence in the Wall Street Journal during the past week. Richard explained the purpose of his trip and the high level support *Georgia Radar Systems* would receive if they were willing to invest some cash in the Radar Division. Chuck received the news enthusiastically.

'Gee Richard, this is just great. The Company has already asked me to look at expanding into the European market and the defence business. Between us two boys, when it looked as if you were going to tie up with *Elsa*, we had some discussions with *Stern*. Nothing agreed yet, but there's definitely some interest there.'

'I don't see why you couldn't pursue both options Chuck. *Stern* product line is in airborne Radar, so they're not really a competitor. Anyway if you're interested in looking at things a little closer, one of our corporate accountants will fly out on Wednesday.'

'Sure thing Richard. Our President and VP Projects fly in tomorrow. I'll brief them and then we can all get together and thrash a few ideas around. I'm sure they'll be very interested in giving it a serious look.'

They talked some more about *AGC's* problems and the advantages of the venture before Trish and Becky arrived and they switched to lighter subjects. After two more pitchers, they took a cab to Georgetown where they ate huge steaks and drank several bottles of Californian wine. Later they danced to a live group in the hotel bar until jet lag set in and Richard and Bex left to catch up on some sleep.

The following day, Trish and Chuck were tied up with *Crow* activities and meeting their VIPs flying in from Atlanta. This gave Richard the opportunity to take Bex around the Capital. They took the Metro to the Washington Memorial and picked their way through the Smithsonian museums, starting with Space and finishing at The National Art Gallery. Until then, Richard wasn't aware just how interested Becky was in French Impressionists. He practically had to eject her from the museum. He was equally surprised just how knowledgeable she was about most of the paintings and her enthusiasm for Pissarro, Sisley, Monet and Seurat. Bex said she was amazed how so many of these wonderful European paintings had found their way into the American gallery. Before they left, Richard made the excuse he was going to the loo and bought her framed prints of Seurat's *Lighthouse at Honfleur* and Pissarro's *Peasant Girl with a Straw Hat.*

'What a pity they're French Bex. Anyway, something to hang on your bedroom wall and gaze at during the more boring moments.'

'Richard, what a lovely surprise. You really are a poppet at times.' She kissed him meaningfully on the lips.

'Careful Bex, we'll be arrested for public disorder.'

They took a cab to the White House and then on to other tourist traps. Exhausted, they eventually arrived back at the *Sheraton* for a nap before meeting up with Chuck and company in the bar at six.

Chuck introduced the two newcomers. Harvey Crawford was the white-haired President. Wayne Harris Jnr was the extrovert VP Projects, who was in about his mid-thirties and looked as if he'd just jumped straight out of an episode of Dallas. Harvey said they would talk turkey tomorrow but he was extremely interested in what Chuck had told him. The dinner was fairly relaxed but businesslike that evening as Harvey had invited along a couple of his *Old Crows* buddies. The Americans reminisced a lot and indulged in talk of the exhibition, the new technologies and personalities. They'd all heard about *AGCs* fate and pumped Richard good-naturedly for details. Richard admitted he was only privy to what he'd read in the newspapers but felt that much of the problem was due to the Board following their hearts instead of their heads. He said that some of the Divisions had caught a cold by trying to do their own thing on civil product diversification. He added that the City commentators had also been very critical over the choice and price paid for their European acquisitions.

Overall, it was a pleasant enough evening and the hosts were careful not to leave Trish and Becky out of the conversation. They spoke warmly of their Scottish heritage and their frequent visits to London and Edinburgh.

The following day, the four men assembled for a breakfast meeting in Harvey's suite. Richard ran through the *Power Point* presentation on the Company, the Radar Division, *Aphrodite* and the current business opportunities.

'Thank you, that was very clear,' Harvey responded. 'So, tell me, how does all this fit in to *AGC's* future planning and strategies?'

'As you're aware, the turnover, profit and order book are well down for the Company as a whole. *AGC* has also made some dubious acquisitions in Europe which has depleted their capital. However, the Radar Division is forecasting a profitable year, with turnover up and a strong five-year order book. We also have a lot of confidence in the future of *Aphrodite*, especially if we win the UK bid. *AGC* is particularly short of cash, so by selling part interest in the Radar Division, they'll be able to bail out some of the other Divisions and hopefully grow them back into profitability.'

'I don't understand you Limies. I can't imagine why your government doesn't give you a head start against any foreign competition. It's crazy. But I guess that's a good point for us if we invest in your Division. What do you think the chances of your success in the competition are?'

'Truthfully Harvey, about fifty-fifty. *AGC* got cold feet about bidding more aggressively because of its preoccupation with the overall Company financial position. They're thinking very short-term at the moment. There'll probably be a chance for a best-and-final-offer and hopefully you'll be on board by then.'

Their debate continued for a further two hours when they discussed the possibility of *AGC* folding altogether, the civil market and the opportunities in Europe and the Middle East. The VP Projects asked many questions about engineering and manufacturing facilities, quality assurance and support. Harvey then drew the discussion to a close.

'Richard, thank you for an excellent session and your straight answers. Chuck's here for a few more days so we'll feed any further questions through him. I gather your financial guy arrives soon, so we'll run through all the detailed figures with him.'

Richard added that he would now leave the debate to the experts and Board members to negotiate. 'From the time I return to the UK on Thursday, your point of contact will be the *AGC* Chairman, whom you've already met, or Sir Anthony Laycock whose details are on these business cards. I sincerely hope our Businesses can come together. Thank you for all your time and attention.'

'Richard, it's been great talking with you. I promise to give the proposal the fullest consideration,' Harvey concluded.

After the meeting, Richard dragged Becky out of bed and they spent the rest of the day at Tyson's Corner shopping. Even Richard, who normally hated shopping, found the malls crowd-free, clean and interesting. Bex was over the moon. She couldn't believe the low prices, wide choice and the helpfulness of the shop assistants.

That evening, Richard and Becky dined alone together, whilst the *GRSC* team attended a *Crows* function. They ate at the Steakhouse in Rosslyn where Becky saw 'the biggest ever steaks in her whole life'. They washed down the huge meal with copious jugs of red wine and fell into bed at ten-thirty.

Becky started fiddling with the TV remote again and suddenly found the adult movie menu. She was particularly taken with the idea of watching '*Debbie Does Dallas*'.

'OK, if you want but it'll be pretty tame you know.'

'So you've seen it before then?'

'No Bex, but I can't believe they'll show you anything you haven't seen before.'

As they watched Debbie's antics on the small screen, Richard was surprised how Becky seemed transfixed and unusually quiet. He was also pleasantly surprised that as the movie progressed, Becky moved closer and wrapped her arm around his waist. By the time Debbie had done Dallas. Bex was visibly aroused.

'Richard.'

'Yes Bex.'

'Could we try that?'

'Try what?'

'Well, you know… that.'

'You mean, like we've been watching?'

'Yes Richard. Exactly that. What did you think I meant, let's go to Dallas?'

'But Bex, you're not into that sort of thing and I…'

'Richard, do you fancy me or not?'

'Becky, I fancy you more than I've ever fancied anyone in my life but I thought that you…'

'Richard, shut the flip up before I change my mind.' With that Becky pulled him closer and kissed him longingly.

Richard responded, at first quite self-consciously.

Although he'd dreamt many times about making love with Bex, he'd never really expected it to happen or for her to take the initiative like this. He took great pains to take things slowly and caress her gently. His hands lightly explored her trim body, stroking, teasing whilst observing her pleasure. He wanted to be sure that Bex was truly ready and wouldn't be put off by too hasty a move. He needn't have worried. It was Becky who eventually took the initiative, rolling herself on top of him and easing him inside of her. She rocked forward and backwards deliberately but agonisingly slowly with lengthy pauses between each intense and consuming movement. Only during the last half minute did she abandon her restraint causing them to climax uncontrollably together in a breathless, burning crescendo.

Neither spoke for several minutes. Both reliving their compelling and intoxicating experience. Bex was first to break the silence.

'Well, I guess that was worth waiting nearly a year for.'

'You didn't have to wait that long Bex, you know. I've wanted you so badly for simply ages.'

'Well, I thought working in the same Company and living together that getting involved with you would only make life difficult. And we got on so well, I thought sex might spoil things. That's why I pretended not to like men. But as I told you last week, there is some truth in that. I had lost interest for a few years now. Then you came along and changed everything.'

'I wish you'd told me earlier.'

'Yes Richard but, remember, you were always having it off with someone else. You really are a tart you know. How do you expect any girl to take you seriously?'

'But as I told you, they weren't what I wanted for the long term. I couldn't have settled down with any of them.'

'Well, you make a pretty good impression of liking

them.'

'I did like them, but not in the same way. I never made any pretence with them that it was for anything else than for mutual enjoyment. They all seemed quite happy with that situation. I promise that I'll be completely faithful to you, if that's what you want me to be.'

'I think that's what I want, Richard, very much. But I realise that sometimes feelings change after people have made love. It makes everything much more complex and I know we'll never be quite the same with each other from now on. I wanted you in Amsterdam and many times since but I always worried how it would change our relationship for the worse. You see I like you as well as love you.'

'So how do you feel right now about things Bex? You know, now that we've done it?'

'Like doing it all over again.'

'Good for me too. I guess the future's up to us Bex. I'm just so relieved that I don't have to pretend not to be in love with you any more.'

Over the next three days, the two new lovers behaved like a couple on their honeymoon. They walked and talked, completely wrapped up in each other. They hired a car and visited Baltimore harbour and aquarium, Annapolis Academy, the zoo and various historical sites. Richard met with Chuck from time to time to answer a number of supplementary questions and was taken for a tour around the *Crows* Exhibition Hall. Becky and Trish found this a good time to go shopping. Each evening, the four of them would try new culinary delights in the endless selection of interesting venues in the City. After the accountant arrived in Atlanta, Chuck began to get some feedback from his boss.

'They seem very happy with your Division's performance but wonder if it will be dragged down by the abysmal overall Company performance. There's also concern that if you do not win the UK Air Defence requirement, you'll find it impossible to sell the *Aphrodite* system elsewhere.'

'Well Chuck, on your first point about *AGC's* overall performance, much depends on the split of ownership on the Joint Venture and hence who controls what. I believe the same applies to the Air Defence bid. From what I hear, it's a close run thing now but if together we could knock another fifteen million off, we'd have better than a ninety per cent chance of winning. I don't think *Elsa* could go quite that far, considering the level of their government's controlling interest.'

'Will they let us revise our prices?'

'I believe that if there is a change to Company ownership before the bid is finally adjudicated, they'd insist on a new offer. Anyway, they always come out with a *best and final* before they announce the winner. It's a way of squeezing the last drop of blood out of the competitors. I don't know why they make such a fuss about closed tenders when they do that.'

'I also believe Chuck, that if you can get *Stern* to be the third partner of the JV, even with a smaller percentage share, it would give the consortium the right European flavour.'

'OK Richard, you speak to your contacts in *Stern* through the back door and I'll contact them through the official route. I've just to find some way of convincing my bosses that the bad news about *AGC* doesn't make a deal with your Division too risky.'

The week simply flew by for Richard and Becky who reluctantly said their goodbyes to Trish and Chuck. By this time Trish had noticed and remarked on the change she had seen in the behaviour of them both.

'So you two seem to have got it together at last Richard?'

'It must be something they put in the food Trish. It just means that we aren't as cutting to each other.'

'Yes, of course that's what it is. So you two think that you can fool your Auntie Trish do you?'

By the time Richard and Becky returned to work, the redundancy letters had been issued. Becky had escaped but Richard received notice that the Company no longer wanted him. He was invited for an interview with Lady Penelope to discuss his future and, in the meantime, was assured that the Company would do everything possible to place him in another post and other such fictional drivel. He knew that Paul had well and truly put the boot in and *AGC* wouldn't have the slightest interest in his continued employment.

'Well it's their loss. I'm not sure I want to work for them anymore now.' Bex was the first to commiserate with him.

'Don't be hasty Bex. There's absolutely nothing to be gained by you chucking it in as well. Put your CV around by all means and go for some interviews. But it's pointless us both becoming unemployed on a point of principle. Anyway, hopefully I can get a job in the area although not many companies in our line of business are recruiting at the moment.'

'Well, I still think they're bonkers when they could save even more money by getting rid of Messrs Hamilton and Petty for a start.'

'It doesn't work that way Bex. Anyway, I've got three months notice so there's plenty of time for me to look around.'

The following day, Richard drove to Headquarters for his interview with Penelope Field. As expected at such a time, the Human Resources Department was under more than the usual stress and her desk was piled high with green personal files.

'First of all Richard, let me say that I'm sorry that your post has disappeared in the organisation. From what I've seen of your performance, I think it's sad that the Company is losing you. Unfortunately, at such a time as this, we've to look at every post individually to decide which ones should remain. And of course the Sales Department represents quite a drain on our overhead costs. Paul has offered up four of the eight sales posts in your Division.'

'Sure. We travel, we entertain and use the telephone on long distance calls a lot, but that's the price of winning orders. If you don't do these things, the order book will fall and the Company will be in an even worse shape. Anyway, the decision has been made and I guess whatever I say today will not change that.'

'No, that is true. It's my job to make it as painless as possible and to try and find an alternative post for you before you leave the Company.'

'What happens if nothing turns up?'

'We'll give you a severance package. For a start, you have three full months from today on full pay. During this time, you can have continued use of your office and site facilities. We'll also offer you resettlement courses and provide any advice you need to help you find a job with another company. I believe it's always easier to find work whilst you're still in a job. I find that would-be employers are less inclined to interview candidates who are unemployed. It's unfair and ungrounded, but that's the way it is.'

'Thank you, I'd like to use all the facilities available. Can you tell me more about the severance payment?'

'We're offering you a package of benefits which includes a thirty thousand pounds severance payment. If you agree to this, you'll have to sign a *Compromise Agreement* which means that you will make no further claims on the Company. We'll pay for you to consult with a lawyer which protects us both from future wrangles.'

'What about my work during this period?'

'With senior managers, such as yourself, we leave this

entirely to discretion. You may well choose to put most of your effort into finding employment. It's up to you.'

'I've already put so much effort into winning the UK competition, I'd hope to see it through before I leave. What about references?'

'Yes, tricky one. Look, normally you choose whom you believe will give you the best reference but if you don't have one from your immediate boss, most prospective employers become suspicious. Why don't you get one from the Divisional Managing Director? I know for a fact that Tony Brooks has a high regard for you.'

'Thanks that's useful advice.' That at least meant Richard didn't have to go cap in hand to Paul and suffer more abuse.

'Right then Richard. Michelle Holmes will look after you on all day-to-day personnel aspects from now on. However, if you've any particular concerns you wish to discuss with me personally, the door is always open. Good luck.'

Richard thanked Penelope for her time, feeling slightly guilty that he'd misjudged her in the past. He next briefed Sir Anthony on the meetings with *GRSC* and told him of the news of his redundancy.

Sir Anthony said he was shocked and surprised at Richard's fate, particularly as he'd tried to influence things on Richard's behalf. However, the Company had set out the ground rules on how candidates should be selected and religiously followed the assessments and recommendations of the line managers. Sir Anthony believed that this was an attempt to stop the victims crying foul at some resulting tribunal. On the meetings with *GRSC*, he congratulated Richard on his good work and said that Harvey had already contacted the Chairman and promised that they would give the matter serious consideration.

That evening, Becky looked more radiant that ever. Some previously faint signs of tension had disappeared making her eyes sparkle and her features even more beautiful than ever. Having this new relationship with Bex took much of the sting out of redundancy for Richard. They both now limited their wine intake to a couple of glasses each evening, preferring to remain sober to enjoy the blissful and passionate lovemaking.

Richard arrived for his meeting with Ian Tucker to find Group Captain Ted Green slouched in Ian's office sipping coffee.

'Don't stand on ceremony lad. Come on in. We'll not bite yee. Coffee?'

'Morning Ted, Ian. Yes please standard NATO.'

'So what's this I hear about t'e bloody company giving yee yer cards then?

'Yes Ted, they don't need me any more. They're going to sell things without leaving the site from now on. Or they'll do it all from HQ by smoke and mirrors.'

'Sounds as if Company's in t'e shit Richard anyway!'

'I don't think you need worry about the Radar Division, that's in good shape. And after the present cost cutting exercise, this year's figures will be excellent. You know from some of the paperwork that passes your desk that we have asked permission to release data to would-be collaborators.'

'Yes. I know ye can't say much about how that's going but I guess that's t'e sort of reassurance we need before placing any more contracts your way.'

'I hope that we'll be able to give you news of that in the not too distant future.'

'So what are your plans Richard?'

'Oh, I've sent out a dozen CVs to people I know around the industry. It'll much depend if there are any vacancies. As you can guess, this is not the best time to go job hunting, especially with all the other rejects from *AGC* on the street. I'll be working for another three months anyway, then I can live on the settlement for a bit. I've got a bit of time to find something.'

'If I hear of anything, I'll put you in touch. Anyway Richard, ye didn't come 'ere te hear me prattling on. I'll leave you now with Ian te talk business. Good luck anyway, I'm sure you'll be fine.'

As soon as Ted was out of earshot, Richard remarked that he wished he'd a boss like that.

'Yes, I'm lucky there. They don't come any straighter. I never envied you working for Paul. That's for sure. So I guess you want to know how things are going on the tenders.'

'Whatever you're able to tell me Ian.'

'Well, you probably already know that we've two serious bids on the table and our technical assessment is virtually finished. We've a few more questions. You know the sort of thing, assurances of how you will meet the spec in certain areas without defying the laws of physics, but I don't think you've any worries there. The existence of your prototype modules and working software helps your technical score a lot.'

'So if the price is good, we're in reasonable shape then?'

'Yes. As always, price will be the main preoccupation of our masters. We've to take the lowest compliant system unless there is a powerful and overriding reason for not accepting this offer.'

'Well, I know that the price envelopes will not even have been opened yet and I'm sure you'll want your usual discount.'

'Most probably Richard. If there are any changes to the Division's structure, we'll also need to know all the details about that, especially if non-UK firms are involved.'

'If I'm still around, I promise you'll be the first to know Ian.'

'And that's about all I can say for the moment. So how's your love-life Richard, still making a complete horlicks of that as well?'

'Not at all Ian. It's absolutely wonderful. My love-life is absolute bloody bliss.'

With all the things happening in his life, Richard hadn't seen Maggie for some time. Each time he'd spoken with her on the phone, she'd pressed him to meet with her. Despite all the other pressures, he reluctantly agreed to meet up one evening.

They met in a bar on the outskirts of Woking. Richard had just ordered a whisky and water, when Maggie joined him and asked him to 'make that two'.

'Hi Maggie, I'm really sorry it has taken so long for us to meet but a lot has been going on in my life.'

'Me too Richard. I've told Georgio that I'm not going back to Sorrento and the kids are staying with me.'

'Really, what did he say?'

'He was pretty devastated and said he wanted the kids and all that.'

'Won't he have a strong claim as they were born in Italy?'

'Probably, but we're not married, so my lawyer says that'll make things difficult for him.'

'Sounds a bit messy to me.'

'Yes. It is. That's why I need your help. I don't have anyone else to turn to in the UK and I can't get my parents involved in this. It will be far too painful and stressful for them.'

'I really don't know what I can do to help, Maggie. I've lost my job in *AGC*. I've just found someone I really like and anyway, I can't see how we could possibly get back together. As things turned out, it was all a big mistake the first time. We rushed into things before and got it all wrong.'

'That was my fault Richard. I made the mistake.'

'Look Maggie. I am happy to keep contact with you but you will have to get on with your own life. I've got enough on my plate as it is.'

'But we are still married, Richard.'

'Yes, but only on paper. And Maggie, I also want to be freed from that. It's not fair to expect me to go back to how things might have been all that time ago. After all, it was your decision.'

'OK, Richard. I said it was my mistake. I should have known you wouldn't help me. I'm going on home now.'

'All right, Maggie, but I hope that you'll keep in contact. Please think again about my wanting a divorce. I know I don't have to have it, but I'd rather do it with your agreement.'

'I'm disappointed, Richard. I'll think about it. Goodnight.'

'Goodnight, Maggie. I really hope things work out for you.'

Chapter Fifteen

Out of the eight job applications that Richard sent out, five regretted that they had no vacancies but agreed to keep his details on file for six months. One was still to reply and two companies invited him for interviews. *Royal Electronics* was a military communications company with an annual turnover of around a billion pounds. *MKT* plc was a much larger company, with about ten billion turnover, and in the worldwide telecommunications business.

At *Royal*, Richard spent the first half hour in the Personnel Section, filling in their standard application forms. As often seems to happen, he found the spaces allowed for his deficiencies were large, and those where he had plenty to say were minute. He then spent another hour doing psychometric tests against the clock. After a further half-hour's coffee break whilst they marked the tests, Richard was taken to meet Bob Hilton, the Marketing Director.

'Richard, I think I've seen you around and about the bazaars. Weren't you at *Asian Aerospace,* Singapore this year?'

Richard's heart sank as he recalled the embarrassing incident in *Raffles Hotel*. 'Yes, the Company sent me on most of the major Defence Exhibitions. It seems to be a very cost effective way of catching a lot of potential customers in one place and finding out about new opportunities.'

'Well, I disagree. Most of them are a complete waste

of money. Half the Delegations don't turn up and those that do are frequently the wrong people or are not really interested. They cost a lot of money and tie the staff up for a week at a time. I only went to Singapore for the last two days of the show, as I happened to be passing through anyway on my way back from Darwin. No, you won't be doing many of those if you get to work for us.'

Richard breathed a sigh of relief. At least he wasn't there for the *Raffles* incident. But he thought it a bit worrying that his interviewer took such an over the top line on exhibitions. Would he be so intransigent on all such matters?

Bob went on to explain at great length the Company structure, their products and their recent contracts. He then asked Richard a lot of mundane questions about his qualifications and experience and his knowledge of communications technology.

'So why are you leaving *AGC* Richard?'

'Partly because of restructuring and partly because it's time for me to move on. I've been in the present job for five years now.'

'Presumably by restructuring, you mean the Company going to the dogs?'

'It's no secret that *AGC* has some major problems at the moment and is downsizing. However, the Radar Division is in good shape. I've always met my own sales targets and seem to be able to work well with our overseas customers.'

'Well we get most of our contracts from our *MoD*. We only ever consider opportunities overseas that we have a very high probability of winning.'

'That must limit your activities rather.'

'Yes well we can learn from *AGC* on that, can't we?'

'I think *AGC's* problems were more acquisition and management related.'

'That's as maybe but we're extremely conservative and

safe. Now let's have a look at your tests. Have you done this sort of thing before?'

'No, never. Are they reliable?'

'Utterly reliable. I swear by them. Since I arrived, all of my existing staff have to take them before they're considered for promotion. Now, let me see... yes, team-worker, somewhat intransigent, independent... can be rebellious at times... loyal, leads by consensus. Tendency to take the least demanding course of action. How does that sound for starters?'

'I've heard those sort of comments on previous appraisals.'

'Good. Told you it works. So how do you get on with Paul Hamilton? He used to work for me, you know.'

'We've very different ways of working and I don't think he likes the way I achieve my targets.'

'Too brash perhaps. Or intransigent?'

'Too decisive but unwilling to be distracted from the key sales task.'

'You feel you know better than Paul?'

'I hate indecision. Most business decisions are not black or white; they're usually some shade of grey. And a decision on pricing or sales strategy is unlikely to be better because it's delayed for a week. I try to keep on top of things, answer my mail on the day I receive it and be prepared for decisions ahead of the time they have to be made.'

'Do you think your previous bosses have felt threatened by you?'

'Only those who were insecure or poor at their job.'

'Mmm. So what do you think are the main qualities of a good salesman?'

'Integrity, tenacity, knowledge of his products, a good listener and the ability to read people.'

'But you've made no attempt to give me placatory answers to my questions today.'

'No, if you don't want me as I am, there is no point. We'd just end up both being unhappy about it in the future. I try to be tactful but absolutely straight with customers in the same way. That's the only way to get their long-term trust.'

The interview carried on in the same vein for a further fifteen minutes, during which time Richard became increasingly convinced that he didn't want to work for this person. When invited, he asked some low-key questions on organisation and product funding, thanked him for his time before leaving to return home wiser, but no closer, to finding a job.

'So how was the interview?' The way Becky asked the question, she was hoping to hear the word brilliant or wonderful.

'Heap of crap really Bex. Strange fish, the Marketing Director. Think he's a buddy, no I mean an associate, of Hamilton. I even believe they'd already spoken about me.'

'What about the Company?'

'Small, inward looking, too dependent on UK government business. Haven't invested much in future technology. Order book reflects it. No, not for me, even if they were to make an offer.'

'Never mind sweetie, you've got another one up North this week. Something will turn up. I'd employ you like a shot.'

'Thanks Bex. Unfortunately, it looks as if I'll be destined to work for Muppets – that's if I ever get another job.'

The city of Newcastle was new to Richard and it was as well that he'd allowed plenty of time to find the Headquarters of *MKT plc*. The building resembled a Victorian industrial factory. A large notice 'Director's

Entrance' was fixed to the newly decorated entrance with arrows pointing to the Staff Entrances at the sides of the sprawling building. Richard noticed that all the car spaces close to the building were allocated with grand titles. The large majority of employees were forced to park in a crowded yard some five minutes walk from the entrances.

The Management Suites were plush and modern and located on a mezzanine floor with an impressive wooden staircase joining the Reception area to the main entrance.

'Richard Bryant. I have an appointment at eleven with Mr Peter Atkinson.'

'Right Mr Bryant. Please complete this visitors form.'

Richard was then given a personalised badge to clip on his jacket and invited to take a seat on the plush sofa. Around the Reception area, inbuilt display cases showed *MKT's* product history going back to the days of telephone switchboards with brass phone jacks and braided leads and telephones without dials. The latest case displayed fibre optics, microelectronics, chipsets, mobile phones and switching systems.

This time, Richard was shown into a small conference room, rather than Peter Atkinson's office.

After few formalities, the ruddy faced, balding Atkinson went straight into the questions.

'So tell me Richard, why do you want to come to this godforsaken part of the world to work?'

'I'm ready for a change and I'm sure you're aware that *AGC* is in trouble.'

'Deserting a sinking ship then?'

'Not exactly. The Division I'm in is doing fine. The Board has made some odd decisions over acquisitions and product development. The Company is downsizing anyway.'

'And Sales and Marketing are easy targets for savings of course. Well, the Company's daft decisions are hardly your problem. It's a tragedy that those at the top don't think a bit harder about the effects of their actions. In these difficult times it can happen to anyone. It's nearly always the guys at your level that come off worse. So tell me what you know about telecomms.'

'Not specifically telecomms but I have a good grounding in electronics, worked for three years as a design engineer on HF communications software, went on to radar systems for another two then, seven years ago, transferred to sales and marketing.'

'Well it's sales people I'm looking for as long as they can get a grasp on the technical bits and we'll always support you with a specialist engineer when necessary. So tell me about what you've sold and where.'

Richard continued answering the series of sensible and probing questions from the down to earth interviewer. It was a pleasant change to meet someone at that level who was so technically aware and businesslike. After lunch with Peter Atkinson in the Executive Dining Room, he was given a tour of the site and promised an answer within the week.

'Well Richard. I've enjoyed talking to you and you're a serious contender for the post. If it doesn't work out this time, I'll keep my eye open for any similar vacancy in other parts of *MKT*. Thanks for coming all this way. Safe trip and good luck.'

Richard thanked him for his time and began the long trek home. He liked what he had seen that day and thought how satisfying it would be to work for a company as professional as *MKT*.

When he reached the flat, Becky couldn't wait to hear all about the interview and Newcastle.

'I've never been that far North Richard. Could you understand them OK?'

'Yes, fine Bex. It amazes me you've been half way round the world and think you fall off the edge if you go North of Birmingham. I didn't really see much of the city but it looked fine to me. The company was impressive. They're doing well and the interviewer knew what he was talking about.'

'So, do you think they'll offer you the job?'

'Better than fifty per cent chance I'd say. He sort of hinted at the end that things had gone well.'

'That's great. I think this deserves a glass of red. I'll save the bubbly 'til you hear you've definitely got it.'

'It's a long journey though. It'll take ages on a Friday night.'

'Worry about that when the offer comes. Until then, let's enjoy what we have.'

'OK. I've been thinking about you so much today and worrying about being separated.'

'Richard. I don't want to think about it. Open the bottle.'

Richard decided that it was time to clear the decks with Kate and Emma. They needed to know that now he was hooked on Becky and not interested in pursuing other females. Richard had always been scrupulously honest in such matters, although he disliked the drama it frequently invoked.

Firstly, he arranged to meet Kate after work in *The Feathers*, a country inn about five miles from the site. It was apparent that Kate was expecting the worst, as she appeared unusually quiet and subdued.

'Kate, I thought it only fair to explain that I've decided not to go out with anyone else now that I'm sort of dating Becky.'

'Not like you Richard, I thought you sort of dated several girls at once and you were happy as long as they were happy.'

'Well, that's true Kate, but I've decided to change the habit of a lifetime and to have a serious relationship now.'

'That's all fine Richard, but are you sure it's not the

change of job that is getting to you and you're just looking for stability in other areas to compensate?'

'Possibly. I hadn't thought of that. But no, Bex is special. I just like to be up front about these things that's all.'

'I expect this is a temporary illusion with you Richard. I'll be happy to take up where we left off when the novelty wears off.'

'If it does Kate, you'll be the first to know, I promise.'

That out of the way, the pair had a civilised couple of drinks. Kate was clearly concerned about Richard losing his job and questioned him about the interviews.

'You'll find it a bit strange *Up North* you know, you don't even speak the lingo.'

'No. I really liked the *MKT* set-up although they seemed to be in the dark ages over their hierarchical class system. Employee relations nevertheless seemed pretty good, even though the workers had to park near Leeds, ate in a different canteen and could only use the side entrances to the HQ building.'

'What about the other one you went to?'

'Oh, *Royal Electronics*. I thought the guy that interviewed me must be a brother of Paul Hamilton. The chemistry between us was terrible. Am I that difficult?'

'Not at all. You rush in sometimes without weighing up the consequences. You wouldn't win any prizes for tact. You appear to take things easy, but you're good at your job and tackle things in a way that requires the minimum effort to achieve the result you want.'

'Well, that's extremely perceptive Kate. I didn't realise you knew me so well.'

'I've been at meetings with you and seen how you operate. *AGC* is stupid to get rid of you.'

'Thanks Kate. I really appreciate your confidence, particularly under the circumstances of our meeting this evening.'

After an hour, Kate made excuses that she needed to leave, pecked Richard fondly on the cheek and left. As he drove home, Richard felt sad but realised it was for the best. He told Becky that he had finished his liaison with Kate.

'What's new Richard? She lasted two months longer than most.'

'I've changed Bex. This is the new me.'

Becky opened the window and leaned out.

'What are you doing Bex?'

'Looking for the pink elephants sweet. Fancy going out to eat tonight?'

That weekend, Richard drove to Woking to see Emma. He had made the excuse that he was going to be in Woking that day and suggested they meet for lunch. Again, he had the feeling that Emma instinctively knew that he was seeing her for a reason and the news would not be good.

However, as soon as Emma arrived, Richard detected from her bursting excitement that she had something urgent to tell him.

'Richard, I'm so happy to see you again. I've something to tell you. I didn't want to discuss it on the phone but I've made my decision. I've accepted the job in Washington.'

'That's great Emma. I'm sure you'll be happy there and soon make new friends. What will you do about the cottage?'

'Let it I think. It shouldn't be too difficult in Woking and I will put anything precious into store. The job's well paid and they provide accommodation so I've no worries there.'

'Well that's absolutely fantastic. I hope you'll be really happy. I'm sure it's for the best.'

'Now, you said you had something important to tell me Richard.'

'Yes. It's rather overtaken by events but I wanted to say that I'm really happy with Becky at the moment and didn't feel comfortable about seeing anyone else. Also I've applied for a job in Newcastle, it's looking good and if I accept I'll be about the same travelling time from Hampshire as you will be in Washington.'

'I guess I was expecting something along those lines. The bit about Becky I mean. She confided in me some time ago that she was struck on you. Not long after we got it together in fact. I wouldn't have got involved with you in the first place had I known but you didn't seem at all interested in her then.'

'I was. I just thought I was a no-hoper, you see.'

'You just don't understand women do you Richard? And why are you going up into the sticks for a job? You're a southerner for goodness sakes. What about the language? What about Bex?'

'It's not the North Pole, you know. I know it's far from ideal, but beggars can't be choosers.'

'Take your time Richard. Don't rush in, you may regret it later. You're a talented salesman and it's not your fault *AGC* was run by blinkered people.'

'I hear you. What you say makes good sense. I do have a couple of months still.'

'If you're still with Becky when I've settled in Washington, you'll both be welcome for a holiday. If you're following your normal pattern and you're not with Becky, you can come on your own. Can't say fairer than that, can I?'

'That's true but you'll probably meet some hunky American anyway.'

They talked for another hour and parted on the best of terms. Richard suffered a few pangs of regret as he drove home but knew he was being sensible and adult for once.

'How was Emma, is she OK about things?'

'Yes, no problem. She's taking the job in Washington

and we're invited for a holiday if you haven't got fed up with me by then.'

'Dream on Richard. I'm not that easy to get rid of. Don't you know that Gemini's mate for life?'

'You've just made that up.'

'I know. But good though, wasn't it?'

'Very good Bex. I just hope it's true.

Chapter Sixteen

It took just a week for Richard to receive the job offer from *MKT*. The salary, terms and package were much improved on what he'd been getting from *AGC*. Richard should have been delighted, but the offer was tarnished by the thought of spending the weekdays away from Becky. However, jobs at his grade and profession were few and far between, especially when twenty odd of his peers from *AGC* were all looking at the same time. He decided to call *MKT* and promise he'd let them have his answer within two weeks.

Becky was visibly pleased that Richard had received a job offer but saddened by the prospect of them being apart.

'I could always try and find a job with you near the North Pole Richard.'

'That would be great Bex but do it whilst you have the security of your present job. In other words, find a job before you quit your present one. After all I'll be on three months probation if I accept and they might not like me.'

'Rubbish. They'll never really find out what you're like in three months. It's taken me nearly a year.'

'Look, I really want to be with you but you have a super job, even though it's with a crap company. Don't throw it away without giving it full consideration. After all, I haven't got much of a track record of attracting gals for the long-term.'

'Rubbish sweetie. You've just been unlucky and particularly crass with your selection of partners. I think you're escaping again.'

'You know me better than anyone Bex, and you know that's just not true.'

'Better not be. They don't call me Becky *Bobbit* Martin for nothing.'

The morale at the Radar Division was at an all time low. It seemed that everyone was looking over their shoulders in case they were next for the chop. The newspapers were still having a field day at *AGC's* expense. Those observers with a degree in hindsight were critical that the Board hadn't realised things were going wrong earlier. The City dislikes surprises more than bad news and several members of the Board, including the Finance and Strategic Business Director, had resigned. Sir Anthony was asked to caretake the Strategic Business post until someone could be found. Paul Hamilton had survived but had become even more uncommunicative and grumpy than ever. Michael Petty's post had disappeared but, of course, Paul had managed to find him a job. He had inflicted him on the Avionics Division as a salesman. Hopefully this would bring Upstart back into the real world with an order intake budget he'd never have a hope of meeting.

Although Richard disliked the atmosphere at the workplace, he continued to work his notice and do everything to help win the Air Defence contract before he left. He felt this was the least he could do for those who had supported him so well over the previous seven years. Kate eventually accepted the split and now treated Richard as a good friend. Rumour had it that she was seen around with an engineer, four years her junior and had a big smile on her face in the mornings. Liz decided to take early retirement in September and was then going to help at a charity shop three days a week.

As Richard was sorting through his files, Clive appeared in the doorway.

'Destroying the evidence Richard?'

'Yes, found some copies of your expenses. Wouldn't want anyone else to see them. Also there's some stuff in here that made extravagant promises on how quickly you'd develop *Aphrodite*. You only appear to be three years behind schedule and thirty million overspent.'

'Really. Can I see them?'

'Come on Clive, lighten up. I've never filed any of your early fiction. How're things?'

'Everything's fine with me but Annie's still in a tiz about the Company. I hear you've got a job up near Greenland.'

'You Southerners. Yes I've had an offer from *MKT* and there's not much else around at the moment. The package is good, certainly much better than here.'

'Well, I suppose you'll get a winter fuel allowance and language training.'

'Truthfully, the job's great but I'm not looking forward to the commute and I don't want to sell the flat in Farnham.'

'Perhaps you'll be able to buy one up there too.'

'It's certainly a thought. I'll think about that when I'm sure they want to keep me and I want to stay.'

'You're well out of it. I can tell you, Richard, Annie's worried sick about things. She's convinced there'll be more job cuts and they'll get rid of the old geezers like me.'

'Nothing's certain Clive, but I don't think they'll get rid of anyone of your experience and low cunning; after all they are well below engineering establishment anyway.'

'I hope you're right. Imagine Annie's reaction if I said we were moving to Newcastle. By the way, did you catch the business news when you were driving in this morning?'

'No, was listening to Classic FM and *Parsifal* was on for pretty well the whole journey. In fact I only had time to catch the prelude by the time I arrived at the site.'

'Well, it seems that there's some strong evidence of insider trading in *AGC*. Apparently somebody dumped five hundred thousand shares the day before the Company's problems became public.'

'That's interesting. Honest Clive, it wasn't me. I've still got my one thousand three hundred and ten share options worth much less now than the price I paid for them. And who'd have thought that the Company was going to the wall anyway. Sounds very suspicious to me. Still, there've been a couple of resignations from the Board; probably one of them.'

'Just hope whoever it is gets their just desserts that's all, Richard. By the way, can you check up on how *Aphrodite's* doing before you go?'

'Sure. I'll give the Ministry a call later today.'

Soon after Richard returned to the office, Liz called out that Margaret was on his line.

'Hello, Richard Bryant.'

'It's me Maggie.'

'Oh sorry I didn't twig.'

'Richard I've some wonderful news.'

'What's that Maggie.'

'I've met someone.'

'You've met someone?'

'Yes. He owns a resort hotel in Florida. I've seen the photos. It's in Orlando, not far from Disney. It's got a huge pool, a spa, a large health club and everything. I'm leaving with the kids at the end of the week. Isn't it exciting?'

'Absolutely super Maggie. I hope it all works out for you.'

'Oh it will this time Richard. I know it's right. I'll send you a postcard. Must fly.'

The phone went dead and Richard heaved a sigh of relief. Maggie was off his back, for a while at least.

'Colonel Bob on the phone Richard,' Liz called.

'Hi Bob, How's tricks?'

'Fine Richard. Look I don't know if you're the slightest bit interested anymore and I can't say much over the phone, but there's been a development here on the Air Defence bid.'

'Yes, I'm still interested Bob. There's been several years of my life wrapped up in that prospect.'

'Well, *Elsa's* agents are in the mire here big time. Caught with their hand in the till as it were. Apparently they were trying to bribe some official and he turned out to be an undercover policeman. General's furious of course. Said he wouldn't take anything from *Elsa* now even if it was free.'

'That's terrific news Bob. Be interesting to see how this impacts on the UK bid. At least it means the French can't get the benefit of the larger production numbers so that should help us a lot.'

Bob asked how the job hunting was going and Richard repeated the pros and cons of the *MKT* offer.

'Well, must go Richard. Hope your luck in your love life improves when you move.'

'It already has Bob. I found the right one at last.'

'Tell me that in a few months. Best of British, Richard and keep in touch.'

'Thanks for calling Bob.'

'Sir Anthony's secretary on the phone Richard. Who's Mr Popular today?'

'It's just that you didn't notice before. You'll miss me when I've gone. Thanks Liz, I've got it.'

'Hello Richard, I'm calling to say that Sir Anthony would like you to join him at a meeting in the Ministry tomorrow. Could you be at the Main Door at quarter to ten please?'

'Fine, do you know what's it's about?'

'No, he wouldn't say. He's become so secretive lately. Always holding meetings behind closed doors and disappearing off for days at a time. Doesn't even tell me where he's going any more.'

'Probably got a bit on the side. I'm sure he's trying to

sort the mess that others have made up there. Seems to me, he's one of the few guys who actually has his finger on the pulse. I'll be there and I'll pack a few notes on *Aphrodite*, just in case.'

'OK, I'll tell him. Glad to hear you've got a job. Must be quite a relief in these difficult times. Guess you'll need a visa for up there.'

'Yes, it's a difficult time to find good jobs. They're few and far between. Anyway, it's really not that far away.'

'Well, good luck anyway. When d'you finish? In a couple of weeks, isn't it?'

'Yes, just over. But it's coming up fast now.'

'We'll miss you Richard.'

'Thanks, I hope everything works out for you with all the changes up there.'

'Thanks. Sir Anthony believes that I'll be all right and he seems fairly secure. So, fingers crossed, as they say. Enjoy tomorrow, whatever it's about.'

'I will. Doesn't really matter much now, does it?'

Richard arrived punctually at the Main Door to the Ministry building. Sir Anthony came through the swing doors within minutes.

'Hello Richard. Glad you could make it. Sorry I couldn't give you more details but everything will be explained when we get there. Let's check in at the Security desk. I'm sure they will have the coffee ready in the meeting room.'

They joined the queue at Security, obtained their badges and, five minutes later, took the elevator to the second floor and Conference Room B.

As they arrived at the Conference Room, their passes were carefully checked against a list before they were admitted.

Once inside the room, Richard grew even more curious. Hovering around the podium was none other than

Charles (Chuck) Hammond and Wayne Harris, the Projects VP. He recognised Ted Green, Ian Tucker from the Ministry Procurement Desk, Vivian Barton from Ministry Contracts and Andrew Fulton from Finance. There were a few other Civil Service types lurking by the coffee pot. At five past ten, Manfred Gunter from *Stern* joined the group and Chuck asked them all to be seated. A few minutes later Nigel Eldridge came through the door with a small posse of dark suited followers, wished the audience 'Morning' and took his seat in the middle of the front row.

'Carry on.' He waved an arm at Chuck.

Chuck took centre stage and welcomed the audience. He then brought up the first vu-graph. It was headed *STRICTLY CONFIDENTIAL* caveated with a warning that any information was not to be released into the public domain until 0900 GMT the following day. The next vu-graph was entitled *FORMATION OF GEORGIA INTERNATIONAL RADAR*.

Chuck quickly explained that the purpose of the meeting was to advise the Ministry formally of the change in ownership of the Radar Division of *AGC plc* which had been signed by all parties the previous day. In particular, he felt the need to advise them on the detail, because of the impact of the major Air Defence bid under adjudication.

He went on to explain that *Georgia Radar Systems* owned sixty per cent of the new Company, *AGC* twenty-five per cent and *Stern* fifteen per cent. The new Joint Venture would be called *Georgia International Radar;* the current internal organisation would remain in tact for the time being with the addition of some secondees from *GRC* and *Stern*. The new Company would cease reporting to *AGC* as from 0900 the following day when they would be managed by *GRC's* Atlanta Headquarters.

The presentation continued with detailed organisational aspects, security and financial controls, the enhanced product range of the new company and so on.

After nearly an hour, Chuck concluded and invited questions.

Nigel Aldridge rose nonchalantly to his feet, complimented *GRC* and *Stern* on their wise investment and asked if the new Company would stand by all aspects of the Air Defence submission as bid.

'Of course Sir,' replied Chuck. 'In fact we'll do better than that. We'll take ten million off the tendered price as bid as a goodwill gesture and to launch this excellent product.'

There were a number of questions on detailed security and financial aspects by the Ministry team which were quickly put to bed by Chuck. The meeting adjourned after the need to keep absolute confidentiality until the due time was reinforced by Nigel Aldridge.

'Well, that was a bolt from the blue.' Richard turned to Sir Anthony who was grinning from ear to ear.

'Thought that would surprise you, Richard. Of course, I couldn't say a thing before today no matter how much I wanted to tell you. By the way, Chuck wants a word with you before he goes off to his afternoon session with the Whitehall Mandarins.'

Richard went over to where Chuck was packing up his briefcase and shook him by the hand. 'Congratulations Chuck. I'm delighted for you.'

Chuck guided him into a quiet corner. 'As I am for you Richard. How does Director Radar Systems Marketing appeal to you? I want you as our man in USA to advise and coordinate the marketing activities of the new Division. There'll be a fair bit of travel to the UK, Germany and the Middle East but you'll be based in the States. I haven't worked out the detailed package yet but I assure you that you'll not be disappointed. And we'll supply you with a house and company car . So how does that sound?'

'Like a dream Chuck. You knew I'd jump at the chance. I'm absolutely over the moon. And so will Bex be when I tell her.'

'Great Richard. I'll see you the day after tomorrow and we'll work out the details. I have to go now with young Nigel and his cronies.'

'Thanks Chuck, you've made my year.'

Before returning home Richard caught the tube to Bond Street to buy a trinket for Becky and stopped off at *Fortnum and Masons* for some food, wine and a bottle of Champagne.

When Becky arrived at the flat, Richard was busy in the kitchen creating an exotic Thai dish.

'Something burning Richard?'

'Very funny, I'm cooking you a special dinner. I've been slaving away for an hour already and that's all the thanks I get.'

'Don't you worry Hun; I really do appreciate you and love food steeped in ginger and lemon grass. I'll go and get a shower. What time's grub up?'

'About an hour.'

'OK. How did it go today?'

'Oh just another boring meeting. Sir Anthony wanted someone from the Radar Division in case they asked a difficult question.'

'They'll miss you when you've gone. They'll regret it then; you mark my words.'

'Thanks Bex. Go spruce yourself up. I went to the deli at Fortnums so we've got nice food and good grog.'

'So what did you think of the news today then. Thought you'd be over the moon.'

'Err… what news Bex?'

'About the insider trading. Didn't you listen to the radio today.'

'No, had the tapes on. So what's new?'

'There's a big inquiry into a Mr Rupert Hamilton,

brother of none other than Paul Hamilton of *AGC* fame, over the selling of large quantities of shares just ahead of the profit warning and all that sort of stuff. You know I don't understand these strange things that happen on the stock market, but I gather it's all pretty serious and rumour has it that Paul has been suspended.'

'Bully for Rupert. Couldn't happen to a nicer person. It's been a really good day today and there's still a few hours to go. Talking of which I got you these.'

'Wow. Long stem red roses. Thank you Richard darling. Who've you been bonking?'

'Can't a chap give the lady he loves flowers?'

'Course you can. Just remember Bobbit.'

'Go and pretty yourself up woman. Dinner'll be ready soon.'

The dinner was by candlelight, soft music in the background. Good wine, excellent food. Richard had really pulled all the stops out.

'That was terrific Richard. What's for pud?'

'Sorry Bex. They're all fattening so I got you this instead.'

Richard took out a small box from his pocket and opened it to show a one-carat solitaire diamond ring.

'Rebecca Martin, can I make an honest woman of you. Will you marry me and move with me to my new place of work?'

'Of course darling. I'd move to the ends of the earth with you. Which I gather is pretty well where we're going.'

They kissed and Richard produced a bottle of champagne.

'To us and the future Bex.'

'To us and the future.'

'By the way Bex, I've another surprise for you.'

'Don't think it can top the last one but go on, do tell.'

'It's just that I met Chuck today. He's offered me a super job in the States. Wondered if you'd prefer that to

Newcastle?'

'America? Live there? Married to you? It's all too good to be true. This has to be the happiest day of my life. Richard, pinch me. I think I must be dreaming.'